COURAGE IN HIGH HEELS

BY
JOYCE S. ANDERSON

PublishAmerica
Baltimore

First printing

ISBN: 1-4137-1616-4
PUBLISHED BY PUBLISHAMERICA BOOK PUBLISHERS
www.publishamerica.com
Baltimore

Printed in the United States of America

To my husband,

B. Robert Anderson

COURAGE IN HIGH HEELS

INTRODUCTION

It has been said that Ginger Rogers danced every step Fred Astaire danced. And she did it backwards and in high heels! Not all the women in this book wore high heels. But they excelled at living and that is what makes each one of them very special.

Women have known about courage for a long, long time. It is not only found on the battlefields of war and in climbing Mount Everest. It is also found in women's daily lives as they meet tough challenges that are dealt them. Raising a disabled child. Surviving breast cancer. Facing a husband's infidelity and betrayal. Courage for women comes in many variations and in different settings. Every woman who has come through the excruciating pains of hard labor and delivered a baby knows courage firsthand.

The glossy magazines today promise women the best orgasm, the deepest cleavage, the ideal man and the perfect color for their lips and nails. Real women know there is more to life than the slick covers trumpet. In millions of two-paycheck families and in single households, women are coping with the multiple pressures of job, children and home. They often feel overwhelmed by life. Flipping through pages of super models in size-4 bare-midriff dresses is an escape and fun. But it doesn't touch their lives. Or give any guideposts for how to make it through the next day.

This book is about eight extraordinary women who have made it through the next day. Each woman has overcome formidable obstacles in her life. And she has found the courage to do this in her own way. Pearl draws on her indomitable will to live. Adele finds strength in psychotherapy. Mamie relies on sheer guts and humor. For Tung-yuan, family bonds give her endurance and hope. The paths they have chosen differ greatly, but they all share an amazing spirit and resilience. Their lives illustrate that there is no one magic formula for courage. And their stories are fresh and compelling — filled with triumph and joy.

The stories in this book are true. They happened to real women who met challenges head-on and came out the better for it. When readers connect with these stories, they will be able to draw on them for inspiration in their own lives.

Courage has many dimensions. The quality of mind and spirit to meet and overcome adversity. Tenacity of purpose and endurance for the long run against hardship. A reserve of moral and physical strength to meet an emergency. Stamina in the face of unfavorable odds. The inherent capacity to rise to a challenge. And fortitude, being able to sustain a severe trial. At different times in their lives, these eight women needed those dimensions of courage to go on. And they found them within themselves.

The situations these women faced defy time frames: family relationships, careers, love and sexuality, marriage, children, friends, financial pressures, betrayal and divorce, serious illness, the aging process. Readers will find themselves in these stories. Their problems. Their feelings. Their own intrinsic courage.

Courage has been a predominantly male province in most of literature and historic lore. Hercules, Ulysses, and the fabled warriors of the Trojan Wars. Ancient tales glorified men for their heroic deeds. Alexander The Great, conqueror of Greece, the Persian empire and Egypt by the time he was 33 years old! Julius Caesar and the Roman Legions who subdued all of the known world. The medieval knights, King Arthur and his Round table. Robin Hood. Fact and myth blend to present the exploits of men of courage.

There were certain women who stood out through the ages. Queen Elizabeth I of England. Joan of Arc. Catherine The Great. All women of courage and vision. But the model woman of long ago was Caesar's wife, best known for her fidelity — for being above reproach. Hers was the more traditional role, that of the dutiful and faithful wife.

Biblical heroes are almost all men. The Patriarchs, Abraham, Jacob and Joseph, made the bold moves. And it is Moses who defied Pharaoh and led the Israelites out of Egypt. Samson, the epitome of strength, is betrayed and shorn by the temptress, Delilah. Women are often extolled, but not for their courage. Rather for their beauty and steadfastness. Deborah, a judge and a prophet, stands out as an exception — a woman of valor.

There are significant woman role models in American history. Harriet Tubman and Sojourner Truth, fighters for freedom from slavery. Elizabeth Cady Stanton, Susan B. Anthony and Margaret Sanger, champions of women's rights in all areas of life. Eleanor Roosevelt, who was a leader for human rights here and overseas. These women are famous and rightly so. They lived exemplary lives and deserve to be admired. Many books have been written about them.

This book is not about famous women. It is about eight extraordinary women whose lives are fascinating and make great reading. They are from diverse backgrounds and from different parts of the country. Each life is unique. And their honest sharing gives firsthand insights into their hopes, passions, struggles, disappointments and triumphs. They are open to change. They welcome new ideas. They see life as a work in progress. They ask, 'What's next?"

Pearl. Mamie. Ruth. Tung. Adele. Sherry. Lillian. Jean. In their stories are woven the tapestry of women's lives — the 'real stuff' of courage.

CHAPTER I
PEARL'S STORY

"If I am not for myself, who will be for me?"
But if I am only for myself, what am I?
And if not now, when?"

—Hillel

"There was a long light and my mother was at the other end. I believe it! Because it was there! It's like a haze at first. And then I saw my mother and I wanted to go to her. But I felt she wanted me to stay. To take care of Arnold. I think that is what pulled me through. That I had to stay and take care of Arnold for her. To do what she wanted me to do." When she was 26, Pearl Mizrahi was near death after a catastrophic automobile accident. It was then that she had the out-of-body experience and saw her mother, who had died five years earlier.

* * *

There is a dramatic thread of fate that begins the day Pearl was born and continues throughout her entire life. "My parents were traveling from Florida to Brooklyn. My mother was pregnant with me and I was the fifth child down. She wasn't due yet. But when she was crossing a street in Washington DC, my mother was hit by a car! She was pushed down and immediately went into labor. I was born in the first week of her ninth month. I weighed five pounds."

While her mother recuperated, they stayed with relatives in their large house that accommodated the Dayan family with four children and an infant. "I became her little baby. She put me in a dresser drawer and that was my crib." The year was 1932. Pearl laughs as she recalls being told that "Roosevelt patted my sister on the head in her little stroller in front of the White House." The family stayed in Washington for almost a year with Pearl ensconced in the dresser drawer.

The importance of family in her life began with these first days and months. Her large number of siblings and the tightly woven network of aunts, uncles and cousins made family the "given" for her in love and security. "Family means everything to me," she says as she shares her life story.

Pearl often leans forward as she talks. She has dark brown expressive eyes and short brown hair with soft bangs across her forehead. When she smiles, her face lights up. Her laugh can be hearty or rueful. She is a woman with deep feelings and an indomitable spirit. She loves to be with friends, with people. She does not like to be alone. She is described by her sister-in-law Margaret in a family anthology as "the person everyone wants at their party because she is so vivacious and full of fun." At times, Pearl uses a cane as she walks. The two horrific automobile accidents she survived in her life have left one leg shorter than the other. This did not stop her from dancing at her grandson's bar mitzvah two years ago. But that is getting ahead of her story.

The family moved to Brooklyn in 1933 where Pearl's father, Saul Dayan, worked several jobs to support his family during the Depression years. "He worked in a linen store and he was a window trimmer at night. My mother, Juliet, was a full-time homemaker with all of us children to raise." Another child was born while they lived in Brooklyn. I ask Pearl how she felt about her parents as she was growing up. "I adored my father as a child because he came home with stories. He was a storyteller about everything that was going on. A lot of times we didn't know what was real and what wasn't real. But we didn't care!" A very vivid memory was not a story but about one night when he came home after trimming the windows. It was three in the morning. He woke all the children and took them into the front room. "We were all lined up on the floor half asleep, except for me. I sat on his knee. Then he said, 'I have to share something with you children, so you will know what it looks like for the future. I haven't had many of these. I want you see it.' And he took out a hundred dollar bill! He had been given a tip for the job he did. It was three o'clock in the morning and he decided to tell us about money. I never forgot that!"

Pearl recounts many happy memories from her early childhood in Brooklyn. "I loved Brooklyn, New York as a little girl. In kindergarten, I was the talker in the class. I used to go home with little notes pinned on me, saying 'I will not talk so much tomorrow.' And my mother would look at it and pat me on the head. I was very outgoing. One day I came home with a small band-aid across my mouth. Yet, I loved school! The teacher picked two kids to take to Radio City Music Hall every year based on merit. And I was one of the two. So she was very fair."

Pearl describes her mother as a very "jovial person". She loved to jump rope with all the children in the neighborhood. Her mother was not Syrian, as her father was. She had blue eyes and light hair and had attracted her father in St. Petersburg, Florida. Syrian Jews usually married only within their own group, as did the European Jews. She was 16 and he was 21. Both families were not happy with the match originally. "He had a lot of explaining to do. But she learned to speak Arabic. She only went to 9th grade and used to say, 'For a woman who only went to 9th grade, I'm pretty smart!' She was very good with languages."

It was not easy to stretch the dollars during the Depression. Pearl recalls it as a constant struggle for her parents. "There's one story I love about my sister Grace, the oldest, who took care of us when Mom was busy. On certain days of the week, people would go to an area that was like welfare to get free food. One day, Mom asked Grace to go. She was embarrassed and went on the back streets. When she got there, she found all the neighbors were there too!" Pearl says she learned that they were the same as other people. At six, she was also very inventive. Each child received a penny a week for candy. She decided she wanted more money. She found used paper cups behind the candy store, filled them up with dirt, planted weeds in them and sold them to passers by as "flowers". She told prospective customers, "My mother is sick and we need the money!" When someone came from the welfare to see her mother, the sidewalk entrepreneur was quickly identified and put out of business. Her mother knew immediately who the culprit was.

The children were taken often to the library by their mother, as well as to the Zoo, the Botanical Gardens and the Brooklyn Museum. And the entire family went to the World's Fair in 1939. "We went to the World's Fair every other day on the subway. And my brother Maurice got lost at the Fair. He wanted to get lost — just as he did on Coney Island. They used to take him somewhere and give him candy. He loved it!" The Dayan family lived in an upstairs apartment with eleven children living downstairs — ten boys and one girl. There was never a lack of playmates. "And Mom introduced us to opera. We listened to the Saturday afternoon broadcasts of The Metropolitan Opera. She wanted us to have a little bit of everything."

The summer prior to leaving Brooklyn, Saul Dayan took a job in a small linen shop in Old Orchard Beach, Maine. Pearl tells me what happened next. "We always talk about that summer when we all are together. My mother had to find a way to get us all up there. There were six children. We had two first cousins and they rented a hearse! We left at night and another child, a cousin, came along. We all got carsick and threw up! Then we stopped at a hospital for my brother. And in Vermont, when we stopped for gas, there was a guy with a huge gun! We had never seen a gun before. It was an adventure! The whole summer was an adventure!" When they arrived, they found they were to live in the top floor of an old hotel. The toilet was in the kitchen and they had to put a big towel up. Pearl is laughing as she continues, "That summer was probably the most exciting adventure we ever had! The pier was raided by the police. The machines were broken open and all of us kids came home with pockets full of things! It was such fun!"

At this point in the interview, Pearl's voice lowers. Her facial expression changes to one of strain. It appears to be extremely stressful for her to continue. When asked if she wants to share what is apparently a very painful memory, she considers this question carefully before she answers. "Yes. I want this in the book. It is part of my childhood. I usually set it aside, but it happened. It affected my life. And it was a terrible thing to happen to a six-year-old child." She then reveals the sexual abuse she suffered at the hands of a 13-year-old cousin over a period of almost two years.

The Dayan family lived at first in Brooklyn with relatives in their large house. It was in the cellar of the house that the boy took Pearl and brandished a knife to force her to comply. He threatened her into silence. "I was afraid! He warned me about telling my mother and I was afraid to tell. He showed me pornographic comic books and other books too. And then he abused me. It went on even after we moved to our apartment. He said I had to come to his house and I went. I didn't know what to do. My mother thought I was out playing."

In 1939 the family moved to Florida, but the ordeal for Pearl was not over. The boy was in trouble with the police and scheduled to go to reform school. Pearl's parents, knowing nothing of the abuse, offered to take him with them to Florida to avoid his being sent to reform school. Once settled in Florida, he resumed his abuse of Pearl. "It was not until he attempted to abuse my older sister that the nightmare ended for me. She told my mother and he was immediately sent back to Brooklyn. And my mother then helped me through what had happened to me. I spent a lot of time with doctors and counselors. My mother was smart enough to know I needed help. She was wonderful! I would never have gotten over it. I know that today."

The Dayan home was a very traditional Jewish home, keeping the rituals and observance of the Sabbath and the holidays. Her mother maintained a kosher home and Pearl does the same in her home today. Her father liked the children to speak English in their home, although Arabic, of his native Syria, was often spoken. Pearl relates how he held a lifelong interest in languages and taught himself to speak and/or write ten languages. He opened linen stores in Florida, but he was not a successful businessman. The family lived in rental houses, mostly in ethnic Jewish and Italian neighborhoods. "My mother was active in the Jewish community and served as president of the synagogue Sisterhood. She believed in helping the underdog — and the less fortunate. We learned from her and we each are interested in social causes today."

Pearl enjoys talking about her siblings and family life. "Grace was the oldest. She always had fun in New York, but she had to be responsible for the rest of us. Victor was the intellectual one, who told us stories like Daddy. But his stories were dramatic stories about people. He read a lot. At sixteen, he was valedictorian of his class. In college, he was a teaching assistant at eighteen. Dorothy, who was three years older than I, was very close to me. She was talented with a beautiful voice. And Siggie was the youngest in Brooklyn, the baby. I took care of him. He went everywhere with me. And he was mischievous too, along with Maurice and me. We three were the ones! I guess I was closest to Maurice and Dorothy, but I adored them all."

Learning was stressed in the Dayan home. "We had to have an education. My father read books all the time. My mother didn't have the formal education, but she was smart and wanted it. She made us promise that each of us would go on in school. That is very strong in my mind. And throughout all my life." With six children, certain events happened to all the children at once. Pearl compares her family with the one in *Cheaper by the Dozen* when the children got their tonsils taken out en masse. "We stood in line in a clinic and each went one at a time. And then Mother took care of all of us. That was how I grew up. Sharing everything. Never had things of my own. Clothes handed down from Grace and Dorothy. All of us were close. We had our fights and arguments. But we were close."

When the family moved to Florida, they first lived with their father's brother in Tampa. They had goats, chickens and a cow which the children had never seen before. "I learned how to milk a goat! A goat moves more and you have to do it right. I wasn't afraid of anything as a child. I was so devilish and tried everything. I was very outgoing." They then moved to Lakeland, on the West Coast, where their father opened a little concession of fine linens in a department store. He also did sign painting to bring in more income. "I liked Florida. It was new. And there were Spanish children in our school. We had a big yard in Lakeland too. My father bartered the linens for food from the farmers on the road. And he had to go to court because we had 100 chickens!" He won the variance and Pearl relates how she learned about many things from the chickens, including mating. They sold the eggs and the chickens. Their life was completely different from

Brooklyn. Then they moved to St. Petersburg, where Saul Dayan opened his own store.

"I always liked school but I was still mischievous. I played hooky from school with my girlfriend one day. We lay on the floor of a house for hours so we wouldn't be caught! Then we went to a milk factory and they called the school. I was ten years old." Pearl describes new friendships wherever they lived. In 1942, during World War II, the Dayan house became a mecca for servicemen. "My mother opened up the doors. They thought it was the USO, our house. The servicemen came out of synagogue and came right to our house which was next door. And I helped." It was in St. Petersburg that Pearl first became aware of prejudice and discrimination — of anti-Semitism and interracial problems. Behind their house was a wire fence that ran between the backyards and divided the black and white neighborhoods. "My mother cut a hole in the fence so that I could go play with the little black girl and she could come into our yard too. My mother wanted us to learn and know. And I did. That's how I learned about different cultures. My father was not tolerant. Years later, he and I had strong arguments as I grew up."

Pearl experienced some anti-Semitism as a child. When she was eight, a non-Jewish girl with long blond curls beat her up for being a Jew. Although Pearl fought back and yanked her curls, she says that she was the worse for wear. She arrived home, bruised and crying, and declared that she was never going back to school again. Her mother took her to the 5 & 10-cent store, bought her a jump rope and told her, "You take this jump rope to school and ask some girls to jump rope with you. This girl will see you are just like she is." Years later, Pearl recalls her former tormentor coming over and apologizing at a class reunion. Yet, she also says, ruefully, that all her life she has had the feeling that she has to prove to others that she is equal or better.

During her teenage years, Pearl often tagged along with Dorothy. Their father did not want them to date non-Jewish boys in high school. "Mom would give in with school dances. But Dad was strict. The Captain of the football team invited me to a dance and Daddy wouldn't let me go. I threw a fit! Many years later, we met at a class reunion. He said, 'You know, Pearl, you were the first one who ever refused me. And I never knew why.' I told him and we both laughed." Pearl took the academic course in high school, with Latin and physiology as her favorite subjects. She was most interested in books on medicine and science. Her oldest sister Grace went to college with the entire family helping with the money needed for tuition or extras. Dorothy joined the Women's Army Corps (WACS) and took courses in the service, specializing in business subjects. Victor, Maurice and Siggie all were graduated from college with the two older brothers going on for Ph.D degrees. Pearl's educational plans were to take a very different turn.

In high school, Pearl took part in many extracurricular activities; cheerleading and the Latin Club were favorites. And she had a busy social life. "We used to date in groups in those days. We also had a military and a naval academy in St. Petersburg. They would take groups of girls over to meet the boys. I met boys and brought them home. They came on Saturday and we would take walks. And there were dances at school where I loved to dance with Maurice. Until I was a junior, then maybe I had a single date. Generally double-dating with Dorothy or a cousin." Pearl also had responsibilities, taking care of her little sister Cecile, who was born in 1941, just when they moved to St. Petersburg. "Cecile is nine years younger than I am. That was a hard birth for my mother. Cecile was a 'preemie' born at home. We all were there. That was an experience!" Pearl smiles sweetly as she recalls the event. "She was a very tiny baby and I took care of her. She was our little baby."

When Pearl was sixteen, in her senior year in high school, her father brought home a young man for Sunday lunch. Harry Mizrahi was in St. Petersburg to open a linen shop for his brother, Maurice, "Chief". He met Saul Dayan, who was most interested in him since he had two daughters of marriageable age, Grace and Dorothy. Harry also came from a Syrian Jewish background and that was very important to Pearl's father. Pearl's eyes are very bright as she tells me how her father met Harry. "My father was walking past the linen store one day on his lunch hour. He looked in and saw Harry getting the store organized. There were no fixtures. My father walked in and started to talk to Harry. He liked the fact that he was Syrian, Jewish and from a good family, the Mizrahis. Right away, my father's mind started clicking. He had three daughters at home. He wasn't thinking of me, rather of Grace and Dorothy." He invited Harry to come to lunch on Sunday to meet the family. He also told him that he had a brother in Tampa with showcases to sell. The scene was set.

Pearl continues with the story, "I wasn't home yet when he came. I was next door at the synagogue teaching Sunday school. I came running in and was introduced. I remember what I was wearing — one of those white peasant blouses that came to the shoulder and a flowered full skirt. And sandals. I came in the house and there was this young man with the most beautiful smile. Dark hair, and he was wearing a beige flecked jacket. He looked terrific to me! And I ran into the kitchen and asked my mother, 'Who's that?' And she said, 'He's not for you!' Harry tells the story that, before I came in, he was looking around the house and saw my picture on the wall. He asked my mother who that was and she said 'That's one of my younger daughters.' He says that he knew then that I was the daughter he wanted."

The family sat down to their usual Sunday lunch, baked beans and hot dogs. Dorothy was there but Grace was away at college. Dorothy liked Harry right away and he offered her a job in the new linen store. Pearl had a double date arranged for that evening in Tampa. She had been planning to take a bus to meet her girlfriend first. But her father offered to take her in the car, a 1927 Hupmobile, since he was driving Harry to Tampa to see the fixtures in his brother's store. "I thought Harry was adorable, but my mother had said he was not for me. Then, while we were driving, Harry, with my father in the front seat of the car, asked him if he could take me out to dinner that evening. And my father said, 'Yes!' I was very angry with Harry. He never asked me! And I already had a date with somebody else." When they arrived in Tampa at her uncle's store, she called her friend and canceled the date. Her father's word was law. She and Harry went out to dinner at a Cuban restaurant in Ybor City.

For dinner, Harry ordered steak and olives, teasing Pearl and telling her that olives were 'passion fruit'. The food was not Kosher and Pearl ate neither the meat nor the olives! She laughs heartily and says, "I almost fainted! I'm sitting there with a guy who is very good-looking. But he really scared me when he said that." Harry had been in the military as a Navy fighter pilot in the Pacific during World War II. But Pearl tells me that he did not talk about that on their first date. After dinner, they went to the movies and then took the last bus home to St. Petersburg. On the way, Harry asked Pearl how old she was, and she said "Seventeen, going on eighteen." He said he was twenty-three, soon to be twenty-four. The truth was that he was twenty-six and she was sixteen. Pearl was worried that her father would be upset that they were so late, after twelve. "I knew where Daddy would be. He used to sit in a chair in the living room that looked right at the door for his daughters to come home. Sleeping, generally."

When they got to the door of the house, Harry said, "Good night," and ran! He did not face her father. Yet, from that day on, Pearl saw Harry every day. Both her mother and father liked him and he was invited to their home often. Meanwhile, Dorothy was working in his store and she was serious about him. Pearl was not at that point. Then Harry asked Pearl out on a date. Her voice lowers as she remembers that it turned out to be hard for Dorothy. "My father told her that Harry wanted to date me. And that was how it was going to be." Then Harry called and broke the date and Pearl says she didn't mind. He had been coming over every night, playing cards with her mother and spending time with the family. When she learned he had a girlfriend who was coming to see him, she was not surprised. But when the phone rang at midnight, she was!

"We were on a very strict schedule — only allowed to be on the phone for three minutes. And then, Harry proposed to me on the phone! He said, 'I have to ask you a question. If somebody just met someone and they really, really liked each other. And they knew that was what they wanted in life, what do you think about that?' And I said to him, 'That would be really nice.' And he said, 'You like that idea? Because I like you a lot.' And I said, 'Yes!' and I hung up the phone. My mother was standing there next to the phone and she took me upstairs in her bed and said to me, 'You realize, honey, that was his way of asking you to marry him?' And I said, 'Wow!' We had not even kissed at that point. And then she said, 'You know, dear, you have to ask yourself whether you can get up every morning and look at him.'" Pearl's laughter is now at full force. "'Oh, yes,' I said. 'He's very handsome!' And then she said, 'When you marry, you have to be able to share lots of things and to be pliable. If there's a problem, you have to talk about it and you have to be honest with each other.' Meanwhile my father is asleep, snoring away while we were talking!" Pearl and Harry had met on December 12. This all happened only two weeks later.

The next day, Saul Dayan was very happy that one of his daughters was going to marry Harry Mizrahi. Every day after that Harry was at the house. Pearl and he spent the winter vacation days together. "I wasn't really sure. I was very young. I said 'Yes' to him on the phone. But I had to get to know him. Both of my parents liked him a lot." Harry had grown up in Atlantic City, New Jersey. He had a twin sister and a brother, ten years older. His father had a successful linen store on the Boardwalk and Harry worked with him, learning to be a salesman and a window trimmer. He grew up in a large home, but his father lost everything in the crash of 1929. Harry attended Atlantic City High School and worked after school in the linen store. He graduated in 1941 during World War II , went to work for DuPont and then enlisted in the United States Naval Air Force. Pearl tells the story, "They were giving exams then and there. He walked in, not prepared, and he passed with flying colors! Very few did. Only two applicants were high school graduates; the rest were all college graduates. But Harry was bright. And he passed!" Harry became a Navy fighter pilot flying from aircraft carriers in the Pacific during the war. When Pearl met him, Harry was in the Naval Reserves.

As their courtship progressed, Pearl's mother wanted her to graduate from high school before they married. But her father didn't want to delay the

19

wedding. Harry had to be in Ocean City, New Jersey for Memorial Day weekend and her father said, "A wife belongs with her husband. And he's not going without you!" Thus, Pearl and Harry were to be married on April 28, 1949. She had to promise her mother that she would complete her education in the years ahead. "I never forgot that promise."

On the day of the wedding, Pearl almost ran away! "That day an old boyfriend showed up. A fellow from the Admiral Farragut Naval Academy. I liked him. I liked his family. And he had said, 'Someday, I'm going to come back and you're going to marry me.' We had sent a wedding invitation to him and his family. But they had been traveling and had not received it. They just dropped in. That day! And he said, 'Why are you getting married? I wanted to marry you.' I said, 'I'm getting married today.'" She did allow him to drive her to the beauty parlor. Then she did not like the set and he drove her to the beach, where she dunked her whole head in the ocean. They sat in the car and talked for a while. And she thought, *What am I doing?*

"When I came home, Harry called and asked, 'How are you doing?' I answered, 'I don't know, but I'll be all right.' And then I went upstairs and washed my hair again to get the sea water out."

Her mother was a calming influence during these last minute jitters. "I think my mother said to me, 'It's almost time, honey. Just relax.'" And Pearl is convulsed with laughter as she relates that her girlfriend pushed her down the aisle. Pearl and Harry were married with the entire congregation invited to the wedding reception. Her old boyfriend and his family were at the service. There were bridesmaids and ushers. Her satin wedding gown was the 'something borrowed' from a neighbor. She wore a traditional headpiece and veil and looks radiant in their formal wedding portrait.

Her mother and aunts had cooked Middle Eastern pastries for days. "We served all kinds of cakes and delicacies. The table was gorgeous, champagne punch, and all along the windows were camellias and gardenias. And all my teachers were there from high school. Afterwards, we had dinner at home for the family." Pearl had told Harry of the searing time of abuse she had suffered as a child. She speaks very lovingly of how he was very gentle and understanding of her needs as they became husband and wife.

Their first years of married life were not to be serene. After a three-day honeymoon, they returned to find that Pearl's mother was pregnant. They went back to St. Petersburg when the summer season was over in Ocean City, and Arnold Dayan was born prematurely in December, weighing only 3 lbs. 6 ozs. He developed pneumonia, which reoccurred several times in the next three months. In May 1950, Pearl and Harry left for the Jersey shore again and moved in with his brother Chief and his wife Lelia. As a very young bride, this was not an ideal arrangement. Pearl shares with me, "I did not want to be there. We stayed with them because Chief had closed the store and Harry wasn't getting paid. He was flying as a member of the Naval Reserve to make money on weekends and on special ferry assignments. And I was pregnant."

On December 1, 1951, exactly two years to the day of Arnold's birth, Jay Mizrahi was born. Pearl's mother, father and Arnold came up from Florida for the Bris, a ceremony that occurs eight days after a boy is born into a Jewish family. When he was two weeks old, projectile vomiting led to a diagnosis of pyloric stenosis, a closed stomach and Jay was operated upon successfully. Pearl fed him every hour on the hour during his recovery. Now, her voice drops and she says with great sadness, "And then, my mother became seriously ill. She collapsed on the kitchen floor and we called the doctor. Everything was total chaos." Her mother was able to return to Florida by train. She was diagnosed with cancer, lymphoma, and was in and out of hospitals until her death in 1953. During that terrible time, Pearl was the one of the adult children who came to Florida and spent six weeks at a time with her mother. She would leave Jay at home with Harry and a caretaker in order to help her mother. Pearl speaks with great love and tenderness of her mother. Her eyes brim with tears. "She continued to help others despite her illness, full of her usual warmth and compassion. She laughed and played with us the card games she loved. Our talks have stayed with me to this day. In one conversation she said, 'I don't want anyone to feel sorry for me. I've had a full life and have wonderful children.'" In hopes of slowing the cancer, two operations were performed, a prefrontal lobotomy and the removal of her pituitary gland. Pearl was there to nurse her after the operations. Juliet Dayan died six weeks after the second surgery. She was 45 years old.

During the time of her mother's fight against cancer, Jay had become seriously ill again, with a brain tumor. This was a frightening time for Pearl and Harry. "Mom was healing from her first surgery and I came home. I noticed that Jay was rubbing his head and not sleeping during the night. After their local pediatrician watched Jay for several months, he recommended seeing a specialist. "He examined Jay and immediately said, 'He has a tumor in there in the center of the brain. And I can't tell until I get in there. As soon as we can, let's get it out.' I said, 'Do you want to do it tomorrow?' He looked at me, walked across the room and hugged me. He said, 'Most of my patients say wait and I don't want to wait with this. I'm proud of you.'" They stayed in the hospital after the surgery. "Harry cried and cried. He was so upset." Jay's operation was successful, although Pearl adds, "The hospital experience was not good. They were short of help. And they gave Jay the wrong anesthesia. They had to pass it out of him. He could have died." But there were no damaging aftereffects. Jay's development after that, at thirteen months, was rapid and normal. He stood. Then he walked almost at the same time. Pearl and Harry felt great relief.

After Pearl's mother's death, she was faced with one of the most important decisions of her life. "My father, like so many men of his times, was not equipped to care for his two young children. Arnold was only three and Cecile was eleven. A few months after Mom's death, Siggie brought Cecile and Arnold from Miami to live with Harry and me in Ocean City, New Jersey. And Arnold and Cecile were a joy to have." Although her older sisters were married, Pearl and Harry were the ones to assume the responsibility of raising the children. "Harry said, 'We can't leave them there. We have to take them.' So I took both kids.I don't know if it was right. But we did it." This selfless decision was to affect their lives profoundly in the years that lay ahead. Pearl was only 21 years old. She had just lost her beloved mother through a traumatic, painful illness. Now she was mother not only to Jay but to her brother Arnold and sister Cecile as well.

For a year they lived in an apartment in Ocean City. Then, with their savings and a Veteran's loan, Pearl and Harry were able to build a house in Margate to accommodate their new family. The boys shared a bedroom and slept in twin beds. "Because they shared the same birthday, joint parties were held and we gave them identical gifts. It was a joy to see these two boys play together. Arnold introduced Harry as his father and Jay as his brother. And of course, me as his mother. But as he grew older, he liked to say he was Jay's uncle!" Cecile had to face her mother's death, the move to live with Pearl and Harry and the roller coaster of her teenage years. Pearl did her best to cope and advise her although she was not that much older herself. When asked how she came through these years, she replies, "I have to tell you. I did what I had to do. You find you have strength. I adored my mother. I felt this responsibility to her to raise Arnold and Cecile."

Pearl describes Arnold as a boy who struggled in school, but as very artistic and filled with imagination. "We bought a fish tank and allowed the boys to buy things to fix it up. Jay bought everything to make it work. Arnold bought everything to make it beautiful, the blue pebbles and greenery."

Cecile reached her sixteenth birthday with a party held a week early since Pearl was pregnant and delivery was imminent. A second son, Jeffrey, was born on June 23, 1956. I ask Pearl if she enjoyed being a full-time mother. "I loved the boys. They were such fun. And Jeffrey was a healthy baby. Cecile was hard at times. But I loved shopping with her for clothes. And I enjoyed cooking, especially Syrian dishes. Harry was away flying often on weekends, but I had a mother's helper in the summers. I loved the beach. Those were happy times!"

On April 9, 11958, while visiting in Tampa Florida during the Passover holiday, the family was in a catastrophic automobile accident. They were all in the car. Harry was driving, with Jeffrey at 22 months wedged between him and Pearl. Cecile, Arnold and Jay were in the backseat. "We were hit head-on in a blinding rainstorm by a car traveling 60 miles per hour on a narrow two-lane road. The driver tried to pass a Mack truck and lost control of his car. I heard Harry yelling, 'I can't get out of the way!' The other driver, who had been drinking, was literally decapitated and the woman with him died later in the hospital. Jeffrey's life was saved by a huge stuffed monkey that he was holding when the impact came."

Farmers who lived nearby heard the crash and ran to help get them out of the car. The Jaws of Life were needed to pull Pearl free. She had been thrown forward violently, with her face smashed into the broken glass of the windshield. They were all rescued just before the car burst into flames and burned to the ground.

Harry's face was cut and his jaw was broken. Jay and Arnold had minor lacerations; Jeffrey needed stitches for head lacerations. Cecile was hospitalized in the same room with Pearl with a knee injury and head laceration. Pearl sustained massive internal injuries and was not expected to live through the night. Only she can tell it as it happened. "Both my lungs were punctured and my heart was punctured. Both my legs were broken when they pulled me out of the car. Everything was broken! My whole left side. My left pelvic bone was split and the femur directly below the knee was fractured and split open. My left ankle was fractured. My right arm was cut completely through the muscle and artery, and was hanging off! It had to be reattached and it had compound fractures. The worst thing was my face. I had gone right through the windshield. I had no nose! My whole face was shredded and all the front teeth knocked out. They just patched me up the first night. The doctors said they had to get the fluid out of my lungs or I wouldn't live. They couldn't set my legs or anything. I remember a young doctor who sat with me through the entire night and blew with his mouth, bringing the fluid out of my lungs. They didn't have the machines they have today. I was going in and out of consciousness. The room was pretty dark. My father came and I saw him standing at the foot of the bed holding a prayer book. I said in a loud voice, 'Don't do that, Dad! I am not going to die!' And I didn't!"

When they had all been brought into Tampa General Hospital, Harry had tried to stay with Pearl. They had to restrain him, strapped to a bed, while they treated his injuries. Then they brought him in a wheelchair to see Pearl. Her voice breaks as she continues, "I remember when they brought Harry in. Telling him that it wasn't his fault. And I remember asking for Arnold of all the children. I was very concerned that he would lose a second mother." Pearl then tells of the out-of-body experience that happened to her during that long first night in the hospital. "There was a long light and my mother was at the other end. I believe it! Because it was there! It's like a haze at first. And then I saw my mother and I wanted to go to her. But I felt she wanted me to stay. To take care of Arnold. I think that is what pulled me through. That I had to stay and take care of Arnold for her. To do what she wanted me to do."

Pearl had been brought in on a Wednesday afternoon and was not taken to surgery until Friday night. They said she would not be able to withstand anesthesia or surgery until her lungs were cleared and her heart was pumping properly. After the original state of shock, she was unconscious most of the time. She does remember the flashbulbs going off as the plastic surgeon took pictures. "I remember him taking the glass pieces out of my eye on Friday night. I talked to him. And I think I fell in love with him that night. He was young and very good-looking. He was adorable!" Pearl is laughing now and I am in awe of her. "I could hear him plunking the glass pieces. They didn't put me out. They were afraid, so I had a local anesthesia. And they had put about 180 stitches in my face."

Pearl was on the critical list for eight weeks and hospitalized for three and a half months. She had blood transfusions for days and was put in traction for her pelvis and leg. Her arm was attached to a special support and the IV tubes were in place for weeks. Through five procedures of plastic surgery, her nose and upper lip were completely reconstructed. She gives enormous credit to the doctors and nurses for her recovery. Harry returned with the children to Margate in the early weeks and would fly down every other weekend. I ask her what got her through the eight weeks. "I was very determined. I wanted to be there for Arnie, Cecile and Jay and Jeffrey. And for Harry, of course. I knew I was going to get well and go home. I handle illness and my physical stuff very well. And I knew I was going to have to work hard to make it happen. I knew I had to do it!"

During her stay in the hospital, Pearl found that helping other patients was important to her own recovery. "The doctor would send people in to talk to me. There was a woman who was hysterical about having her tonsils out. Never had surgery. There was a man who was burned very badly. They would look at me in traction with no teeth and all stitched up. I couldn't move too much. My head was kept straight. And I would talk with them and encourage them in any way I could." When asked if she was ever frightened that she would not go home, Pearl says firmly, "No! I knew I was going to go home. I didn't know when. They told me at one point that I would never walk again. And I looked at the doctor and said, 'We'll see.'"

Pearl was in traction until four days before she came home. She describes her worst day in the hospital. "I was going up for plastic surgery. They were going to give me a new nose. I was in the traction bed and had been given some anesthesia to prepare me. The doctor said they would put me in a room by myself and I could not talk to anyone — or laugh! They wheeled me to the elevator, and the bed could not fit into the elevator. I could hear the nurses talking. I was under sedation and kind of flying. I yelled, 'Saw off the bed! I want to have the surgery now!' And they got a carpenter who sawed off the long pole attached to the bed. But I had to wait until the next morning and that day I was hysterical. The doctor sat with me and said, 'I promise to do it tomorrow.' And he did."

Pat, the patient who shared the room with Pearl in the early days, became a lifelong friend. And Ed, the hospital mail man, also became a special friend to Pearl. "He was a college student and he came up to the room one day and said, 'I have to tell you I have been delivering mail for some time now and nobody as gotten as much mail as you! And I had to come see who you were.' And from that day, he came in every day. He read my letters for me and wrote some too. I couldn't write. And every Friday he borrowed five dollars and paid it back by Tuesday! We had that going on for months." When she went home, a separate suitcase was needed to carry the letters.

On the home front, life went on. The three little boys caught the measles and Harry had to nurse them back to health. He wrote with lipstick on the bathroom mirror to keep track of the times they needed their medications. Cecile graduated from high school in a wheelchair since her knee had not healed. And they waited the many months until Pearl's return. When asked if she was apprehensive about leaving the hospital, she replies, "Well, yes. I was leaving the medical support system and the people. When you're there that long, they become your friends. They become your family."

When Pearl finally came home in July, she weighed 68 pounds. Cecile, who had been staying with neighbors, returned to help in many important ways. "She made milkshakes to build up my stamina and washed my hair. It was all hard on her as a teenager. She was good with the children and I appreciated all she did. Jeff was a young toddler. He would not leave my room. He wanted to stay with me all the time." Harry took over caring for the children when he came home from his job.

Pearl speaks of her neighbors and friends with deep affection and appreciation. "To this day, I have to thank all of them. One friend came over while I was still in the hospital. He bought a freezer and filled it with meat and food. He filled it up. A whole side of beef. He knew we had lost the car and had many bills to pay." The women of the B'nai B'rith chapter, where Pearl had been installed as president in absentia, bought a hospital bed for her return. While she was confined to bed, two friends who were doctors would come and check her. The cooking was done by Cecile and a network of friends. They were able to find a young girl to help with the children during the first summer.

By October, Pearl was able to maneuver on crutches and a walker. "It took a long time. As a total, to really recuperate, it took me six years. Before I didn't stop falling. I used to fall a lot. As for my appearance, it never even bothered me. And the plastic surgeon said something I will never forget. 'You're going to go home and put makeup on. So you'll wear a little more than you used to. And I never want you to worry about paying my bill. You'll pay what you can when you can. You go home and take care of those children.' They were not covered by the right insurance and it took years to pay the bills. As she looks back at that terrible ordeal, Pearl adds, "Two years after the accident, I flew to Florida to see my doctors. They were very pleased. And I did see the doctor who told me I would never walk again. I walked into his office — still with some help. And he was thrilled!"

The decade that followed the accident, from 1958 to 1969, was a very demanding time for Pearl and Harry. During the initial recovery period, Pearl worked with physical therapists to restore the strength and mobility in her legs and her right arm. "I was in and out of bed the first year. I used crutches and a wheelchair to get around. It was not easy." They struggled financially, with Harry flying on weekends as well as working in the linen stores with his brother. One summer they rented the house and lived in a small basement apartment in Ventnor. Pearl also worked part-time in a women's wear store to make extra dollars. She ran the household and raised the children. Cecile had enrolled in the University of Florida at Gainesville. When Harry was away flying, Pearl had the full responsibility and there were hard problems to cope with. "There was a lot of turmoil in my house. The older boys were 7 and 9 when I came out of the hospital. Jay was having stomach pains, finally diagnosed as colitis. Arnold had both physical and emotional problems. He was not growing as he should and he was a child who worried all the time. My father would come and visit and that would confuse Arnold. He was also disruptive in school. I had my hands full!"

And she had not forgotten her promise to her mother to go on with her education. She pursued her high school equivalency diploma first, taking courses at the local community college. Pearl describes how she felt going to college. "I was scared. But you know, all those things I just did. I got up. I made a schedule. I used to cook for the week. I was going to school and raising the kids at the same time. I studied when I had to. I did not like exams. I had to learn how to answer questions and write a theme. I knew that I could do it. And I liked the idea of being with the young kids." She did successfully complete the requirements and receive her GED. It was an important milestone but just the beginning. In the years ahead, she would complete a four-year college degree and work with pre-school children, first as an assistant and then as the head teacher.

The importance of her friends was crucial to Pearl during these years. "It was my friends who brought me through. Since my family was scattered and far away geographically, my friends were very important to me. Always have been. I feel badly that a lot of my problems and pains were transferred to my friends." The most serious problem Pearl and Harry faced grew worse during Arnold's teenage years. Pearl describes him as "a good, kind boy, but very troubled and disturbed." They consulted with doctors and counselors, but his depressed behavior became more pronounced. He was diagnosed as "being disturbed", but anti-depressant drugs were not in use at that time. Arnold attempted suicide several times, putting plastic over his head once and trying to set his pajamas on fire another time. Pearl and Jay found him each time. The effects upon Jay, of course, were profound as they were for Pearl as well.

Pearl continues talking with great difficulty. "We took him to counselors for years. His teachers would say, 'He's so smart, but we can't get him in the right direction.' He had us and he loved us, but his father kept showing up. And he had his father's last name, Dayan. It was very confusing for him. He was worried he would be taken out of our home. And physically, he wasn't growing right. He was worried all the time."

A family decision was made that Arnold would spend the summer with his oldest brother Victor and his family in California. Pearl goes on, "We had to separate the children and that was hard. It was hardest on Jay. His colitis became severe and we had to take him to Children's Hospital. The doctor told us that with Harry away a lot, it was becoming too hard for me to cope by myself." After living with Victor for a time, Arnold moved out to be on his own and tried to continue in school. He hitchhiked home the summer he was nineteen. "He only stayed for a brief time. He left as quickly as he came. And when he got back to California, he checked himself into a mental hospital because he felt he needed help. He wrote us from the hospital." A week and a half after he was discharged from the hospital, Arnold Dayan took his own life.

Pearl sighs deeply as she shares this tragedy. "Victor called me. They found him in his apartment. We flew out to California. It was worse than anything that had ever happened. With my mother's death, I lost so much of a mother. But she was so ill — it was a relief to know she wasn't suffering anymore. With Arnie, he had his whole life ahead of him. He was only nineteen years old. That really hit me hard. And I felt I had not fulfilled my mother's wishes. We lost him. When we got home, I was alone a lot. I would walk back and forth in my house. It was November and it was dreary. I couldn't concentrate. My head was spinning. From that day on, it was six years before I entertained in my house. I had no heart for it." When they found Arnold in his sleeping bag, he had letters to Pearl and Harry and from them in his hands. And he had left poems that Victor found and copied and sent to Pearl. She comments very sadly that Cecile and Jay were both deeply affected by Arnold's death with reverberations to the present day.

In 1969, Pearl went back to Atlantic Community College and took a psychology course with Dr. Gino Baruffi. During a lecture on suicide, Pearl couldn't stay in the room and waited outside until the class was over to talk with him. He became a friend and a counselor to Pearl during this stressful time. She speaks of him with the highest regard. After she received her Associate Degree, she went on to Glassboro, a four-year college. Pearl had been teaching in a pre-school program as an aide. Then she became a head teacher at Friend's School. She liked working with the young children. Her mood lightens as she says, "They were so honest and open. You're not dealing with lies. This is it. They're real. I had my hair cut and asked them if they liked it and they said 'No!' It was refreshing to work with them." Pearl also wanted to work with children with big problems. "I had a need to take care of these kids. And I worked hard at it."

She took on a very demanding schedule with the three- to five-year-olds, teaching two different groups; the morning and afternoon sessions. She also drove children to school to raise extra money. "Preschool is very physical. You have be on your toes running after the children. You feel the responsibility for their safety. The class size ran from 12 to 15, and if you had one who is a problem, it's like having four extra in the class. When I came home, I was very tired. Exhausted! And then I had the meals to prepare." Pearl chuckles as she recalls how she became the head teacher at the Friends' School. "I got that job in one day, because they were desperate!" When the school closed, she moved to a private religious academy where she taught for ten years until 1983. Pearl took courses at Glassboro while she was teaching, including some night classes. She found the driving hard, but she persevered. In 1983, she left her position and enrolled full time at the college to complete her degree. She had never forgotten her promise to her mother.

Jay and Jeffrey had been graduated from college and Pearl had more freedom and less family responsibility. She took a clerical position with South Jersey Airways because of the 'perks'. "I wanted to travel! And we did. We went on our only cruise. And we visited my family too in different parts of the country." Harry had stopped flying. He had worked at Wheaton's Glass for years and moved up to a managerial level. He also became a partner in a small hobby shop, growing out of his interest in model trains. Their financial situation had improved considerably. Pearl laughs as she says, "Those were the happiest times!" And they took many trips in the years that followed.

Pearl has always been active in her community. In addition to working in many activities in her synagogue, she has taken the literacy course to tutor students one-on-one in English as a second language. All this work is done on a volunteer basis. She coordinates a group of women who cook and deliver meals to people who are ill or in a period of bereavement. She dons her apron and does the cooking as well. And, according to the Jewish tradition, she washes and dresses the body of a woman who has died and sits with the deceased for a proscribed period of time. This difficult endeavor is a 'mitzvot' — an act of goodness. Her family and friends confirm that her response to others is always to help and give of herself in their time of need.

Margaret, Pearl's sister-in-law, writes in the memoir, "Pearl is best known for her love of family. She is ready at the quick to attend a wedding, a bar or bat mitzvah or sadly at times a funeral. When she arrives, if help is needed in the kitchen, she whips up the Syrian delicacies for which she is famous. Nieces and nephews love to visit their home and come often to celebrate the holidays. It is their home away from home."

Jay Mizrahi married Cheryl Laco in 1984 and their son Daniel was born July 3, l985. He is Pearl and Harry's only grandson and they have nurtured him in many ways since he was a small boy. For years, he spent the Sabbath eve with them and that was a very special time of sharing. He spent vacations with them when his parents went on trips. Pearl speaks of him and his many achievements in school and in the sports world with great pride and love. Jeffrey, their younger son, who lives in Boston, also wrote in the family memoir. "My mother believes we must strive to learn. She is dynamic and thoughtful, remembers what is important in the lives of others — a birthday, an anniversary, a new baby, a departed loved one. My mother stressed to us the importance of giving to those who are less fortunate."

Fate was to intervene again on January 30, 1992. Pearl and Harry were in California visiting her brother Victor and sister-in-law Margaret. They were

driving in a car with a friend, Claire, at the wheel. It was 8:30 at night —
twilight. "We were stopped at a red light waiting to make a turn to the left.
I was sitting next to Claire and wearing my seat belt. The light changed and
a car came that was down at the bottom of the hill. Claire started to turn and
he hit us full force on the right side of the car."

When asked if this was like the first accident for her, she says, "No, this
was very different from the first accident. I was aware of everything
happening around me, but I didn't know what. I heard things. And I saw
flashes of light. It was total chaos in my head! Everything around me was
spinning!" Pearl was thrown forward into the windshield and the entire top
of her head was pulled back, what the surgeons later called 'de-gloved'. She
had to be freed by the Jaws of Life from the wreckage of the car. Neither
Claire nor Harry, who was in the back of the car, were injured.

"I heard the whirring of the helicopter. I was in shock, I guess. I was so
cold. God, you feel cold! *Please just make me warm. Make me warm*! They
kept talking to me in the helicopter to make sure I stayed conscious. They
asked me my name and how old I was." Now, Pearl laughs heartily as she
continues, "And then I said, 'Oh, I always wanted to go for a ride in a
helicopter!' and they all laughed. I was in and out after that. I felt them
wrapping me. I don't remember arriving at the hospital, a special trauma unit.
I felt those men saved my life. I was bleeding heavily. They were quick.
Efficient. It was almost like a movie — but it was happening to me."

Pearl was very badly injured and listed in critical condition. But the
internal injuries were not as severe as in the first accident. She suffered
broken bones, the fibia and tibia in both legs. The bone directly below one
hip was shattered completely and had to be wired together or she would have
lost her leg. A long metal bar was inserted as well as clamps. One ankle was
badly smashed and one hand had serious damage to the ligaments. And, of
course, there was the major surgery to repair her scalp and forehead. It was
to be almost four months before she would return to her home. She would
spend weeks in three different hospitals for recovery and rehabilitation.
Harry would fly back and forth to be with her as he had 34 years earlier.

Pearl remembers the day when it hit her hard that it was all happening
again. "It was the day my friend Ed came to see me. He had been the postman
in the Florida hospital and he now lived in California. In fact, Harry and I
had lunch with him and his wife a few days before the accident. They called
Ed and he came to visit. He turned white when he saw me and he sat in a
chair and passed out — literally!"

It's hard to believe that Pearl is laughing as she describes the pictures that
were taken and how she looked with the myriad tubes and the casts and the

bandages. However, once she was moved from the ICU, she relates that she felt apprehensive about how long it would take until she could go home. She speaks very highly of the people in the rehabilitation unit. "They taught me how to walk. First, I had to crawl because I couldn't use my legs. And it was scary! They would put me on a mat and say, 'Crawl!' The most important thing was to develop my arms so they would be strong. They told me it would be difficult because I had weakness in my legs from before. But they never said I wouldn't walk again."

Pearl and Harry flew home, where she was confined to her bed for many months and pursued therapy for her hand to successfully avoid an operation. She spent months as an out patient at a local rehabilitation center and counts her recovery as taking the full eight years since 1992. She was in a wheelchair first, then crutches and a walker. She still uses a cane to assist her in maintaining her balance when she walks. One leg was left shorter than the other as a result of the injuries and she wears special shoes with a lift on one. She adds, "It was only three months ago that I could walk down the steps using two legs. But I want you to know that I danced at Daniel's bar mitzvah! It was in 1998 and I had a wonderful time!"

Pearl has had eight operations since she left the hospital in 1992, including lung surgery and taking the metal bars out of her legs. She also underwent plastic surgery to remove the scars on her face and calls it "the worst thing I ever did!" The surgeon wanted to operate on her reconstructed nose as well and Pearl calls it "a disaster". Her breathing has been impaired and a follow-up attempt by another surgeon to repair the damage was unsuccessful. She says with great regret, "I should never have let him touch my nose!" Pearl perseveres with exercise, walking and doing therapy in a pool when possible. And she and Harry started to travel again, taking their first trip to Europe in 1997. They visited Pearl's niece in Rome and then drove north to stay with friends in a villa they had rented in Tuscany. Pearl's face lights up as she talks about the decision to go. "That was my great trip! It was good. And that was before the leg surgery. I said to myself, *What the heck. How much can I hurt? I'm going!* And I did go."

And then, she laughs deeply as she tells how she climbed the steep path up to Orvieto, one of the famous hill towns. "We didn't know that we could park the car at the top. It was a mile and a half, we found out later. And I'm going up with my cane and I'm saying to Harry, 'I don't know if I'm going to be able to do this, Honey'. I had walked around Rome, where it was flat and I didn't have any problems. Then we reached the halfway point and saw cars parked! Now I'm really dragging and Harry is pushing me and pulling me. But we got to the top! I did it! I loved Italy. We went to Siena and

Firenze and toured the museums. We sat in the famous squares and watched the people. We ate that delicious food. And we shared all this with our dear friends. It was a marvelous vacation!"

When Pearl is asked, "How do you feel about yourself?" she replies, "I don't know. I've made a lot of errors. I didn't do it on purpose. I think I took on more than I could chew and didn't realize it. And I do good things and I know it is beneficial to me as well. My mother was a helper and I think that is imbedded in me. Does that make me a good person? I don't know. I think I have done almost the best that I could have done. Would I have done the same things again? Yes. Absolutely! I think I made decisions not always with my mind but with my heart. And that may not have been the best decision. But you don't know until the future whether it was good or not. I do know that I am strong—with what I have overcome." Pearl considers herself a religious person. "Probably. I enjoy practicing our faith, Judaism. I think it's a very fair religion with its humanistic emphasis on reaching out to care for other people. If someone is bleeding, you help!"

Pearl loves to cook and experiment with new dishes. She recalls how she grew up in a kitchen where her mother cooked for ten people and numerous other guests. She roars with delight as she recounts how Harry is a good sport when she produces new culinary creations. "He doesn't want to hurt my feelings. He's so good about this. And I'll say, 'If you don't like it, just tell me! But he doesn't.'" Her favorites, her passion, are the Syrian dishes that she and Harry do love. Another special activity for Pearl is her newfound proficiency on the computer. Originally, she learned in order to build an expanded recipe file, but now she has branched out in many directions. Most important, she sends and receives e-mail messages that link her to her relatives across the country. This has given her an additional way to further her ties to her extended family.

As Pearl has told her story, her husband's character and strengths have also been brought to light. She shares her picture of him. "Harry is a man who is very happy with his life. He is compassionate. He is very stubborn about things he believes in. He has set ideas about a lot of things. In terms of the differences between men and women, he is a definite man. He doesn't ask for directions! Harry is 78 years old. And he can still fit into his uniform from World War II — except for the hat. He has always kept trim. And, so very important to me, Harry has always encouraged me. He encouraged me to go back to school. He encouraged me to drive in a car again after the first and the second accidents. He encouraged me to overcome my fear and drive a car again. He has always been there for me." Jeffrey writes of his father in the family memoir, "Quiet and peaceful, Dad works hard to provide for his family, without complaint and comes home with a smile. He has taught me to be grateful, to count and remember my blessings. He always said, 'Give a man a chance to be true to his word and don't stand in judgement of him.'"

Pearl and Harry celebrated their fiftieth wedding anniversary on April 28, 1999. She has told her story and of their years together. Asked about the future, she replies, "I don't think about the future. I take every day as it comes and I deal with it. And that's it!" Perhaps, her response is not surprising, based on the events that have happened over the past years. And the mountains she has climbed to reach today.

As an afterthought, Pearl shares a special way she has helped herself come through some of the bad times. She calls it 'finding a safe place'. "I learned this from one of the therapists — using imagery. And when I was going in for one of the big operations I used it for the first time. My wheelchair was facing the wall and no one was around. I felt very isolated and lonely. I didn't know the operating room was right across the way. I just knew I was alone. So, I looked for a safe place. I imagined I was in a boat in the water with people I love, Harry and my brother Maurice and his wife Sissie. And Ed, my friend, was driving the boat. I was with people who loved me and cared about me. And then, I began to feel better. I wasn't lonely anymore. I had found my safe place."

Chapter II
Tung-yuan's Story

"You have your brush and colors.
Paint Paradise and in you go!"
— Nikos Kazantzakis

Tung-yuan Chin was born into an aristocratic Chinese family in Manchuria on October 10, 1920. She was one of twelve children, each of whom had a special nurse or amah. Her childhood, teenage years and early adulthood took place against a backdrop of political upheaval and enormous changes in China. During our interviews, she talks about her life and how it was affected by the historic events of those years. She speaks of a different and fascinating world.

Each time we meet, Tung, as she is called, greets me graciously with a warm smile. She is a petite woman filled with energy. Her home is in Boston near one of her daughters and she visits with each of her other three daughters and her son periodically. Her oldest daughter lives in New Jersey in a beautiful lakefront home where the interviews take place. We are seated in the living room, where one of Tung's fine Chinese water colors hangs on the far wall. She is wearing a wine knit dress and small black Tahitian pearl earrings. Her short black hair is accented with streaks of grey. She seems eager to begin. As she recalls her earliest memories from childhood, her dark eyes are luminous. She speaks slowly with deliberate emphasis and tone.

"We lived in a big compound with houses and square courtyards and gardens. A high wall ran around the compound and during the night we had watchers outside to make sure we were safe. It was an old tradition for landed families to hire these guards. We were in between a large city and the Army camp of Chaing Kai-shek's soldiers. This was the time when the Japanese were moving into Manchuria. I was in elementary school. There was no limitation on age and I had started very early, before I was five years old in the same class as my older brother. And I still remember one night, when I was about ten, that we came home from a play about nine o'clock. Then in the middle of the night, we heard the bong! bong! bong! The watchers were warning us of trouble. In the morning, we learned the Japanese had overwhelmed Chaing's soldiers and taken over our entire area in one night!"

It is not surprising that this frightening night is the first memory Tung shares. The Japanese occupation of Manchuria in 1931 was to affect every member of her family in the years ahead. She also tells of the earlier years living in the compound with her brothers and sisters. "I lived in a small two-room house with my amah. I liked living apart. My sisters and brothers lived in other houses with their amahs. Some of them slept in bunk beds. There were originally six boys and six girls, but one brother died as an infant." Tung was number five in the birth order, "right in the middle." Most of the days in early childhood were spent with the amahs, including meals. "We did not see our parents that much. It did not seem strange to us. We played with each other in the courtyards. Games children play. Girls skipping rope. Boys playing basketball. We had fun together. There were so many of us. And, of course, there were musical instruments at home. Once we started school, there was serious reading and study." Now, Tung laughs, "I'm not so humble. I loved to study and in the family, they called me a 'bookworm'!"

Tung has strong memories of her grandparents. "My mother's parents lived in the country side and would come to visit and stay for long periods of time. There were bandits roaming around at that time. It was not safe. It was dangerous. Lots of trouble! My father's father, I never met. He worked for the royal court and was Governor of a province at the end of the Ching Dynasty. I was told he lived in a fortress. This was in the early 1900s, before the time of Sun Yat-sen." Known as the 'father of the revolution' of 1911, Sun Yat-sen founded the Kuomintang Chinese Republic. He was a statesman as well as a revolutionary leader and changed China forever. Tung was born the year Sun Yat-sen died, in 1920. During her childhood, his successor, Chaing Kai-shek, assumed the leadership of the government and led a civil war against the fast growing Communist movement. This internal turmoil stretched from 1927 to 1936, when the two factions joined forces in opposition to the invading Japanese. Tung was seventeen when the official outbreak of hostilities was declared between China and Japan in 1937.

Tung describes her parents with respect and deference. "My mother was pure Manchurian. There are six variations and she is pure. She was very petite and elegant. She wore very beautiful jewelry; jade bracelets and earrings and necklaces. And silk tunics in all the lovely colors. She had been married in a traditional ceremony and wore the red embroidered silk that was the custom. Her dowry of linens and silks was so large that some of the pieces were never used in the years to come. My oldest daughter is told that she looks like her. My father was tall with high cheekbones. And, of course, a full head of hair, as Chinese men are not usually bald. He was not home too much since he worked for the government. My mother was in charge of the household."

Tung recalls the year she was ill and out of school, studying at home. She attended the provincial girls school and says, "My hair was all gone and I didn't want to go to school. Younger girls wore pigtails. But in high school, we would put it up in the back in a bun. I was sick during the eighth grade and I learned by myself at home. There was no tutor. I had been skipped in an earlier year and I was younger than the other girls in my grade. It was a very hard year for me."

High school years for Tung were concentrated on her studies. The curriculum covered history, science, mathematics and language. She began to learn English in junior high school as well. This was the time when the civil war was raging across China between Chaing's soldiers and the growing number of Communists. She and her brothers and sisters lived at home and attended high schools in the province. The family remained in a fairly secure position based on their wealth and influence. They were away from the cities and still secure in their walled compound. Her father had escaped to Nanking since it would not have been safe for him to remain at home. Tung tells how she looked ahead to continuing her education after high school. "In Japan, where some of the wealthy Chinese had sent their sons, there were no girls in the university. So, I left home to go to college in China where girls attended the university. But I did not go alone. I left Manchuria with my third older brother to go to college in Nanking, which was in central China. I was only sixteen."

In order to enter college, Tung had to take the national entrance exam. She laughs and says, "I'm so lucky that I got in. The national examination was very hard. I'm not so humble. But I got in! But the Sino-Japanese War had started. And before I had finished my freshman year, the whole Northeast University had to leave. We all went to Xian. The war was very bad! The Japanese were moving in. Then we moved again to the west to Sze-Chuan." Tung felt torn when she left for college. "I missed my home and my mother and father a lot. I was on my own for the first time. There was no going home for a visit. It was too dangerous to travel. And no letters could be written. And no telephone. I was worried about my mother. She really hated the Japanese! But we knew officials and she was safe in the compound. At the college, I lived in a dormitory and it was very comfortable at first.

Two people in a big room. But later when other universities also moved to escape the Japanese, more students came and squeezed in with us. After a while there were six girls in the same room in double bunks!"

Tung's major course of study in college was economics. She also learned standard and professional English in the four-year program. And she met Chang Ming Chin, a fellow student who was to become her husband. When she talks about how she met him, she laughs. "It was half and half arranged. Chang came from a scholarly family. His father was a famous historian who taught at the University of Beijing. And in China, the scholars are considered of the highest status in the society. Some of his father's books have been translated and are used today as references at Harvard, Yale and other universities in the United States." Tung laughs heartily as she relates what she thought at her first meeting with Chang. "It was half a family match. And half, we were school mates. My brother and uncle were in Japan and his family was in Japan and they knew each other. But, no I did not like him immediately. It was during the war and the family wanted the girls to be married and settled and safer. Chang was very intelligent. He had been in Japan before war and he was able to leave and come home to China by way of Hong Kong. It was a very hard trip. And once here, his father wanted him to go to college and, of course, he did."

"Chang had been in engineering school in Japan. Now the government in China brought the engineering school together with the national colleges to consolidate and meet their budget. So Chang and I were students in the same overall university. There was the medical school and the law school too. All together at that time." She describes their courtship. "We went out with other students. Sometimes to the theater. And we got to know each other. After our junior year, several years later, we were married. It was 1940, during the war, and we had a very small wedding. Just classmates and a few relatives. My parents were not there. My mother was still in Manchuria. And Chang's father was away on an important university appointment. I was twenty years old and Chang was twenty-two. It was not a big traditional Chinese wedding. Just modern clothes. Very simple. And we were to live in my father-in-law's house while we continued our schooling." Tung pauses before she responds to a rather personal question, "What did you think marriage was going to be like?" And then she breaks into her deep laugh again. "I don't know! I don't know! I guess I was very innocent. I didn't know what to expect."

During this time, the Communists were building their movement in the country and in the colleges. Tung and Chang did not become involved at their school. "We were not interested in politics. Some classmates became part of it. But we stayed with our studies. And our feelings were concentrated

38

on the Japanese. That was our main concern." After graduation, Chang became an instructor of architecture and design at Chunking University. Tung was also graduated and they moved to the faculty dormitory. Their first child, a daughter named Sha, was born the next year. Tung looks back at how she felt on becoming a new mother. "I don't know! I was twenty-one. I didn't know how to take care of her. When the baby was sick, I didn't know what to do. But there was a maid in my in-law's house. And this was a big help. And I learned how to take care of her."

After the war was over in 1945, Tung and Chang took the baby and went with a group of friends to travel around the countryside. "We wanted to go with the young people. It was curiosity. An adventure! To Xian and other places. My father-in-law had flight tickets but we wanted to go on our own. We had a lot of fun! The baby was little, about two years old, and the only child in the group. We went by bus and truck and then finally by train. Stayed in little inns. It was a real adventure! And at times, we had to hide from the Communist guerillas. It was like the time when we had to hide from the Japanese bombing when I was a student in Chunking. Then we went into the bomb shelters. Now we hid in the little inns or in a tunnel, wherever we could take cover to be safe. Finally, we left the group and made our way by train to where my family's house was in Manchuria. I remember that night so well. I had my little girl with me and it was dark when I came to the street to find my house. I saw short walls, not high walls and said, 'This is not my house. Why are the walls shorter? This is not my house!' I went to the neighbor and she said, 'Is your last name Su? That's your house!' Then I knocked on the door and a woman came to the door, looked at me and asked, 'Who are you looking for?' It was my mother! She did not recognize me and I did not recognize her. It was ten years since we had seen each other!"

Later Tung learned why the walls appeared shorter to her. During the war, to be safe from the Japanese bombings, a tunnel had been dug inside the compound and the dirt piled up outside against the walls. On the inside, the walls were still tall, but Tung was correct that the walls were indeed "shorter" when she saw them for the first time in ten years that night. Since she had left home at sixteen, she had earned her college degree, met and married her husband and become the mother of a little girl. "Much had happened to me since I had last seen my mother."

Tung's father was in Xian with his work and they went to see him as well. They lived in the compound for several months. Then they moved to Beijing since Chang was teaching in the Northeast University. The Communists were gaining control of the country at this time. In 1949, Mao Tse-tung established the Central People's Government. Chang and Tung Chin made the enormous decision to leave the mainland and move to Taiwan. They did not see their future at home any longer. Both sets of parents remained in China. They would never see each other again.

Tung tells how it happened. "Chang went first to find a teaching position. Then I brought my daughter to Taiwan. Our parents stayed in China. They were too tired to leave. From the many years of civil war and from World War II. But we wanted to escape from the Communists. And our parents said, 'You young people go!' And we left." Tung speaks of their life in Taiwan. "It was so poor. The Japanese had occupied Taiwan and taken the best from the island. They took everything to Japan. We could not get milk. We had to buy the powdered milk. We lived in a house on the campus of the university and I had a cleaning lady. And when I had my babies, three more daughters and one son, I had a full time maid. My husband was teaching architecture but the professor's pay was very low. I had to sell some of my jewelry for extra money. My days were spent taking care of the children and running the house. It was hard at the beginning to adjust to taking care of the house and the children. But after a while, I became used to it. We lived there for eleven years. And I did miss China." In Taiwan, Tung explains, the spoken language was different. Pronunciation is different for all the Chinese dialects and understanding the Taiwanese dialect was another hurdle she had to overcome. At the beginning, she spoke some Japanese, which the Taiwanese people had learned from the years of occupation. She notes that the written language was the same.

The next major step for the Chin family came when she and her husband decided to leave Taiwan and emigrate to the United States. It was in the early 1960s. The children were seventeen, eleven, ten, seven and two years old. Chang was able to secure a teaching position in architecture at The Virginia Polytechnic Institute. "My husband wanted more Western knowledge and he wanted to do research in the United States. His position was to be part research and part teaching. Again the adjustment at the beginning was very hard. Especially the communication with the people. Of course, I had studied English in school but it was not the same. I had no chance to speak in those years." Now Tung laughs, "Sometimes, I forgot my own name!" She says that the children picked up the language very fast. She worked as an assistant at the elementary school to facilitate the transition for the children. She would take her two-year-old son with her and he would sit at the table in the library or the cafeteria with his crayons while she helped the teachers. "I enjoyed this work. It was a lot of fun! And during the lunch time I helped the teacher watch the children. I learned something too."

The Chins rented a house and Chang stayed in this position for about two and a half years. Then they chose a location to move to and bought a larger house. "We have to consider the schools and this location had very good schools. That was the main reason we bought the house there." Tung had no maid to help her in Virginia. "I was so busy! And no help as I had in Taiwan. Five children. Seven people. Cooking and shopping. And taking care of the household. It was hard. A big adjustment again. My husband had a car but I did not drive at that time. Sometimes my husband helped with the food shopping and we went together. I was so busy! No extra hands to help." Tung was fortunate in having neighbors next door who were both friendly and helpful. She laughs when she recalls that her neighbor was visiting one day and discovered Tung at the ironing board. "With seven people to take care of, you don't have to be ironing sheets!" Tung adds, "But I still ironed them. I wanted everything to be just right for my family."

Chang left the teaching position after several years and joined an architectural firm, where he was to remain for the rest of his professional career. He became a senior designer with the firm. Tung's daily life continued to focus upon raising her children and running her household.

As Tung talks about their family life, her daughter, Sha, joins us to add her insights to the interview. It becomes clear that Chang was a traditional Chinese father, a strict disciplinarian who expected the best behavior and achievement from his children at all times. His daughter relates that he would say, "If you don't listen, I'll break your leg!" We believed him. We didn't want to take any chances. And we listened!" The Chin children were strong students and usually brought home straight A report cards. Even then, Tung smiles when she notes, "He would say to them, 'So, how many other students in your class had straight A report cards?'" But he also praised them for their accomplishments and always expected them to do well. And he told them stories as he did with his students when he was teaching. Chang was a great storyteller; often his stories had the moral of pursuing education to reach a happy ending.

After dinner in the Chin household, Chang led family discussions. His daughter emphasizes that he was modern in the sense that they were allowed to argue with him and take a different position on politics or religion or philosophy. "In that way, he was liberal. He liked the challenge. He loved to argue and hear our opinions. But he always wanted to win!" Now, she laughs when she adds that it really depended on his mood. "If the cooking was good, his mood was good. And then he loved to argue more!"

Tung served as a buffer when problems arose with the children. She states with great emphasis, "I always told them to come to me and tell me everything. I wanted them to trust me. That they could share whatever they wanted. And if anything was wrong, they should tell me first. Then I would talk to their father about it. We would talk about the day after dinner, but I told them if there was a problem to come to me first. And none of my children were drawn into the drugs that some of the other young people were experimenting with. I am very proud of that. No LSD. No smoking pot. They did none of that! I trusted them." Now, she laughs. "But I tiptoed to check!" She also told them, if there was a B- on their report card, that it was "okay" sometimes. She believed that you could not always push children too hard. And that each one was different from the other as well. "There was a lot of competition among the second, third and fourth daughters. They were very close in age. At times it was good. Not always. But all the children concentrated on their studies and were strong students."

Tung explains that she and the other members of the family became United States citizens at different times. "I think our family did this one by one. The children, until they grew up, they decided for themselves. My oldest daughter was the first one. When she married, her husband was in the Army and they were stationed overseas. And she had to be a citizen to get a passport to travel with him. The second daughter became a citizen next; she needed it for her job. I was the third one and became a citizen in 1977. The mainland of China was now open and we could go home to visit. Of course, we needed the passport. Therefore we needed to become citizens. My husband and my son were next. When my son went to the university, at that time they applied together. We all became citizens in Virginia.

"It was important to us to become citizens. We had learned the culture. And the language. We did not apply right away. I think it was at least five years after you come, you become a permanent resident. My husband had a special code as a permanent resident. I do think people should know the culture before they become citizens." Tung smiles, "I had to decide if I wanted to be a citizen. We learned different knowledge. And told the children they had the freedom to decide for themselves. There was freedom in the United States and Communism in China!"

Tung also shares some aspects of family life at home before the children left for college. When asked if she was a good cook, she breaks into gales of laughter. "I feel very bad. I am not a good cook. My husband was a good cook. But the children and all the family were not hungry to death! After we came to the United States, my husband had no time for cooking. The architecture department is very demanding. Not like other departments. The students have the projects with the time limits. Sometimes they work through the night to finish the design. And often, he stayed with his students all night. And when he joined the firm, he would often work during the weekend since he was the senior designer."

"My interests always were in reading, especially in classical Chinese literature. But there was very little time for reading or music or painting in the days before the children went to college. When that time came, I had more time for the other interests in my life." Tung does share the love she had of gardening when she lived in Virginia, with natural perennial flowers, daffodils and deep orange day lilies that spread through the large yard every spring.

The importance of education runs as a strong connecting thread throughout her life. First for Tung herself in her childhood and school years. Learning was always of the highest importance to her. "I loved to read!" From her earliest days, when her siblings teased her as the 'bookworm', to her college years, when she tackled and mastered the daunting major of economics. Then she married into the Chin family, where the main endeavor was one of scholarly pursuits. As she and Chang raised their children, they chose an area to live in based on the quality of the local school system. Then she assisted in the schools to facilitate the transition from the language and customs of Taiwan to their new life in the United States. And their mastery of the English language. Finally, they encouraged their children to follow their education to the highest possible levels and graduate degrees. "Some reached the Ph.D. degrees and we said, 'Go to the post doctoral level!'" Tung is very animated when she speaks about education and love of learning being at the the core of her family history. She emphasizes that it was the number one value they transmitted to their children.

One of the deepest interests that Tung turned to when her children left for college was Chinese painting and calligraphy. She describes her style as "a combination of traditional and contemporary. I use water colors and black ink. I tell you the truth — I did not learn it. I taught myself. I paint scenes from nature; birds, flowers, trees. And I have given many of my paintings to my children. They hang in their houses. When I paint, I get the inspiration first." She smiles sweetly and makes a graceful wave of her hand to her head. "In Chinese painting, you do not do a sketch first. You just use a brush and paint. You cannot correct it. It has to be right the first time. I love to paint!" Tung had two shows of her paintings in Boston a few years ago. One of her paintings is hanging in her daughter's living room. The subject is of gourds hanging from a tree, brushed in varied watercolors that contrast with the black ink calligraphy running vertically along the right hand side. The painting is both soft and striking, and very beautiful. When she receives a compliment, Tung, is very modest and laughs gently.

With a little urging, she shares insights into Chinese painting and her work. "I mix my colors first and, of course, we use the rice paper which absorbs the paint immediately." She gestures to the painting on the wall. "This was done from memory of a scene on my grandmother's farm in the countryside. It is autumn and the yellow gourds are hanging among the leaves and twisted vines on the tree. Notice that there are many shades of green and some black over the green of the leaves. And the veins on the leaves are painted when the under color is almost dry. I must paint fast. I touch my brush first with one side and then with the other. And the gourds are done with shades of yellow and some red and brown to highlight. There are many colors here. The calligraphy is the title or legend of a painting. This calligraphy translates to 'During the autumn time is the farmer's pleasure. Everything is ready for the harvest' And below that is my signature or painter's name. In Chinese painting, the painter has a separate name. Mine is Sin Ying — the closest translation would be 'Intelligence shines through'. And there is a stamp below it, in this case in red ink, that is made by the carved ivory or stone 'chop'. That is part of my signature as well."

Tung became a widow in 1983 and she speaks of that time in a calm, soft voice. "My husband died after an illness. We had been married for a long time, 43 years. It was a very hard time for me. I was only twenty years old when we married and that was my whole life with Chang for 43 years. First in China. Then the years in Taiwan. And, finally we came here and spent all our years here. Raised the children together and saw them off to their colleges. Three years after my husband died, our son graduated from college and went on to his graduate degree. After my husband died, I moved to Boston and lived near one of my daughters."

Since that time, Tung has led a very active life. "My life. I never just sit and do nothing! I enjoy the classical Chinese literature. I have time to read my books now. Of course, my painting is very important to me. And I travel. I travel a lot. Mostly with my children. They go to Europe or Asia and I go with them. And two times I traveled with my friends. One time on a cruise to Alaska and the other time a cruise in the Mediterranean to Turkey, Greece and Italy. We returned from Rome. And I visited my son in Switzerland. Oh, I liked Venice so much and Austria and France. I've been there a few times. I love the countryside in France and the French people are so nice to meet. We rented a small house in Provence for some weeks one year." Tung does not paint on her trips. "No. Chinese painting requires a lot of equipment. It would be very hard to take what I would need with me when I travel."

Tung also goes back to China often. "Sometimes, once a year; other times less often. I go back to visit my relatives. At the beginning, I felt very bad about their lives under the Communists. Now, they live much better. Since about 1985 things have improved and they are more comfortable. When I went back to find my mother's house, I found that the house was completely torn down! All the houses on the street were torn down. There was also the incident of the history that was written by my father-in-law, Chang's father. He had worked for the Kuomintang government under Chaing Kai-shek, but never joined the party. And he worked for the Communist government and never joined the party either! He was always a scholar and a historian doing his research. He was not a part of the political party in power."

"He taught at Beijing University. He wrote a history in ten volumes. It is translated and used as a reference at universities in this country. My in-laws' house had been sold in Beijing but the deed is missing. When I was in China, I wanted copies of the history, the set of ten books, for each of my children. The officials said they could not mail it to my five children. It would be too much money. And I said, 'You have to! Because we had a contract. We paid the money for the house and now I have no house. I want the books!' Finally, they said they would send them. But they only shipped one set. We are still waiting for the others! We have been waiting for three years!"

Since Tung was born in 1920, the Millennium year of 2000 would mark her 80th birthday. Her children decided to surprise her with a party in advance in July of 1999. The party was planned at the Connecticut home of one of her daughters and an elaborate ruse was designed to bring her there the day of the event. "They told me we were going to the Chinese opera in New York. We would drive down from Boston. I said I was not interested in the Chinese opera. I only kept my husband company when we went before. They said the tickets were very hard to get. And very expensive. You have to go! I didn't want to disappoint them. It is part of my personality that it is hard to say no. So I said okay, okay. And that day, my daughter told me I had to wear something very special to the opera. I said, 'It is not so special to see the opera.' But I dressed up a little bit.

"Then, they said we would stop in Connecticut. And we walked into the yard and I saw the big tent. I thought it was for the neighbor. And we have to go to a party! How will we get to the opera in time? Suddenly, I saw all the people. I was in shock! I was so surprised! I saw all my children. And my grandchildren. I saw my husband's students from all over! I almost cried." Tung covers her face with her hands. "I realized all the people were there for me. I was in shock! And then I saw the in-laws from my children's families. There must have been more than seventy people there. And the caterer served beautiful food and wine. Of course, I feel a warm surprise all the time. Even my six-year-old granddaughter who lives very near to me knew and never gave the secret away! She did not tell me! Not one word. And in the car, when I thought I was going to the opera, they kept calling on the car telephone. And saying, 'The traffic is very bad.' But I didn't guess. I thought they were talking about being late for the opera. It was a wonderful day!"

Tung has ten grandchildren and often travels to visit with each family. The youngest in Ohio is two years old. The two oldest grandchildren are in their twenties, already graduated from college and pursuing their respective careers in design and management. She speaks of all of them with great warmth and pride. Tung also shares that she is optimistic about the future. "Yes, I am optimistic. The children all have good lives. They are independent and stable. All the family, they have followed in their ancestors' steps. To get a good education. And the grandchildren too. They all work hard and are doing well. The grandchildren, everybody behave. I don't have to worry a lot. So far, so good!"

Tung becomes very animated when the subject turns to what her passions are in life. "Art is my passion! Nobody push me. That's my interest. I love it! Sometimes I feel the inspiration to paint immediately. If the inspiration is not there, I do not paint. And I go to the museums in Boston all the time. I take all our visitors first to the Art Museums. You know Boston is a fine cultural city. In 1985, there was a special Chinese exhibition at the Boston Science Museum and I served as an interpreter. There were traditional woven tapestries and embroidered silks. They were the finest examples and very beautiful. Some of the panels were embroidered on both sides in lovely colors, most unusual and mounted on moveable frames to be seen from the front and the back. Other displays were of pottery and clothing. There was also a booth where acupuncture was explained and demonstrated. This was a great hit with the visitors!"

When Tung looks back over her life, she says forcefully, "I have no regrets! In my whole life, being in the United States is the largest time. I have lived in different places and met so many interesting people. And the people where I live now are good neighbors and friends. Most of the people are Jewish and very warm. At least once a year, we get together. We have a block party and we go from house to house for courses of the dinner. It is very enjoyable."

She pauses and then reflects upon the sweep of years and events that served as the background of her own life. Her voice is clear, almost buoyant. "I feel very good. In my whole life, you can say, I go through! The years of terrible civil war in China — I go through! World War II — I go through! And living those hard years in Taiwan. Then coming to the United States. To this wonderful country. Raising my children. And they are all fine and accomplished. You know, I am very proud. I go through!"

CHAPTER III
RUTH'S STORY

Ode To Ruth

I cannot say I am your best friend;
you are your own best friend
and you have others before me.
I cannot say I'm your child alone
because you have others beside me.
I cannot say you love only me
because you love all things:
people, flowers and abstract art.
You have deep feelings for humanity;
every day you spoke to me of
reaching out to others.
And all of the things I could not see
you showed me in your song.
You put me in a magic circle
and I blossomed like a flower in the
rains of April.
You are a great shepherd in a
world of aimless sheep.
— Anna Frangedis, '75
Task Force/Project Direct

Ruth Stein is very animated as she talks of her past, present and future. Her green eyes are highlighted by just the right amount of shadow and her silver hair is styled in a very short sophisticated boy cut. Handmade silver earrings, bracelets and rings are signature jewelry. She smiles often and laughs easily. At 82, she is accomplished, poised and ready for the next adventure in life. "I want every day to bring something new," she says. "I am happiest when

I am busy and productive." Along the varied paths her life has taken, she has never lost the sense of adventure.

Her mother always insisted, "She sang before she talked!" Ruth Marsha Levaur was born on April 1, 1917. A little twin brother did not survive the birth. She was the youngest of the four children of Louis and Mamie Levaur. Her brothers Samuel and Herman were much older; fourteen and twelve years, while her sister Louise was almost seven when Ruth arrived. She would be called 'Baby Dear' for many years by both parents, and Ruth remembers being embarrassed as she grew into her teens when her friends heard the pet name. Her mother still used this term of endearment even when she became an adult.

By the time Ruth was five, her brothers were off to school and work; she saw them on visits. Most of her time was spent tagging after Lou, who called her "a little brat", and playing with the Lapin kids next door. The family moved to Atlantic City, New Jersey when she was eight and she remembers Lou taking her to the beach, a favorite playground, and to the movies. Ruth loved the movies; Theda Bara and Rudolph Valentino were stars. She also recalls that she thought the actors were behind the screen and would come out after the movie was over. She says Lou told her with big sisterly disdain, "Don't be so dumb!" Being the youngest had its advantages and its putdowns, of course.

Music was an important part of her life from her earliest years. Her mother used to say, "Ruth was always singing." She made her first public appearance at the age of 5, dressed as a little boy singing to a little girl, "Away From You". Her mother made her a costume of "black satin pants and a white ruffly shirt." The family owned a Victrola, and opera recordings with such legendary voices as Enrico Caruso were often playing. Ruth was taken to concerts of classical music presented on The Steel Pier, where she also loved listening to the Creatore Band. They played rousing songs similar to John Philip Sousa. "I was about five and would curl up in one of those big wooden rockers with the cane seats. I told my mother, 'I'll stay right here and you all go see the other shows.' And I did. It was safe to leave a child in those days." Ruth began piano lessons at age eight on the baby grand with Mrs. Adams. About four years later, Mrs. Adams said to her mother, "Do you know that Ruth has a beautiful voice? I think she should have voice lessons."

With her mother as her greatest booster, Ruth began her studies with Mrs. Klara Kase Bowman in Philadelphia. She says with great feeling, "I loved her. She taught me so many things about voice: posture and projection. These lessons were the most important part of my growing up." In school, Ruth belonged to Glee Clubs, singing and traveling across the state. She also sang in quartets; always a mezzo soprano. In the larger groups, she was an alto. In high school, she was a soloist for both Class Night and Graduation. She reflects on these early years about music and the role it has played in her life. She would spend hours each day at the piano and with her voice lessons. "It was a passion for me then — and it is now!"

Ruth and her husband, Walter, live in a fourth-floor ocean front apartment in Margate, New Jersey. They have lived there for over thirty years, enjoying the ever changing seascape of the Atlantic Ocean from their large windows and extended balcony. In the spring, Ruth plants her favorite geraniums, petunias and impatiens in a spectrum of pinks, purples and reds. By summer, the flowers spill over the sides of the terra cotta pots and provide a luxuriant enclave for eating meals, reading or reflecting. Both Ruth and Walter make the most of their space and their world class view of the beach, the ocean and the sky. She remembers her early childhood apartment in Atlantic City with the same setting and expansive view.

Ruth's parents came from very different backgrounds. Her mother, Mamie, was one of the five children of Herman and Louisa Beeckel, an affluent German Lutheran family in Philadelphia. He was a very successful designer of fine mens clothing; an original partner in Hart, Schaffner, Marx and Beeckel. Ruth describes her grandfather as "a man of infinite taste." Mamie, who was her father's favorite child, often took trips with him across the country. Ruth has pictures of her mother as a young woman, wearing beautiful jewelry, a sealskin coat and carrying a chinchilla muff! She remembers going to her grandparents' home when she was only 4 or 5 and seeing the "beautiful things, the china and silver and cut glass vases." This was a household where the dressmaker lived in as well as the other servants. Some of Ruth's earliest memories are of "watching the man go down the street to light the gas lamps. Going to the corner store with a bowl to be filled with scoops of ice cream. And hearing, "Don't open the ice box !" from Mrs. Craig, the housekeeper. "I was scared to death of her!"

Ruth's father, Louis Levaur, was one of nine children in a Russian Jewish family who came to America from the Ukraine in the 1890s. His parents were Samuel and Marsha Levaur; the family came in several shifts, as did many immigrant families of that day. They settled in Pittsburgh, where Samuel opened a jewelry shop. Louis was next to the youngest of the children. Both of her Levaur grandparents died long before Ruth was born. Her middle name was in memory of her grandmother, and her brother Samuel was named for his grandfather. Ruth was the youngest of the Levaur cousins. She rarely saw them, since they lived in Pittsburgh and she grew up in Atlantic City. Sometimes they would come to visit and see the sights at the seashore resort.

Mamie Beeckel and Louis Levaur met at a spa in Mount Clemens, Michigan. They were attracted to each other and, as Ruth relates, "fell in love despite or because of the differences in their families' social positions and religions." When they met, Louis was running a very successful business with one of his brothers, the Globe Stamp Company. A forerunner of today's Green Stamps, they offered premiums to the customers who accumulated their stamps. The premiums were very beautiful objects that people collected for their homes such as imported hand painted, gilt-edged china plates. Ruth has several of them hanging in her living room today. After a year and a half of courtship, Mamie converted to Judaism and they were married in 1904. Ruth showed me the fine tape-lace collar from her mother's exquisite wedding gown. Mamie's parents gave her a diamond pin in the shape of a horseshoe to hold her veil. The couple received beautiful and luxurious gifts, including a magnificent chest of sterling silver service for twelve.

Ruth speaks of her mother lovingly. "She had such manners as if she had gone to finishing school. And she loved beautiful things so...." And then Ruth sighs as she says quietly of her mother, "She did not make a wise marriage." The Globe Stamp Company did not last as a profitable enterprise and the partners lost their sizable investment. Louis Levaur was to pursue different avenues in the years ahead; always a salesman and often traveling away from home. "He was thinking all the time and he always worked for himself," Ruth relates. He created the 'Ruise' Company, named for his two daughters, and had mirrors made, the frames decorated with intricate rosettes made of mirrored pieces. He sold stocks and bonds for a while. Always a salesman. And usually on the road. "He always came home with presents."

The family would take trips on the sleeper train from Pittsburgh to Atlantic City for vacations. Ruth loved these excursions. "I would sit up and wave to other conductors and my mother would say, 'For goodness' sakes, go to sleep. I'm paying for that berth!'" There was a famous horseshoe curve on this route and if they were in the front of the train, she could see the last car as they rounded the turn. Ruth remembers tucking her baby dolls into the hammock in the car; she thought that was supposed to be their bed. On their trips, her mother, who had rheumatic fever as a child, felt better "in the ocean air." She suggested moving to the seashore and Louis agreed. He entered into a venture of selling stock for the Brigantine Hotel and they moved to an apartment facing the ocean in uptown Atlantic City. Whether the climate actually helped Mamie's health was not clear, but once they made the move, they stayed. The stock venture, however, was not a success and Louis felt he never recovered financially from it.

Ruth looks back on her childhood with mixed emotions. There were wonderful times with her friends and there were too many times when her mother was concerned about paying the bills. She would say, "Don't answer the door. We owe the laundryman." Or, "Don't answer the phone today." It is not surprising that Ruth holds ambivalent feelings about her father. And there is no question that she adored her mother, who was always loyal to Louis. There was no disparagement of their father to the children.

Ruth laughs when she remembers the times she had with her friends. She was about ten when the Lapin kids won first prize in the Baby Parade. "Their father had dressed Libby up as a pirate with her baby sister in a trunk covered with gold coins. And the first prize was a pony!" Those were the days when horses and ponies were on the beach for riding. Mr. Lapin made a deal so that the pony would be available for his children and friends for riding on the sands. Every Saturday morning there was horseback riding and Ruth says, "I looked down from the horse and it seemed like nine hundred feet. And then the horse took off for the ocean!" In addition, "My mother bought me tweed jodphurs that itched! I came up with an excuse every Saturday. One complaint after another. 'My throat hurts.' 'My head hurts.' I hated those horses! They smelled!"

A favorite treat happened on Wednesday afternoons. The Apollo Theater on the Boardwalk had all the first run musicals and dramas before they opened on Broadway. Ruth's mother felt it was important that Ruth learn to appreciate the theater. Thus, every week, "She pressed fifty cents into my hot little hand. I sat in the peanut gallery, of course. But after a while people noticed me. I was about ten. And they said, 'Save a seat in the front row for the kid.' So I saw *George White's Scandals* and Helen Hayes as an ingenue in *Coquette*. I would think about how I could stay in the theater until the evening performance. Maybe hide in the Ladies' Room. But then, Mother would come looking for me, saying — 'Where's Baby Dear'!" Ruth loves the theater to this day and credits her mother's wisdom in instilling this at an early age. And then she adds with a teasing lilt, "After a matinee performance, I still think about how to hide and see it again in the evening."

Ruth became a teenager during the Great Depression. Her high school years were centered on studies, singing and working during her junior and senior years as a waitress to add to the family's income. "I watched my father gradually take the sterling silver, fine china, marble figures and cut glass vases down the street to the pawn shop. And my mother's beautiful diamond bar pins disappeared in the same way. Those were very hard times." Ruth recalls sewing up the runners in her stockings to make them last longer. However, the voice lessons in Philadelphia continued with Mrs. Bowman. She did not charge when the money was not there. She told Ruth, "This is my investment in you." As for dating in high school, Ruth says she had little time or interest in boys then. Decades later, several former classmates said, "I was in love with you. But you were too busy doing your school work and singing!" Ruth adds, "I did date. Sure. But the big worry then was whether I would have to kiss them good night!"

By the time Ruth was a senior in high school, she had already been doing some professional singing at the hotels in Atlantic City. She loved it. "My mother always sat in the first row when I performed." Her great desire was to go on to college and study as a music major. But the year was 1935, the depth of the Depression, and this was not to be. The money for tuition and board was not there and the wrenching decision was made that college was not possible. The one thing that Ruth knew she would not do was to "stay in Atlantic City and work in Blatt's Department Store." She tells of how she moved in another direction. "I was always interested in medicine. And that is not unusual, because music and medicine are very compatible. Many community orchestras are made up of doctors and dentists. And they are great supporters of music and the ballet." She had wanted to go to the Temple University Music School. Now she began to investigate schools of Nursing in Philadelphia. She chose the Mount Sinai School, "because they were interested in me as a person. Atlantic City High School had sent my records with all the emphasis on my voice and singing. And when I interviewed at Mt. Sinai, they indicated that music could still be a part of my life while I was in the program. This was the deciding factor."

The three-year nursing program was rigorous and strict. In the dorm by nine p.m., one day off a month, no smoking, and no food in the rooms. Time was on a tight structure: classes, practical work on the floor of the hospital, and homework. "The head nurse didn't like elaborate hairdos. She would say, 'Miss Levaur, you must remove that curl! You must try, my dear. You are such a good student.' Every spare moment, Ruth would rush to Mrs. Bowman for a voice lesson. Then rush back to the hospital, jump into her uniform and appear on the floor. On her day off each month, she would take the ferry to Camden and the train ($1 fare) to Atlantic City to see her mother and dad. And she adds, "I dated a little, but not interns." She found that "Mt. Sinai was proud of my singing. There were holiday programs of the traditional carols. And tickets to the concerts at Robin Hood Dell if it worked in your schedule. And of course, they allowed room for my voice lessons. I never gave up my music!"

While in training, Ruth would listen whenever possible to the Saturday afternoon radio broadcasts of The Metropolitan Opera from New York City. She relates, "Did I ever want to get there. And I did! We had three miserable months at Allentown Hospital for The Mentally Ill. I had saved my pennies from the $5 a month salary we earned at Mt. Sinai. And I finally got a Saturday off. I took the train to New York City. The opera was *Tannhauser*. I sat transfixed in the top tier of seats. The opera ran almost four hours. What an introduction!" Ruth was graduated with her nursing diploma in September of 1938 and awarded the prize in Pediatrics. Only seven of the original class of eighteen made it through the program. She was 21 years old. Fifteen years later, Ruth was to return to Mt. Sinai to give a concert for the Nursing School staff and students. "They were so receptive and happy to have me sing for them. They were so proud."

After graduation, Ruth returned home to Atlantic City to spend some time with her mother and father, who had not been well. She had been offered a position at Mt. Sinai Hospital but she was restless and wanted to try something else. "I was unsure of what I wanted to do next and I went home to talk to my parents." Romance was the farthest thing from her mind. When she walked in the door, her mother embraced her and said happily, "Oh, Baby Dear, we're going to have such a wonderful time with you home. And I must tell you, a young man will be calling you." To which Ruth replied, "Oh, Mother— please, I don't believe you did that!"

"Well", said her mother, "you have to go out with him, even if you only go out with him once. Because his aunt is a very dear friend of mine and if you don't go out with him once, it might break up our bridge game!"

Ruth remembers saying, "Mother, I certainly wouldn't want to do anything as important as that. So, yes, I'll go out with him."

A few hours later, the phone rang and Walter Stein introduced himself and asked, "Are you busy tonight?"

Ruth smiles at her first impression of Walter, "That evening, in came this young man dressed in a black overcoat, a black hat and a cigar a mile long. He looked for all the world like an undertaker. But he was kinda cute. He was tall and slim with beautiful skin and very blondish hair. Just a very good-looking young man. But I was annoyed. My mother making dates for me. It was humiliating!" Her mother told her older sister, Lou, after they left, "Baby Dear will never go out with him again, because Baby Dear hates cigars!" She was, of course, very wrong about that.

The couple went to the movies first to see *Marie Antoinette* and Ruth looked over toward the end of the film to discover that Walter was asleep. She was unaware that he woke every morning at five to go to work and assumed he was bored. After the movie, he announced he was going to take her someplace else. Ruth was becoming interested. "To begin with, he had a car. It was 1938 and everybody didn't have a car. And he had a Buick! So

55

he drove and drove to a place, and I'll never forget it, The Spread Eagle Cafe. And I was very impressed. People began to send wine over and food over. And everyone was saying 'Hello, Walter.' 'How are you, Walter?'" By this time, Ruth admits that she decided Walter was a real winner! On the way home, driving very fast, he was stopped for speeding. For Ruth, this was not a bad sign. "I was very impressed. He has a car and he has money to go eating. And he's a daredevil and isn't this exciting! I'm beginning to like him a lot." At her door, he asked "What are you doing tomorrow night?"

Walter took Ruth to the Penn Atlantic, the next night, a trendy hotel dining room where he ordered crab salad with capers. She laughs, "I always thought capers were when you kicked up your heels in joy." Again, he was greeted by many of the diners and the waiter came over with complimentary drinks. She remembers the evening clearly, "Walter was very sweet and very nice. Not, as we used to say, fresh at all. We talked about his job; at that time he was a purchasing agent at a large restaurant. I told him about my training at Mt. Sinai and went into a long spiel about opera and how I liked it an awful lot. And he said, 'You, know, I bet I could get to like it too.' He held my hand, and I think it was a kissy good night." Then he said, "What are you doing tomorrow night?" All Ruth recalls about the third date, rather than where they went, was what Walter said. "Well, listen. How would you like to marry me?"

And she replied, "Marry you! I don't even know you."

He laughed. "Well, you'll get to know me. You'll love me. Everybody does!"

Ruth was stunned. Next, he asked to see her finger and took out a piece of string to measure it. She thought, *This man is nuts!* When he asked her out for the following night, she declined. She was becoming "a little afraid." Walter persevered, " My birthday's next week and I would like to ask you something. Would you go with me to my mother's for lunch in Philadelphia? And I'm taking my two aunts." Ruth shares that she wasn't too thrilled about that but she agreed. She did not tell her mother later about the proposal and his measuring her finger.

The luncheon at his mother's was lovely in all respects and Ruth liked his mother immediately. His sister Blanche was also there and Ruth sensed "a lot of action and undercurrents in the air." Then his mother produced a diamond ring! "So I looked at that diamond ring. I was 21 and I had been cooped up in that nursing program for three years. This was getting exciting!" Walter then put the ring on her finger — without asking if she agreed. She had never said she would marry him. He just assumed it was a "done deed". And it was. Ruth returned home wearing the ring and told her mother, who promptly "got the vapors" and went right to bed. Ruth told her it was all her doing. If she hadn't made these arrangements with "this lovely young man," it would never have happened. Their courtship had covered less than ten days.

Ruth was slated to take the nursing state boards the end of November and Walter suggested they marry Sunday, November 27. Her parents were very upset at first with the whirlwind courtship, but they liked Walter very much from the outset. They knew his family, and each time he came, he brought lovely gifts; fruit, sweets and once a "great big turkey." Wedding plans were modest Ruth explains, "It was 1938 and nobody had any money. So we decided to marry in the rabbi's study and just the family and a few close friends would come back to my parents' apartment. And that's what we did." Ruth wore a rust three-piece suit with a beaver collar on the full-length coat. Her brother Samuel had sent her a check to choose something special. She carried a bridal bouquet of violets. All went according to plan, except the newlyweds did not count on the blizzard that struck on November 27. They canceled their honeymoon plans of driving to Florida and took a train to New York instead.

They went to the theater and to *Siegfried*, a Wagnerian opera. "A terrible thing to do to him on his honeymoon," Ruth now admits. Walter soon fell asleep and the woman next to her said, "Would you please tell him to stop snoring!" And Ruth replied, "I don't even know that man." But Walter redeemed himself. They enjoyed New York, and then went on to Washington DC to see the sights there. They were most anxious to return home to their apartment, which they had completely furnished before they left. "The shelves were lined. It was a one-bedroom; it was adorable. And there was a marble hall in the building!" Ironically, in the hall was a marble pedestal and statue that had once belonged to Ruth's parents. Now, 'The Lady', as Ruth had always called her, was a bittersweet reminder each day of the beautiful objects lost during the depth of the Depression.

The pace of their lives quickened when Ruth became pregnant. Walter teases Ruth and says, "Judy was born nine months and ten minutes later!" Actually, "a few weeks later," Ruth corrects him. "This precious little baby, a dumpling baby doll that we played with like two children. She was chubby, with pink cheeks and blond hair. And alert and fun." They moved to a two-bedroom apartment, where they lived for about a year. Then, like everyone else, they faced the war clouds on the horizon. Walter tried to enlist in 1941, when war was declared, but was turned down due to nearsightedness. "He was very smart. He went to aircraft school. We put our furniture in storage and lived with his parents in Philadelphia." Very quickly, he was hired by the Navy and they moved to government housing near Hatboro, a small

Pennsylvania town which Ruth detested. Walter did well in his job and advanced rapidly to becoming a supervisor. But at home, their lives became very complicated. "My brother decided it would be a good idea if my parents, both of whom were ill, should come to live with us. And Walter agreed. It was a nightmarish time. My mother had heart disease and my father had cancer behind his eye. My father had many operations. Except for Judy, it was a terrible time."

Ruth used her nursing skills to care for her parents. And since the couple had no car, it was necessary for Ruth to walk with Judy a mile into Hatboro. Whenever she had a chance, she went into Philadelphia to a museum or to the library. Then, she saw a little notice that the government was going to open a child care center so that the women could work in the factories and they wanted to hire people. Ruth thought of working an hour or two and applied for a nursing position. "How terrific that would be!" She sat down with the Superintendent of Schools who was doing the interviewing. "Little did I know how impressed he was with me, that I was a nurse. The next thing I know, I either got a call or a letter that I am the Director of the Child Care Center!" She took the train to Philadelphia and got every book in the library she could find on Child Care. She pored over the books and learned fast. "My first task was to hire the entire staff: dieticians, teachers, assistants, cooks. I was hiring people who had master's degrees and I'm in charge of this program. I had my little RN!" The Center was right up the street and Ruth planned to take Judy with her. But Judy, four years old, didn't like it there. She wanted to stay home with her grandmother. The Center was open from six in the morning until eight at night; there was also an after-school program for the older children. "I loved working with the staff and the children," Ruth shares. "And the evaluators from Harrisburg gave the program high marks."

The Center was open for three years. Ruth tells what happened next as if it were today. "The day after the War was over, the notice came. Over! Done! Finished! Kaput! And the aircraft plants were shuttered immediately as well. Walter's job was kaput too! I couldn't wait to get out of there!" Instead of the two salaries they had been drawing, they now had neither. It was 1945 and Walter returned to Atlantic City to look for a job. Ruth remained behind with Judy and her parents. When he was set in a purchasing job at a large restaurant, they found a small house in Ventnor, where they were to live for 21 years. Ruth settled in, "with the little girl, with my mother and father needing 24-hour nursing, with the cooking, the shopping, the cleaning, the ironing!"

Then, "One night we went in to Philadelphia to see Lillian Hellman's drama, *Watch On The Rhine*. And I always say, I went in there an ordinary young married girl and I came out a woman. Lillian Hellman opened doors for me in that play of standing up and being counted. And doing what you believe in. I just loved her and all my life I read everything she has ever written and followed everything she ever did. Now I know she was not a perfect human being. But I loved that she had the guts! I loved what she did in the Fifties to stand up for what she believed in!" From that time on, Ruth says, social justice was a burning concern for her. She was to become deeply involved in the Civil Rights Movement in the Sixties; attending meetings, marching and in every way committed to eradicating prejudice and discrimination in our society.

Ruth coped with her demanding responsibilities at home. And they lived on one salary. She comments, "We didn't have much money. None for a car, certainly. But we never had an argument in 61 years of marriage over money. Never! That's what it was. That's what we worked with!" Now, Ruth is laughing, "Sure, we had arguments — like 'I hate those shoes! And you don't know how to put colors together, Walter!' 'Can I help it if I'm color blind?' Important issues!" From that subject, Ruth turns to one that had lain dormant since she left Philadelphia in 1938. "One day, my sister said the smartest thing she ever said to me. 'You don't ever talk about singing?' And I said, 'When do I have time to sing?'"

Lou replied, "There's a Judean Choir that meets on Tuesday nights and I told them about you." She auditioned with Abigail Hoffman, who became a lifelong friend, and was accepted on the spot. In the first concert, Ruth had a solo and the Rabbi from Beth Israel Temple was there. He asked her to be a soloist with the Beth Israel Choir, a professional group of singers. After she auditioned successfully with the director of the choir, Nathan Reinhardt, she began a "rich period of almost thirty years of singing at Beth Israel on Friday evenings, Saturday mornings and the Holidays. They wanted to hear me. I became a fixture there and very important to them. I was singing again and I loved it!"

Ruth became friends with several of the other singers in the choir. "A marvelous soprano came to us, Roberta Weining, and we began to sing together. It was as though we were created for each other. When we sang, our voices meshed. And we became fast friends as well. She was a few years older than I and had a marvelous career in New York. People used to come who were not Jewish to hear our special concerts. For the High Holidays, I brought in singers from the Metropolitan; that had never happened here before. We had a quartet for a time that was really glorious. I sang there for 30 years. The only time I ever missed was if I were sick or took a vacation. I loved it!" Ruth relates how she went to New York and spent days choosing music that was different from the ordinary music. "We did gorgeous contemporary synagogue music by Kurt Weill and Leonard Bernstein. Then people began asking, 'Who is that alto? Does she do any programs for women's clubs?' That was the start of an entire new direction for my singing career."

Ruth went back to Mrs. Bowman and worked with her again for several years. Then she adds, "I knew I had to make a move. She was very disappointed but I went with another teacher, from The Met in New York, Madame Rose Landver. She was wonderful. She was marvelous. I took coaching with her. And staging. Different from technique. Coaching is your interpretation. She thought I was very talented. And I was doing a lot of singing. Weddings. Sunday evening musicals at the fine hotels in Atlantic City. Strictly professional engagements. The community was proud of me." At this point in her life, both of Ruth's parents had died. Her daughter was 13, entering high school. And Ruth was 35, "when one's voice reaches where it ought to be. So, imagine the guts of me! I decided to audition for The Metropolitan Opera. When I told Madame Landver, she just said, 'What are you going to sing?' She didn't get real excited. And we worked on the "Seguidilla" from Carmen." Ruth auditioned for a man she describes as "very nice", but nothing happened. Then Madame Landver asked Ruth if they could sit down and talk. This conversation was to be a turning point in Ruth's life.

Madame Landver said, 'You are married and have a good marriage and have that darling little girl. I want to tell you something, Ruth. You have a very beautiful voice and you are a very talented girl. Very. But, you know, they are pounding the streets in New York.' She asked, 'Are you making any money?' and I said 'Yes, I am.' She said, 'Sometimes, it's much better to be a big fish in a little pond. You have your family. Do you want to sacrifice your family? Do you want to move to New York and run from one audition to another?' And she knew how supportive Walter was. I said, 'I can't move to New York. I can't do that.' Then she asked, 'Do you enjoy what you do?' And I said, 'I love it!' 'Then, just keep doing it', she said. A very wise woman." Ruth adds, "The more I thought about it, I knew it wasn't for me. I was 35 years old and not in my early 20s. And I thought, *Let me do what I'm doing.*. The phone never stopped. I was singing in all the hotels and making very nice money. I was a soloist at Beth Israel. And by then, I had an agent who booked singing engagements up and down the Eastern seaboard. My self-esteem was soaring."

At the same time, a friend of Ruth's told her that they needed nurses at Atlantic City Hospital very badly. "And I thought, *I put in all that time in training. I'm not going to be singing forever.* I was forty. So I went in, saw the supervisor and asked if there was a refresher course. And she said, 'You'll go on the floor. That'll be your refresher course!' And I did, naming my own terms of working several days a week. I liked it very much. I was always fascinated with medicine. But I never gave up my singing." When Judy left for college, Ruth increased her days at the hospital. Walter had become Vice President of Atlantic Beverage with his beer distributorship.

After seven years at the hospital, in 1965, Ruth's career path would take a major swing. "I pick up the paper and I see the government is starting a new program called, Head Start. I was always interested in kids and child development. I went up to see the woman in charge and in two minutes she said I want you to be the nurse on this program. And I was ready to leave the hospital. I didn't want to move up there. So I resigned. I wanted something new! "Now I am fired up! What is this going to be? I love new things!"

Ruth rapidly discovered there were few guidelines. When people came from Washington and asked what she was doing, she told them she was making it up as she went along. They assured her that they were counting on that! "I was examining the children every day. And if they have lice or don't feel well I take care of them. And I'm giving lectures to the parents on nutrition and child care and all that stuff." After the summer, the program was funded but not for the nursing position. Ruth decided she would stay on without pay and worked from September through November. She visited each of the satellite centers in churches and schools all over Atlantic City— without a car. "I wore white boots and uniform and the kids would say, 'Here comes the Go-Go nurse!' They were adorable, three and four year old pre-school children. I loved them! I would say, 'Anyone have kisses to fill up this pocket? I need them for all day long.' And how they would giggle and laugh!" When a director arrived, Ruth was given back pay for the months she had worked and funding for the nursing position was put in place. She adds, "I had wonderful new experiences with Afro-American people. We had great rapport and they were great to work with."

The director, Jane Flipping, promoted Ruth to Medical Director and Consultant. "We used to go to New York together to attend meetings. I had to talk to other Head Start Centers and I was reading every book I could get my hands on. It was all new and I loved it! Then we had to go to Washington and meet with the national director. It was a great experience. I was flying high. I was there over two years. And I became the Director of the Cape May Center and got my own car. A lot of driving. It was a very, very demanding job." At that point, Ruth recalls, "Earl Johnson, the principal of Pennsylvania Avenue School, says, 'Ruth, I want to ask you a question. There's a very big

61

program coming up in the school system and they're going to need a nurse. I think I'm going to be the director and if I am, I want you to be the nurse. A million-dollar program.'" Ruth, as always, was ready for a new challenge and Jane Flipping encouraged her to apply. "I was interviewed and hired on the spot!" It was l968.

Ruth's eyes light up as she describes Project WILL, a program aimed at improving interracial living and learning among students in the Atlantic City School System. A task force of high school students lived at The Traymore Hotel after school every day, from Monday to Friday. "They slept there. They ate there. They had programs there. They went home on weekends. The room assignments were interracial, two to a room." The program lasted six to eight weeks, with different groups of students over a period of three years. The emphasis was on self-esteem, health, interracial understanding, sensitivity and attitudes toward each other. Evaluation from Washington took place all the time. "The kids, of course, loved living at the Traymore. I did not stay overnight; there was a special staff who did that. Sometimes, I stayed until 11 at night and Walter would pick me up." When asked if she felt WILL was a successful project, Ruth replies, "It's hard to measure what goes on in people's minds and attitudes. But I met a woman the other day who stopped me and said, 'I was in Project WILL and I never got over that program, Mrs. Stein!'" Ruth's involvement with the teenagers also heightened her interest in drug prevention. She staged a large scale Drug Fair to reach students from the high schools in the area. Officials came from the Narcotics Bureau in Trenton to present the programs.

In l969, Ruth decided to go back to school and earn a college degree. Glassboro State College offered a special program for nurses giving credit for two years and Ruth entered it part-time at night, driving with several other women to take the courses. "I was very fascinated with that too. Getting back in the classroom and writing papers. And I must tell you, I was one of two summa cum laude and didn't even go to the graduation. I had a meeting and it was raining cats and dogs. I just wanted the degree! And Judy said, 'Oh, Mom, you're going to get your master's before I do!'"

It was then that the Superintendent of Schools asked Ruth to write a project on drug prevention. Ruth came up with a completely new idea and was successful in getting the funding. She did not concentrate on the marijuana plant itself, which was the focus of most programs at the time. Her voice becomes hushed as she confides, "I thought there's something more to this. Why don't I tackle this from the idea that if you like yourself, you don't have to put that stuff, marijuana and heroin, into your body? And this program that I called Project Direct stimulated a lot of interest. The core was building self-esteem, a fairly new concept at that time. They ran down from Trenton to watch what I did. It was aimed at elementary and high school students. A task force of high school students was trained to go out into the elementary schools. We used the Magic Circle, a wonderful activity, with the children to build their self-esteem. I selected the classes that would take part based on the teachers I felt would follow up on our visits. It was a tremendous amount of work for everyone involved and I feel it was very successful. We were funded for several related mini-grants as well as the yearly grant from Trenton."

During this period, Ruth enrolled in a master's degree program in Human Growth and Development, offered at extension sites by Fairleigh Dickinson University. "It just fit in because I could use everything I was doing at the time. It was a very creative program. The professors came down to Atlantic County. I completed it and received my degree." When Project Direct was over, Ruth was offered a position as a nurse in the school system which she took. "I was so bored with those inoculations. I threw those kids into a Magic Circle. They never had such a good time in their lives! 'Why are you going to the nurse?' 'Because I love that nurse!'"

While Ruth and Walter worked hard those years, they also loved to travel on their vacations. "We went to Europe, New Zealand, Canada and many times to Mexico. We just loved to travel! We had the most wonderful times! Sometimes we planned our own trips, sometimes on a tour as we did to Israel and Greece. We went to Italy all on our own, from Milan down to Capri. We went to the opera in many cities." And now Ruth's eyes sparkle, "I always say I want to go to the opera and make love in every capital city of Europe!" They also went to the opera in New York. "We would come home from work, jump in the car, drive to hear The Met, get home at three in the morning, and go to work the next day! We weren't just working ourselves to death. We were having a wonderful time!"

The year was 1976, a year that would bring a shocking and unexpected event in Ruth's life. She speaks of this harrowing time in measured, low tones. "In the meantime, I didn't know that I was sick. But I was. I became very high-strung. I would do tests on myself and I couldn't remember the names of things. Like the little plants on the window sill." At the same time, she decided to have cosmetic surgery to remove "the bags under my eyes" and it went very well. When she returned in November for a follow-up visit, the doctor complimented her on her appearance. But she told him, "I don't feel right." She related some of her symptoms and he immediately referred her to a neurologist, Dr. Haase in Philadelphia. "He had a cancellation and Walter and I went to the office. He took me through a whole series of tests including a Cat Scan and an EEG. The nurse told us to wait and then Dr. Haase came out and said, 'You have a brain tumor. And I would like it out as soon as possible.' And I said, 'I'm going to Mexico and when I come back, I'll call you.' 'No', he said, 'You are not going to Mexico. This is Friday. I want you in here on Monday. You'll meet the surgeon, Dr. Simeone. And the operation will probably take place on Tuesday.'"

When Ruth heard this, she says, "I was very calm. And so was Walter, so very positive and supportive. I wanted to call Judy and our lawyer. I didn't cry or anything. And when Dr. Simeone saw me, he told me, 'I can't give you any guarantee, but from what I see in the Cat Scan, I don't think it's malignant. The shape of it and where it is.' We went to a pre-Christmas party and everyone was very sweet. Judy came running down and was very, very upset. Walter said, 'It's going to be fine, dear.' And it was. I was out of bed the next day after the operation and stuck red Christmas bows on my bandaged head. Dr. Simeone told us several days later that the tumor was benign. It was the worst winter in years, but Walter was there every day. I got to listen for his footsteps in the hospital hall. They had shaved my head. I had long, luxuriant hair, and when Dr. Simeone took off the bandages, I looked in the mirror and all I could think of was The Three Stooges! I was there about ten days. When I got home, I found that Walter had kept my hair in a plastic bag in his dresser drawer."

Ruth was home only a few days, walking as much as she could, when her leg began to pain and she said to Walter, "I think I have phlebitis." Her diagnosis proved to be correct. She was hospitalized again in Philadelphia. "It was very serious. Deep clots. I was listed in critical condition for ten days. Much more dangerous than the brain tumor operation itself. I had to give myself heparin injections in the abdomen for months afterwards." When asked how she dealt with this, again her spirit and sense of humor shine through. "While I recovered, I played Scrabble with Judy and she won. 'Oh, well,' I said, 'I just had brain surgery.' And she replied, 'You use any excuse!' Judy also kept me laughing when she told me Dr. Simeone had said to her, 'There may be significant changes in your mother.' But Judy told me that I was as fresh as ever!"

Ruth always looks to the future. She shares with me the yellowed sheets of paper, dated May, 1977, that are headed Lifetime Goals. Next to each goal is a note and the date she reached it. The first was "To teach Psychology on the college level in a humanistic way, and attempt to enrich the lives of others." The notation reads, "Yes! Will start 9/12/77."

In the Fall semester of 1977, Ruth began to teach at Atlantic Community College as an adjunct instructor. Coincidentally, she had received a call the day she came home from the hospital. Ruth was to teach at the college for ten years; Human Growth and Development I and II as well as General Psychology. Sometimes more than one class section, on the main campus and at the extension center at Atlantic City High School as well. When she was observed by the Department Head, she received top evaluations. She developed her own class syllabi. "I loved teaching there! Another new experience for me. The students were all ages and from all parts of the community. It was wonderful! One cold winter night at the high school, we were locked out! Most of the instructors dismissed their classes. I told my class to get in their cars and come home with me to my apartment. They sat on the floor. We had crackers, cheese and wine and covered the night's lesson. They were blown away! And my supervisor was floored when I told her!"

Throughout these years, she continued her singing. "After I left Beth Israel, I joined the Festival Chorus." They were a group that formed in Margate and as a singer with a strong reputation in the area she was welcomed. In fact, Ruth became the first president. "I sang with them for years and made wonderful friends there. I loved it. We did a variety of beautiful programs and I was a soloist." On the 25th anniversary of the Chorus, Ruth was awarded special honors. She was also serving as the president that year as well. "It was really full circle for me." A musical opportunity arose in 1989 when Ruth joined a choral group that traveled to Spain and Portugal to sing in different cities for two weeks. "Walter, of course, came with me and we were told later that we held the group together. It was a great experience for both of us!" In 1993, Ruth had one of the starring roles in *A Little Night Music*, staged by the Margate Little Theater. She played Madame Armfeldt, a role that had to be sung from a wheelchair. "I just adored playing Madame! She was a sophisticated, elegant, worldly courtesan. I wore the lace collar from my mother's wedding dress and twirled a long gold cigarette holder. And the music was beautiful. The cast exceptional. Such fun! It was really a swan song for me."

Ruth says, "Music will always be my passion in life!" It reminds her of lines from T.S. Eliot's Four Quartets.

"Music heard so deeply
That it is not heard at all,
but you are the music.
While the music lasts."

Another favorite pursuit of Ruth's grew from her love of laces and linens. In her living room, very delicate lace-trimmed linens grace the tables. An antique paisley shawl is draped over a slipper chair. "I learned all about laces from my mother. She would say, 'Baby Dear, bring me the napkins with the Val lace.' Or, "Isn't that a pretty collar with the Pointe d' esprit lace?' She loved beautiful things and so do I. In fact, about fifteen years ago, I started to buy and sell laces and linens. I had read books, visited museums, learned a great deal and decided to write to three dealers in New York, sending pictures of certain of the pieces I had. I was amazed that all three answered and expressed an interest in meeting me. Away Walter and I went to New York, and that is how I began searching for antique laces and linens. I watch out for tag sales, read the newspaper ads and have built up contacts over the years who refer people to me. I have met the most interesting people doing this. Women who have stacks of table linens and runners and odd pieces of lace folded in tissue paper in big boxes in the attic. And handkerchiefs with the most exquisite lace. I adore handkerchiefs and often keep them for myself!"

This subject leads naturally into the subject of clothes."I love pretty things. Especially natural fabrics, wools and soft cottons. I love to mix pieces together. I usually wear very tailored clothes. In fact, my trademark is an antique lace handkerchief in the pocket of my tailored suit jacket." Then she laughs, "If I go out without it, people say, 'So, where's your handkerchief, Ruth?' And I love high colors, reds and purples and black, of course. I wear a lot of black. And I love gray too, but always with something bold that tops it off, gives it an edge. And I adore beautiful accessories and I never throw any out. Never! I have bags and gloves, scarves and costume jewelry. I don't part with any of it. It's good forever. I've had some lovely silk scarves for 35 years! Yes, I do love clothes."

When Ruth talks about her family, she smiles. Judy retired after teaching in the New York City school system for 25 years. "She also taught several courses at Queens College for a while and then decided to really enjoy her freedom. She is a terrific person! An individual! And John, our wonderful grandson, who is taller than Walter, is enrolled in the New York School of Culinary Arts and loving it! Several years ago, he and Walter took a five-day cruise up the St. Lawrence River to Canada. Just the two of them. They both said it was a very special trip. I remember when John was a little boy, he would come and stay here with us for a few days and we would do all sorts of fun things. One time, when he was getting on the bus to go home, he said, 'Grandma, who are you going to play with now?' He graduated from the High School of Performing Arts and decided he wanted to be a chef. He is a fine young man and we are very proud of him."

Ruth and Walter celebrated their 60th anniversary in Paris with an evening cruise on the Seine. She speaks of Walter very lovingly, "He has been a most loving supportive husband. Any idea that I wanted to do, and some were pretty far out, he would say, 'Go for it! I want you to do that.' And when I received my master's, he was so proud. He said, 'I want you to go on for your doctorate." Then she laughs. "I said, 'Walter, I would be on Social Security by that time! I don't think so.' He has always been a loving, attentive father to Judy. She absolutely adores him. He also has a wonderful sense of humor and has often been referred to by many people as 'the last gentleman'. I agree with that wholeheartedly. His kindness to other people is legendary. He would never, never refuse a friend anything. If they need transportation, if they need help, if they need money, he is the first one to say, 'How can I help you? What can I do for you?' We have had many rough times, with much illness in the family and with financial setbacks, but he is a very positive person. He has always said, 'This is just a passing thing. We will work this out together.' And indeed we always have. Walter and I share our love of so many things, opera, travel. We've been to Elderhostels all over the country, our love of history and museums. And especially, our love of people."

Ruth's current interests are broad base. She became computer literate several years ago. "A new challenge!" She is active at Richard Stockton College as Vice President of The Friends of The Performing Arts. "My work there in charge of membership is very satisfying. We've broken all kinds of records. I also have worked very diligently at the local library. And I am co-president of the Festival Chorus." When asked where she gets the energy to do all she does, she replies, "I take a two-mile walk every morning. But my best time is the afternoon and it continues into the evening. And I love living here near the ocean and the beach. In the summer, I swim whenever I can. I love coming in on the big waves. Sometimes I just sit on the rocks and watch the sea and meditate. This gives me inner peace and strength. And I am nurtured by beautiful things. Walter and I will go to New York and see an opera or a wonderful play and I will say, 'This will feed me for quite a while.'" Ruth adds another insight into how she often becomes emotionally recharged. "I will meet someone from The Project Direct Task Force or from my Atlantic Community College classes and they will tell me how that experience changed their lives. Or they tell me of a crisis they have faced when they think, *What would Ruth say?*

"I met a former student from Project Will in the men's department at Macy's and I said, 'Kim, what are you doing here?' He told me he was the manager and I said, 'That's terrific!' 'Well,' he replied, 'You told me I could do anything I wanted to, didn't you? Isn't that what you taught us? Just do it! Get your mind in focus. And that's exactly what I did!' In later years, I learned he had been promoted to a position over many stores. I was thrilled."

Ruth comments on her sense of fulfillment. "All these people I meet, whom I worked with over the years, give me a wonderful feeling of fulfillment. I knew them as children or teenagers or adults, all at significant times in their lives. Turning points. And I was there to help them. I met a woman at Stockton last week who had been in Project Direct. She said, 'You know, Mrs. Stein, I've never forgotten those days and the things you taught us.' And I feel greatly fulfilled with my music too. I know I cannot do the things I used to do with my voice. The choral group won't hear of it when I tell them I'm going to leave. I met the singer who was the Count in *A Little Night Music* and we remembered the pleasure of singing together. He said, 'Your voice, Ruth, was like velvet.' Another sense of fulfillment for me comes from all the friends we have made over the years, people we love and are close to. From our travels, from the Festival Chorus, from my nursing years, from our love for opera. People of very different interests and pursuits — from all over. They're interesting. They're bright. I don't suffer fools gladly. I just love people who are honest and direct. And comfortable to be with. Our friends are very dear to us."

Ruth thinks of herself as 'a woman of a certain age'. "This means to me a woman who is not young anymore but is determined to pursue a fulfilling life. And to me that includes the outdoors, when Walter and I go hiking in the state parks and the county parks. I love the trees and I love flowers. Just sitting looking out at the ocean. So lovely. So beautiful. So innocent." When she looks again at the yellowed sheets of paper with the Life Goals she had written in 1977 after her brain surgery, several goals seem most significant:

"To grow each day in all areas of self: Intellectually. Emotionally."
"Improve my relationship with all those I love (and like!)"
" Not to stagnate anywhere!"
"To live a full, productive satisfying life."

Ruth feels that these goals are as true today as they were when she wrote them. The smile is there and the green eyes are on fire. "Yes, they are as true today as in 1977. And I hope in the future that I will have things that will stimulate me. I see something and think, *Oh, I would like to do that or try that.* I'm forever looking for a challenge. An adventure. Something new! Something exciting!"

CHAPTER IV
MAMIE'S STORY

"Rosie is a person who has a life that she fulfills in her own special way....

Without Rosie, life would not be so meaningful."

—Diane Pantalena
November 21, 1986

When Mamie Pantalena was first asked to share her life story and be in this book, she laughed heartily and dismissed the idea. "Why would you want me in your book? I haven't led a very interesting life. I never even went to college like the other women you are writing about."

I replied, "You let me decide who should be in my book. Going to college is not relevant. You are one of the wisest women I know. And one of the most remarkable mothers. You belong in the book. Will you do it?" After some further discussion, she reluctantly agreed.

At the beginning of each interview session, Mamie would raise the question again. "Are you sure that I belong in the book?" And I would reassure her that she did indeed belong. She met the two important criteria. First, she had overcome significant obstacles in her life with courage, dedication and boundless love. And throughout the extraordinary day-in and day-out demands that she coped with, she had maintained her zest and her humor. Making the big decision and staying the course.

Mamie and her husband Anthony, whom she calls 'Babes', have four daughters. Rosie, the oldest, now in her forties, is retarded. Mamie has raised Rosie as an integral part of their family and has built a life for her through the decades. This monumental decision is at the core of their family life and has had profound effects — both positive and negative. Mamie's story is a deep and moving tribute to one woman's determination to give her retarded daughter the best possible life she could have. Through some terrible times, she has never given up this goal.

71

Mamie has been my hairdresser for over thirty years. She has become my friend as well. Beauty parlors can be intimate places, where women exchange bits and pieces of their lives with each other. Often, there is sharing of frustration, elation, worry, hardships, jokes, and the daily events that make up the skein of our lives. After three decades, one learns the measure of a woman's character. There was no question that Mamie's story belonged in this book.

Our interviews take place in the dining room of her comfortable two-story home. Plates of cookies and fruit are set out on the ecru embroidered cloth as tempting treats. She is a gracious hostess. And once she begins, she tells her story with ease and unsparing honesty.

Mamie talks about her parents, both of whom were born in Italy. "My father, Lorenzo Maccagnano, had come to America first and worked at odd jobs as a cook in the big hotels in Atlantic City. He saved enough money to buy two small row houses in what was called Liberty Terrace. He then sent for his mother, two sisters and a brother. Both sisters died of pneumonia on the boat. His mother and brother survived." Mamie relates how her father and mother, Carmela Allegra, had been betrothed in Italy before he came to America. "She was bequeathed to him. That's how it was done. It was an arranged marriage." Her mother had to wait nine years until she could come at age 35. She was from Messina in Sicily and had been educated there, finishing high school. "She didn't speak very much about her childhood. She never really told us anything about herself. But as we were growing up, we heard her talking to other people. Like the census bureau." She knew how to read and write and wrote letters for her neighbors in the Terrace. She read the newspaper, *Il Populo Italiano,* and spoke classical Italian. She didn't speak English that well. Mamie smiles as she adds, "But when I had problems with algebra in high school, she helped me with it. She helped me with algebra in Italian. I never knew she was that well educated."

The language spoken at home was Italian as Mamie and her older sister and younger brother grew up. When Mamie was born, she was christened Domenica which means Sunday. Her mother nicknamed her Mimi, which turned into Mamie when one of the cousins announced that Mamie sounded "more American." "As a little girl, I felt Domenica was too Italian. I wanted to fit in. But when I went to high school, my home room teacher, who also taught Italian, said 'Your name is Domenica. You're foolish.' But I stuck to my guns. I said, 'My name is Mamie!'" Mamie's older sister Maria also wanted to fit in and when she reached high school, she changed her name to Debbie. Paolo, three years younger than Mamie, was called Paul.

Her early childhood memories are vivid. "My mother used to take us

COURAGE IN HIGH HEELS

down to the beach. She always wore a dress and carried an umbrella. She would tuck her dress between her knees and the three of us had to hang on to her and play in the puddles! We weren't allowed to actually go into the water. She was fearful of anything happening to us." Mamie's father faced a layoff every year in the winter when the resort industry in Atlantic City closed down. "Every Christmas, my father lost his job. And we were without any money. It was hard. They would wait to buy the last tree on Christmas eve. The world's worst tree. Probably cost a quarter. Horrible! But we had a tree!" She describes how her mother first learned about Santa Claus coming down the chimney with toys. That year, her mother called the girls to the foot of the steps and threw down their presents, big plastic dolls.

Mamie shares her feelings about her mother as she grew up. "She was not taught how to keep a home, because in Italy, she had maids. She was from an aristocratic family and always felt my father was beneath her. He wasn't as educated as she was. And she always put a great value upon education." Mamie remembers that her mother tried to learn how to cook and bake without much success. But she had "remarkable hands for sewing and embroidery". She made tablecloths, bed spreads, pillow cases. She had brought huge dowry chests full of linens from Italy that she had worked on all the years that she waited to come to America. Then Mamie comments ironically, "She never used any of them! They were too special. They were always in the chests. When she passed away, we couldn't believe what we found." She also became an excellent seamstress and taught her two daughters to sew as well. "She used the sewing machine with the treadle and later changed to an electric."

As children, Mamie's mother was ever vigilant and fearful that something would happen to them. "We were not allowed off the porch in the front of the house! We did have a small backyard. She bought one bike for the three of us. We just went round and round in the yard." Yet, there were luxuries that her mother deemed important. She bought ice skates for each of the children, white figure skates for the girls and black hockey skates for Paul. Every weekend, she took them to the ice skating rink in Convention Hall. "She bought the best skates there were. They cost $25 in those days. She bought them big so we wouldn't grow out of them too fast." They would spend the entire day there, skating and having lunch in between. "She sat there all day and watched us."

Mamie hated being cooped up on the porch as she watched the other children running around the terrace. It was an enclosed area, but her mother was fearful. The children constantly complained and Paul at times climbed over the gate. "She couldn't control him. I was very good. Too good. I didn't want to make my mother unhappy." Mamie describes her mother, "She was always crying. Her brother died in Italy at a very young age and she wore black for a long, long time. And she cried because they were very close. He was a lawyer. She wanted to go back to Italy and they couldn't afford to go. She didn't like it here because she had to learn how to cook and clean a house. She thought this land was going to be full of gold!" Mamie adds sadly that she rarely remembers her mother laughing.

Mamie learned that her mother had come from a High Episcopal family but she took the children to the Catholic church every Sunday. Her father, on the other hand, was not observant of traditional rites and rituals. "My father didn't go to church on Sundays. He wasn't religious. He had a belief — 'I shouldn't go to confession to a man who is the same as I am.'" Mamie remembers that she liked to go to church. "This is part of your life until you get older and see that some things do not make sense. I felt quiet in church. And I tried to be good. Because we learned early from the Catechism that if we weren't good, we would go to Hell!"

The three Maccagnano children attended Catholic schools, which were free at that time. They were taught all the Italian songs and the grammar of the Italian language, reading and writing. They learned some of the prayers in Latin. The parish priest at St. Michael's was also the head of the school. "You had a little fear of him. You had to be respectful." Mamie recalls liking school and observing other children. And wanting to look like some of them. "I hated my thick straight hair. I was a fanatic! I spent hours trying to get all of it into a barrette. My mother would call up to me, 'Mamie, you're going to be late for school!'I ran three or four blocks every single day to get to the school yard in time." Mamie recalls the incident in grammar school when she and her alto voice were not chosen to be in the choir. As a result she was given a low mark in music. She then decided to go to the choir rehearsal after school, where the nun asked her why she was there. "I said, 'If I don't sing in the choir, I won't get a good mark like the other girls.' And she started to smile and I got into the choir. All I heard her saying was 'Piano, Mamie. Piano!' Meaning soft. Because when I sang, I sang loud!"

Mamie and Debbie slept in the same room and were supposed to be quiet and obedient. But when the radio played, Mamie loved to dance around the dining room table and pretend she was a ballerina. Their mother found money for roller skates as well as ice skates. "It made her feel wonderful to give us that." She took the children to nearby Columbus Park, where they skated and played with their bike. And they also all went on the Boardwalk every Sunday. "She used to make my sister and me our clothes. We dressed alike. Suits with cartwheel hats and little white gloves. There was a navy blue dress and a cape with a shocking pink lining. I loved it! She probably made the outfits for Easter and we continued to wear them. She was quite talented. But she used to bargain for the material in the stores. That, we found very embarrassing." After the Boardwalk promenade with an ice cream treat, they would go to the Marlborough Hotel to meet their father as he left work.

Affection was not expressed openly in the Maccagnano household. "Parents today are always loving and kissing. We had none of that! They didn't give us that hugging and kissing as we grew older. Why, I don't know. It didn't happen." And their mother was the disciplinarian. Their father, when he came home from work, was tired and often had more than one drink as he relaxed. There were arguments and fighting between the parents about his drinking. "But my father never laid a hand on any of us!" Spankings were administered by their mother when she felt they were deserved. "But I loved my mother. We were taught the Ten Commandments in school — to honor your parents. We loved our parents. Maybe we took them for granted."

Mamie tells how different cousins came to stay with them for extended periods of time. She loved having the company and how this affected her mother. "My mother became a different woman, enjoying and laughing when other people were there. And I loved Sunday dinners too when visitors joined us because she wasn't sad then. But she always wanted to move from that house. She wanted a bigger house and she wanted to go back to Italy. But that wasn't ever going to happen. She died in that house at age 84."

As they grew older, the three children were responsible for cleaning the house. "We did all the housework. My sister did the upstairs and I did the downstairs. The neighbors did the same thing. Some of the mothers were working. This was during the Depression. We did the wash with a scrub board! " Money was tight in the family and Mamie, Debbie and Paul also worked outside their home. "I lied about my age. We all did. I was only thirteen. We were supposed to be fourteen to get a work permit. I worked on the Boardwalk in a 5& 10. Behind the counter as a salesgirl. Rows and rows of merchandise. But I really wanted to be on the beach having fun."

When they became teenagers, Mamie, Debbie and Paul attended Atlantic City High School since the Catholic high school was not affordable. "I think the best time of my life was high school. I joined the tap dancing group. I joined the Leader Corps. I was in the Drama Club. I loved all those activities. I experienced things I never had before in Catholic school. It was bigger and there were all kinds of kids there. And I always enjoyed observing."

Mamie describes the freedom she felt in high school, not having to prove herself to the people she had grown up with. The students were from different neighborhoods and she enjoyed her expanded social and intellectual horizons. With her mother's encouragement, she took the classical course, with three years of Latin as a requirement. She loved algebra, trigonometry and solid geometry. "Math came easily to me." Literature was another favorite subject. Mamie and Debbie were good students but college was not discussed as an option in their home. The money was not there and it would be necessary to graduate and start bringing in an income.

Socially, Mamie was a part of a group of friends who worked in the summer and gathered after work at The Steel Pier on the Atlantic City Boardwalk. "We used to go home and wash our hair and meet everybody by six. We would go to the movies, see the show and dance for hours. I loved to dance. We were jitterbugs!" Her mother was still very strict and insisted that Mamie go with her sister, never alone on a date with a boy. And she arranged for someone she knew to bring them home. Mamie describes herself as "very trusting as a child and teenager. She felt secure in her family and neighborhood and with her friends. "I didn't know there was anything evil out there! I trusted everybody."

This was also the World War II era and Mamie tells of a particularly harsh incident that occurred in their home. Mamie's mother was not a citizen. "The police came to our house and took our radio and destroyed it. Then they looked around the rest of the house. We had to stand at attention. I didn't know what was happening. My father said, 'What are you doing? I am a citizen. How dare you!' " Mamie recalls that it happened very fast and they were not frightened. There were no more intrusions into their home. Mamie was fifteen when the war ended in 1945.

When Mamie was fourteen, she met her future husband. He was part of one of the groups who congregated at The Steel Pier to socialize and dance. "Babes was fifteen. He went to Vo-Tech and he used to stand there with his cousins and look at the girls. We were all in groups, but we did pair off. And I paired off with him. Tell me why I liked him? Because he was a good kisser!" He was a waiter at the time but moved to a job at the gas company. They went together off and on until she was twenty. Most of their dates were to the movies, walking on the Boardwalk and dancing on Steel Pier. And they both enjoyed ice skating. Now, Mamie laughs heartily and says, "There was no money to go out to dinner."

In 1951, Babes proposed and she accepted. "I couldn't be without him. I loved him." Her parents came to know Babes and his cousin, who was to marry Debbie, when they helped her father make wine in his cellar. Although it was against the law, everyone in the Terrace made wine in the fall. It was one of the communal events of the Terrace. Another was the three-piece band that Mamie's father organized with his friends who had come from Italy.

They played guitars and the mandolin and drank their homemade wine as the music swelled through the Terrace.

Mamie and Babes were married in Saint Michael's Church, with a brunch at a hotel following the ceremony. "I wore a long white lace dress and a traditional veil. And in the evening there was a party complete with a band." The couple paid for most of the wedding expenses from their gifts. They set up housekeeping, and Mamie, who had completed secretarial school in record time after she had graduated from high school, continued working. One of her first jobs had been as a bookkeeper part time at a fine women's clothing store on the Boardwalk. After she was told to go downstairs and pick up pins from the floor, she quit on the spot. "Here I am on my hands and knees picking up these pins! And I wasn't even getting paid for the time. I just told them I had another job even though I didn't. Where did I have the nerve to leave? "

Mamie next went to Convention Magazine, where she worked for about a year. Then, one of the owners asked her to come into the office after dinner. As she was reviewing the books, she found out that he did not have work in mind. "He closed the door, grabbed me and pushed me over the table. I yelled, 'What's going on? What's happening?' I didn't know what to do! But I pushed him away, ran, opened the door and got out!" Mamie never went back there again. And she never told anyone what had happened that night. "Nobody talked about it in those days." She found a position as a bookkeeper at an insurance company where she stayed for five years. This was the job she held when she married Babes.

Mamie speaks openly about her husband. "He's a good man and a good father. But he isn't basically a happy person. Something happened in his childhood that was tragic and they didn't have therapy in those days. His mother was very sweet, loved her two children, was a good housekeeper. His father fooled around with women. One Christmas, his father gave his wife a fur coat and his girlfriend a fur coat. His wife found out, went into the bathroom and swallowed Mercurochrome. She was rushed to the hospital but they were unable to save her life. She was thirty-three years old when she died. Babes was eight." After his mother's death, he lived with a succession of relatives; his grandmother, uncle and sister when she married at eighteen. "He never talks about what happened to his mother. He never will."

Mamie's life was to change in the most profound way with the birth of her first child, Rosie. But she did not know this when Rosie was born. "She looked normal to me. She was very tiny, four and a half pounds. But she was a hyper baby. We were up with her all night long. She never went to sleep. And then her head didn't grow normally. The doctor called me in at eight months and he told me she was microcephalic." Mamie went to Children's Hospital in Philadelphia, where the diagnosis was confirmed. She was told that there was nothing she could do. Rosie would be retarded. "I couldn't believe it! It was awful."

Mamie had become pregnant again when Rosie was six months old. Now, she had to cope with a very difficult baby, knowing she would never grow up to be a normal child. After several months passed, Mamie went back to Children's Hospital once more. "I took the bus. I was by myself, very pregnant, and with Rosie. The hospital was in a very bad neighborhood. I was so frightened! I went up there and had all these questions written down. But they didn't want to hear about it. No cure! No nothing!" Mamie went home, devastated by what the doctors had told her. "Crying! Couldn't see straight for a week. Babes was quiet. He always felt that all his life, nothing goes right. And I couldn't help him and he couldn't help me."

Rosie's pediatrician said that in twenty years, there would be a cure, but the government was spending its money on space, not on medical research. "That really hurt me. That didn't help Rosie!" There are surgical procedures that are done today for babies whose skulls stop growing to allow the brain to develop normally. Rosie was born before those medical advances came to be. The pediatrician recommended placing Rosie in a home for the retarded. "I looked into Vineland. I went there. They wanted $6000 a year! My husband wasn't even making $6000." There was no government subsidy at that time. And they did not know what her level of development would be. In later years, Rosie was classified as 'trainable', a lower level than 'educable' on the retardation scale. Mamie taught her the motor activities like ice skating, hoping this would improve her cognitive skills. This was not to be. "I treated her in the early years the same as the other children. Her motor skills were very good. I took her to the parks. She learned by imitation. She saw another child do a somersault. She did a somersault. I gave her gymnastics lessons. And she always loved to dance. She loves music."

Mamie's second child was a boy. But, tragically, he was stillborn. "I felt it two weeks before my due date. I turned on my side and just felt this clump. Not an easy movement. I went to the doctor and he said the child had died. No heartbeat!" Mamie went through labor without any anaesthetic in case there was a chance for the baby's life. "I didn't name the child. I should have." When asked how she dealt with the terrible shock of losing the second child and having Rosie to raise as a retarded child, Mamie says, "I didn't come to terms with it immediately. It took me years. I used to go to church every Sunday before I had children. I sang in the choir. But after the second baby, I drifted away."

She did not wait long to become pregnant again. Julie arrived three years after Rosie, Diane another three years later. They were both completely normal in every way and Mamie built her life around her family and her work. She had become a beautician in the 1960s. She liked working as a hair dresser and she could balance her days using baby sitters. She had obtained her license and traveled to the New York shows to learn hair styling. "It was glamorous and fun in the beginning. Hard work. I was meticulous. My first boss said I was good. Of course, first I washed heads and swept the floors. Then I graduated to doing heads. I wanted to set the world on fire!" Mamie recalls that many of her customers came right from the beach, transients who just walked into the shop after six and the operators had to stay until ten or eleven. "I learned a lot about cutting hair and sets. I wasn't doing color at that time. I was a novice. I was paying the baby sitter eight dollars and I was earning eight dollars!"

Mamie progressed through several jobs building regular customers along the way. She blended her responsibilities at home with her days at work. Then, a serious accident occurred when Mamie and Babes took a skiing vacation in Vermont. Mamie had taken a bank loan to go on the trip — their first in years. The accident happened on the last day when she fell and both legs were broken as they twisted in the skis. On their return, she asked the bank for a loan extension since she would not be able to work. "My sister and sister-in-law helped me take care of the kids. I don't know how I survived. But I managed. It took three months until I could get around on crutches with a cast still on one leg. It was a nightmare!" Mamie describes how she kept her house clean, bumping up and down on the steps with both legs in casts. She washed the floors as she crawled around. Her legs healed slowly and she went back to work while she was still on crutches with one leg in a cast.

Paul, Mamie's brother, established a beauty parlor and she joined his staff in the mid '60s. She worked five days a week at first and brought in a good income. She enjoyed the people she met and the culture of the hairdressing world. "Those were the days of the up-dos, and the curls and the beehives. All hairdressers learned how to do the beehive, where the hair is teased and then pulled back and coiled around. I did do some of the Miss America contestants. And I went to the hotel to do Miss America, and put on her crown. It was fun and it was good pay — $75." Mamie relates that many of her customers were older women who spent the summers in Atlantic City while their husbands worked in Philadelphia and Baltimore. She describes the single male operators leaving with these customers to spend an hour in their apartments. "There were a lot of good-looking young guys in this business. This was a big time for hair dressers. Like the movie *Shampoo*, with Warren Beatty!"

Another dimension of being a hairdresser is that customers share their most intimate problems and worries. With the 'regulars', this occurs on a weekly basis. They expect a combination great listener and psychological counselor along with skillful attention to their hair styling. "All the women confided in me. They had me to talk to. For some, their husband died and they had no life. Or they were divorced. They asked for my advice and I gave it. They were women left alone and the more they were alone, the more they talked to their hairdresser. They opened up to me a lot. They told me who they went out with. And all about their children. But no one asked about my life. They never knew I had a retarded child."

Mamie also recalls unusual one-time events. "When the beehive was big, the head of the modeling agency, who had ears that protruded, wanted that hair style. I got glue that we use on wigs and glued her ears back. The next day, she couldn't get her ears unglued! We almost had a lawsuit!" Mamie laughs at this point and then she talks about the humor she finds in life. "There's so many things that set me off. Certain people invite humor. One woman was never happy with how I did her hair. She brings her husband in and says, 'My husband says my hair looks terrible!' He replied, 'I never said that!' She then told him to 'Get the hell out of here!'" Mamie shares that she also likes to laugh at herself.

As Mamie raised her daughters, Rosie, of course required the most attention and care. Each developmental step for Rosie required enormous effort and patience. Things had to be taught repeatedly until she was conditioned to do so. To feed herself, to become toilet trained, to dress herself, to brush her teeth, all the basics a child needs to learn. For Rosie, each was a mountain to climb. Diane wrote a paper about her childhood and her sister. It gives insight into how it was growing up with a retarded sister. She writes, "Training Rosie for the first five years was the hardest thing my parents ever encountered. To accomplish this, it took a great deal of patience, hope and love. My parents knew that an institution was not the right place for their firstborn, so they ignored all professional advice and raised their mentally retarded child themselves."

Toni, the fourth daughter, was born five years after Diane. The family considered Julie the oldest in terms of responsibility. As they grew older, all the sisters were expected to take Rosie with them when they played and visited friends. She was not accepted by other children and her sisters tried to protect her from the cruelty of other children. Rosie looked and acted different. She had very limited speech. Diane writes very movingly of the feelings she had for her sister. "Every summer, my parents took us to the lake for Rosie's birthday. Rosie and I were in the lake swimming, when this redheaded girl began calling Rosie names, 'retart, idiot, dummy!' Rosie did not understand, but I did. I felt like drowning that girl. I felt like a knife stabbed right through my heart, feeling hurt for her and for me because my sister was not like other sisters."

Diane also shares that there were times as she grew up that she resented Rosie. "I began to feel that society would not accept me because of her. It's a horrible feeling growing up resenting your sister because of the pressure and rejection of others. I felt embarrassed and refused to take Rosie anywhere with me. She would ask, in a sad way, 'Can I come?' and I would reply, 'No' without any explanation. I felt guilty all the time but I didn't want people to look at us and laugh." Diane's paper was written in 1986 as a college sociology assignment. When Mamie read it, she was deeply disturbed. She had never realized the depth and extent of the impact upon the three sisters as they grew up with a retarded sister. "I cried! Diane's the quiet one, the sweet one, the giving one. I never knew how she felt." Years later, Mamie also learned that Julie blamed her for placing so much responsibility upon her for taking care of Rosie. "She feels I took some of her childhood away from her. She always had to do something in the house instead of being out playing with her friends."

When asked if she ever went to a therapist to deal with what she had learned from her daughters, Mamie replies vehemently, "No. Absolutely not! I could handle it. I told Julie, 'I had to do what I had to do. If that interfered with your childhood, I'm sorry.' That's it. A lot of things happen in your childhood that you have to accept." Years later, when Julie's little girl Stephanie was very ill, Mamie and Julie were sitting at her bedside together. Mamie said to her, "'Now, you've become a mother. You're here worrying about your child. Imagine how you would have felt when you came home from the hospital with your first child who is retarded for the rest of her life. And then you lose your next child.' Well, she was in tears. She couldn't stop crying. She said, 'Oh, Mom, I never really understood.'"

Rosie was enrolled in a Catholic school, the only one at the time that would accept her. Progress was very slow. After two years, she learned to spell her first name and count to ten. When she was seven, Mamie prepared for Rosie's First Holy Communion. She bought her the pretty white dress and veil, rented a room for a party and sent out invitations. In school, her teacher, Sister Andrea, explained as simply as possible the meaning of receiving the host as "Jesus coming to her." Rosie learned to make the sign of the cross and to genuflect at the altar. "Sister Andrea was most kind and generous with Rosie. But then, we had a meeting with the priest, who said Rosie had to make confession. She had to say 'Bless me, father, for I have sinned.'" Rosie could not learn to say this and the priest refused to allow her to take part. Sister Andrea talked with him and told Mamie that she could participate. Rosie practiced with the other girls and boys walking in the processional in the church. Mamie continues, "The day arrived and Rosie was in the line with the other children, when a nun came and took her out of the line. She took her to the back of the church into the sacristy. I never found out what happened there. We left and went to the party."

Rosie moved back and forth in special classes between the parochial and the public schools through her childhood and teen years. She never learned to read. A particularly poignant episode was when Diane asked for a blackboard at Christmas. She tried to teach Rosie with almost no success. "I just wanted her to learn like me, so people wouldn't make fun of her. Rosie always enjoyed playing school with me because to her it was like having a playmate. The attention made her happy."

Rosie had pronounced mood swings. At times, she smiled and was very loving, hugging everyone in the family and saying, "I love you." At other times she had severe temper tantrums, yelling and hitting anyone who was nearby. Her strength would increase and she would become almost uncontrollable. It took two people to hold her down. Those were the years before tranquilizers were in use. Mamie and Babes accepted the terrible episodes and coped as best they could on a day-to-day basis. Diane writes, "I hated those times because it made me extremely upset."

Mamie relates that she was very strict with the girls as to their jobs in keeping the house clean and doing other chores. "I had no choice. I had no other help."And she was determined to give Rosie as many opportunities as she could handle. "She had speech therapy for six years. I paid a fortune for that and I don't know how much it really helped. I gave her skiing lessons and she won Special Olympic medals. She had swimming lessons and won medals in swimming as well. And she excelled in the track events." Diane wrote of these important moments, "We were extremely proud, not just because of her medals, but because she accomplished something on her own." Mamie relied on the three sisters to love and take care of Rosie. Looking back, she now knows that this took its toll on them in different ways. However, she believes it also taught them to become more compassionate adults.

When she looks back at raising her daughters, she says, "We were not the Brady Bunch!" Yet she recalls that the girls were well behaved and never fought with each other. "They knew there was something not right and they tried not to make waves." There were birthday parties and Christmas parties and sleepover parties. And the family went skiing every year. Mamie put aside the $400 dollars for the trip, lessons and the ski outfits for each of the girls. During the summers, Mamie took the girls to the Ocean City Boardwalk, the rides and of course, to the beach. Babes didn't enjoy these outings. Mamie was following a pattern her mother had set with her own children a generation ago. And she encouraged them to pursue their education as her mother had done with her. Julie, Diane and Toni all earned college degrees.

Mamie always wanted to travel. Babes did not. She particularly wanted to see Italy. When she was fifty, one of her friends told her about a trip she was taking to Europe for about $1200. "I wanted to see something. I was desperate, you might say! So I was determined to find a way to get the money and go." Mamie knew there was no money available, but they had some bonds with her name on them. She also knew her husband would never approve, but she felt she had to go. She told Babes that she had won a ticket to go to Italy. She then cashed the bonds and bought the ticket. "It was something I felt I had to do. I told my kids the truth and they gave me a little extra money to spend. I went on a shoestring. I was like a cat out of the cage. I stayed out all night. Went to sleep at four in the morning with my next day clothes and makeup on. The best was always waiting for me. I loved it! I was having such a good time. I never called home once!" The two-week trip toured France and Switzerland as well as Italy. Rome. Florence. Geneva. Paris. It whetted Mamie's appetite for future travel. She never told Babes about the bonds.

Five years later, Mamie took a trip to California with another friend. She told her, "If the plane goes down, make sure you tell my husband the truth about the bonds!" They saw Big Sur, the Hearst Castle, San Diego and Los Angeles. Five years after that, there was another chance to go to Italy. By then, there was more money to save and plan vacations. "In high school, I had Ancient History and I knew about all the ruins and buildings. And I speak Italian fluently. I wanted to go there. I loved Florence and Rome. On the second trip, I went to Capri and Sorrento. It was breathtaking. I loved it!"

In addition to traveling, these were the years when Mamie planned weddings for Julie, Diane and Toni. They were big weddings, over 200 people at Julie's wedding. "We had a lovely dinner in the evening after the church ceremony during the day. Beautiful restaurant room at Copsey's. And the second wedding for Diane, we had a sit-down dinner at the Buena Vista Country Club. Three choices of roast beef, crabmeat or fish. It was delicious. For Toni, we had about 160 people at the Holiday Inn. They all had beautiful wedding receptions." At this date, Mamie and Babes have seven grandchildren. Julie has two sons and a daughter and Diane has four daughters. All of her children and grandchildren gather at her home for the holidays. She prepares traditional Italian dishes like manicotti in homemade sauce, and sausages and peppers in addition to the turkey and the ham centerpiece dishes.

While her sisters were attending college, Rosie started spending her days at the Opportunity Workshop, a state-supported facility for disabled and mentally retarded adults. She is taken to the bus each day and joins other adults who work in small groups doing tasks that they can master. There is a small stipend for the jobs they perform. Mamie compares the current activities as very positive to years ago when there was little for them to do with their days. Rosie refers to the workshop as 'school'. This daily contact also provides a social context for the adults who attend. In addition there are dances once a month, which Rosie began attending in her late 20s. Mamie relates that Rosie in her late thirties became very close to one of the young men who was also mentally retarded and small in stature. "Johnny and Rosie would eat lunch together and take walks. And they hugged and kissed on the cheek. Rosie called him her boyfriend. Especially when her sisters talked about their boyfriends. And they danced at the monthly dances. They won all the contests. Johnny would say to me, "I'm going to marry Rosie and come live with you."

Their closeness lasted for about five years. An incident occurred that was to drastically affect Rosie and radically change her behavior and personality for over two years. At one of the dances, Johnny turned his attention to another girl, asking her to dance and spending the evening with her. Mamie relates that after that night, Rosie became a completely different person. "It was like Dr. Jekyll and Mr. Hyde! She became violent and angry at all times. She talked all night about Johnny and when no one was in the room. She wouldn't get on the bus to go to the Opportunity Workshop. She yelled and ran out into the street at night. She spent hours in the bathtub scrubbing her arms and talking to herself. She never smiled. Just walked around with a mean, angry look. She went from sweet to horrible!"

Mamie's voice carries deep emotion as she talks about this terrible time in their lives. She began taking Rosie from one doctor to another looking for an answer. And she tried to drive her to the Workshop. Each day was a struggle, with Rosie refusing to get in the car. The few times Mamie was able to get her there, she was so violent they called Mamie to take her home. All facets of her behavior changed. She insisted on wearing layers of clothing and refused to brush her hair. Mamie would take her to the beauty parlor during the day, where she stomped about, talking to herself. Friends and some of her family wanted Mamie to place Rosie in a group home. And Babes blamed Mamie for bringing this on with her encouragement of Rosie's friendship with Johnny.

Different doctors prescribed different medications to quiet Rosie. None of them worked. Psychologists interviewed Mamie and tried to talk to Rosie as well. Mamie told the same history and story to each professional she visited. After two years, she was referred to a psychiatrist at Family Services. She told her the same story and Rosie's history. About the radical change in her behavior after the night Johnny chose another girl. The psychiatrist diagnosed Rosie's problem as a drastic chemical imbalance brought on by trauma. "She had felt loved and that was gone! Johnny even refused to talk to Rosie at the Workshop. It sent her into a tailspin and her chemical balance was affected." The psychiatrist prescribed a particular drug for this type of disorder.

Mamie obtained the drug and gave it to her in the morning. She then took her to the beauty parlor. Archbishop Bevilacqua from Philadelphia was one of Paul's customers and he was there that day for a haircut. He talked with Mamie and then called Rosie over to give her his blessing. Mamie tells what happened next. "In the morning, the change in Rosie was remarkable. She was calm. She dressed in normal clothes and brushed her hair. She was smiling and talking as she used to. 'What should I wear, Mommy?' And when I brought her to the beauty parlor, she came through the door and started to sing and dance! I will never know if it was the pill or the blessing from the Archbishop!" Since that day, Rosie has been 'herself' again. Mamie comments, "We went through hell for two years! All of a sudden, she was my Rosie again! The stranger was gone."

Mamie has faced her own physical problems over the years with the same open mind and guts she drew on during the ordeal with Rosie. She looks for solutions and hangs tough. For over thirty-five years she suffered from increasingly severe heart palpitations. The episodes would last for many hours and they became more and more frequent. "The doctor kept giving me stronger and stronger pills to take. But they didn't stop the racing heartbeat. It would happen during my sleep and when I was awake. I would stand at work cutting hair and feeling my heart pounding in my chest. It was not easy." One afternoon, while watching television, Mamie saw a commercial from a Philadelphia hospital about a procedure that was used to cure severe rapid heartbeats. She immediately called the number and asked for information. When she received the brochure, she read it and arranged to go in for the procedure. Her own cardiologist, when he learned she was going to do this, recommended a doctor in Philadelphia at the University of

Pennsylvania Hospital. Mamie asked him, "Why didn't you tell me about this? It has been in use for eight years? I had to discover this watching television!" She went into the hospital with complete optimism and confidence. And she emerged — completely cured. "They just zapped my heart and that did it!"

She has also coped with two broken wrists after a fall while roller skating. And several years ago, she had to have a knee operation due to a loss of cartilage. "I had pains. It was hard. I could barely stand up and work." The surgery was successful but it ended her favorite sport, playing tennis in a foursome of women. But again, she sweated out the recovery when she could not work, and never lost her equilibrium. She does not feel sorry for herself. "If I couldn't play tennis, I would find something else. And I did. I took up golf. And it's fun." Mamie loves to have fun, especially with her friends. This includes taking bus trips to New York to see a show and have dinner. She plans these jaunts many months in advance. On a more regular basis, she finds ongoing entertainment at the casinos in Atlantic City. She allocates a certain amount of dollars that she will spend at the slot machines and does not go over her limit. Steady attendance has given her the extra perks, tickets to shows in the cabaret theaters and dinners at the casino/hotel restaurants. She goes to the casinos with her friends and with Babes who has joined her in recent years. Along with millions of others, she says, "I get a kick out of the thrill of playing the slots and winning — sometimes!"

Mamie turned to the Philadelphia hospitals again when Rosie developed ongoing vomiting. Doctors diagnosed a hiatal hernia and surgery was strongly recommended. Although this would involve great difficulty explaining to Rosie what was going to happen, Mamie moved ahead with scheduling the operation. She did not know what the aftereffects would be with Rosie. Whether she would be psychologically upset. "What I did know was that the surgery had to take place. The vomiting wouldn't stop!" Mamie takes full responsibility for Rosie and does not rely on Babes or her daughters at these times to make the hard decisions. The result of the surgery was that Rosie was cured and there were no negative aftereffects.

Two of the hardest questions posed to Mamie are, "Have you ever seriously considered placing Rosie outside your home? And what will happen to Rosie after you and Babes are gone?" She replies, "I considered placing her once, those two years when she had the nervous breakdown. The chemical imbalance. When she was not sleeping; roaming the streets. It was horrible! I was advised to place her at that time. But I knew she was sick and I was not going to do that. I couldn't do it! She was still very much part of our lives. She had all these nieces and nephews that she loved very much.

And before her sickness set in, you could take her anywhere. She was sweet and would eat like a lady when we took her out to dinner. Yet, during that awful time, her sisters urged me to put her in a group home. I needed help — not advice! And it was during that awful time that I realized that I couldn't expect them to take care of Rosie when Babes and I would be gone." Mamie does not want her daughters to have Rosie in their homes. And she believes strongly that they would place her in a group home. Her solution is to enter into an arrangement with the Church, giving them her home, with the stipulation that Rosie would live there for the rest of her life. The contract has not been finalized at this time, but that is her plan.

Lest she be seen as a completely serious person, Mamie shares some of the "funny" things she has done over the years. "You only know one side of me. When we had the little kids, my husband wouldn't buy me an air conditioner. I was so mad! I'd fix him! I cooked the whole dinner without any clothes on. He was there while I was cooking. While I served the kids. They were little. They didn't know. He said, "I'm not going to get it for you!" She then went out and bought a secondhand unit. She tells of another time when she went to a movie with her friends. As they waited on line, they saw a man at the booth gesturing toward the cashier. Mamie strode to the head of the line and said loudly, "What's the hold-up?" He looked at me and ran! He had a gun under his coat and had threatened the cashier. The police came. I was a heroine!"

There were also the incidents with her husband's co-workers. Babes used to tell them, "My wife is a bitch! She doesn't do this. She doesn't do that! He always complained. I understood, he was never happy." One day, he brought home two young men for lunch. Mamie decided to tear her nightgown at the shoulder. She came downstairs and started to fondle Babes. "And I said to him, 'Let's go upstairs.' The two guys were bugeyed! They kept eating and I kept rubbing Babes. I was in my early 30s." A final anecdote Mamie tells is of when she saw Babes working with some other men on a gas main in the street. "I stopped the car, rolled down the window and called to him, 'Boy, you were terrific last night. The best sex we ever had!' The guys hit him on the head. Ever since then, the men became my friends. They would call and tell me when the dinners and affairs were. They loved my sense of humor!"

Mamie loves a good time. She and her friend Marion, who is her co-worker as a beautician, learned how to be belly dancers. "We went to class. I had made my costume , the silver bra with the chains hanging. I was real thin then. The skirt and the veil. I enjoyed doing it. I used to practice in the house. And Rosie used to go with me to the lessons. She loves to dance. One night the teacher took Marion and me to the Arabic restaurant in

Philadelphia. We did our dancing. Marion was limber. She made six dollars. I only made two! They stuck it in my hip belt. I loved it. I felt free. The movements were sexy." In Florida a year ago, Rosie joined the belly dancer at a Moroccan restaurant and won applause from the crowd.

Mamie says she is happiest when she feels free. "When I'm having fun. My girl friends tell me that. Trying out everything I can think of — to get a taste of living. Not to wish you had done it and find out it is too late." She recalls her trips to Europe when she was part of a group that traveled by bus. "The others said I was always late. I decided to buy a bottle of wine for the whole bus and everybody enjoyed the trip. I was away from home and I wasn't worried about anything! I had all of these places I wanted to see." The other times she is happiest, she shares, are with her grandchildren. "They are very special to me. I am proud of each of them for all they accomplish. Most of all, for who each one is. They are really nice, kind kids. I love them all!"

Mamie describes herself as a practical person rather than a spiritual person. "There are so many people who depend on religion to get them through the day. I depend on me and my efforts to get me through the day. To get me through the crises." Her comments about death are direct. "There may be a heaven. And you have to die in good grace. I don't feel going to confession and saying your prayers necessarily makes a good person. Only God knows if you're a good person. If I go to a sick person's house and do her hair at home, that's doing my church. That gives me grace and comfort."

Women friends are very important to Mamie. "If you're a friend, you have to be a friend. It's a mutual understanding. I have a very dear friend who needed me when she was going through chemotherapy. I couldn't handle it. She felt I was more upset than she was. Then there was my friend Irene, who died of cancer. She was very brave in the years of her illness." Mamie tells of one incident when she rented a limo with other friends so Irene could go to New York to see a show. "We stopped at Saks Fifth Avenue and Irene jumped right out and ran into the store! She had just come out of the hospital that day." Mamie is usually the one who arranges trips with her friends, to go skiing or to visit Disney World with their families. "We took sixteen, eighteen, twenty-five people to the Poconos for the skiing. I would work late Saturday, then come home and pack all the bags. At five in the morning, we were off!"

Her response to how she feels about herself as a person is honest and straightforward. "I could stand to be improved. I'm just an ordinary person. I feel good about what I've done in my life. I couldn't do it any differently. I have to accept that I did what I did because that's how life came my way. I think I could have improved on my marriage. I think I could have improved being a better mother." There are parts of her life she feels good about. "I could have been a teacher. I once helped a boy pass algebra. I am good at my work. Or else I wouldn't have people coming back to me. It gives me pleasure when my work turns out the way I want it to be. But it is a man's world in hairdressing."

As far as how she feels about the aging process, Mamie is vehement. "I feel terrible! I look in the mirror and say, 'What happened? Where is that little girl! Where did the years go?' I think of that often. It makes me very upset!" In terms of her feelings about the future, she has a more optimistic outlook. She has started computer classes and enjoys working with the computer. Her granddaughter, who is five, helped her log on America On Line. "I was thrilled that I was able to do it. I felt great! I did it! I have to know what is going on. I don't like being in the dark."

Mamie has definite ideas about how she should spend her time. She does not think she should be a babysitter for her grandchildren as some other women are on almost a full-time basis. "I brought up four children and I'm still raising Rosie. I'm not going to have to baby-sit. I want to be able to do what I want, when I want, without being obligated. I want to be free." She shares that she does feel guilty sometimes. "It's the old Italian way of thinking." When she wanted to learn how to drive, her husband discouraged her. But she took lessons and learned. "It felt terrific when I got behind the wheel and drove! And I bought my own car on my own credit. I picked out a purple car at first and when Babes objected, I went back and got a bigger, better car — royal blue." Mamie confesses that she has had nine accidents. None were serious. She finally realized she needed a cushion to give her more height to see properly through the windshield.

She and Babes moved to their current house after she put down the deposit on a lot and chose the design. She was determined to move from their semi-detached home in Atlantic City and Babes was reluctant to make a change. "I said, I am moving from here. And I put the $500 deposit down without his knowing it. When he found out, he was so mad!" Mamie wanted to buy another house as an investment, but there was no money to follow through on that idea. Mamie secured a mortgage and sold their former home. "When the house was being built, I made do with the money we had. I wanted hard wood floors and a garage. It was an extra $1000 at the time." Once the house was built, Babes accepted the move. Their youngest child, Toni, was in middle school. The girls were teenagers and Mamie felt that having the bigger house in a nicer neighborhood was very important to the entire family.

When she talks about being fulfilled as a person, Mamie, as always, reveals her original take on life and her wonderful sense of humor. "I don't feel fulfilled yet. I don't know if you ever really feel fulfilled. If you do, then it's time to go!" And she laughs. "There are things I want to see. I want to see England. And things I want to do. So I'm not fulfilled. But I don't know how I'm going to do it, to get to these things. My mind is always thinking, *What am I going to do next?* I want to go to Italy again. It's going to happen for me. I'm going to do it."

Mamie looks back and sees definite turning points in her life. "The years have gone by without my even knowing what happened to those years. Rosie's birth was definitely a turning point. And the stillborn baby was a sadness. Even now, I feel terrible that I didn't name the baby and have a funeral. The priest told me I didn't need to do that. He was baptized. The worst thing was I didn't want to see him. I resumed my life. It happened. But I went on and had other children. They tell me I was gutsy. To me, I just went on. After Rosie, I could deal with these things. I am a survivor. And the years have been good to me with Rosie. When Archbishop Bevilacqua blessed Rosie, I asked him to bless all of us in the shop. He's a Cardinal now. And I told him the story of how Rosie was refused Holy Communion when she was seven years old. Whenever I go for Communion, I take her with me and she receives Communion. To this day, Sister Andrea asks me how Rosie is doing. And now, Rosie is back to her sweet loving self. She says, 'I love you, Mommy.' And I think to myself, *I want her as she is.* I wouldn't trade her for anyone else in the world."

CHAPTER V

ADELE'S STORY

*"A New Orleans woman said to me in 1961, 'I don't know how to
figure out these rich kids. They're something. ... They could be
dropped on an island in the middle of a big ocean and they'd know
what to do, and if they didn't have anyone around to be pleased with
them, they'd be all right because they'd be pleased with themselves.
And it wouldn't take them long to know where to go and what to do on
that island because they are so sure of themselves, and they always
have their chins up, and they're happy, and they know where they are
going, and they know what's ahead — that everything will come out
fine in the end. When you have that kind of spirit in you, then you'll
always get out of any jam you're in, and you'll always end up on top,
because that's where you started, and that's where you believe you're
going to end up ... and if you're willing to work hard like these kids
are ... then you just can't lose, and don't these kids know it, I'll tell
you!'"*

— Robert Coles
Privileged Ones

Adele, at seventeen, looks out of the pages of her high school yearbook with
classic beauty and an air of confidence. She is described as "...blithe ...
beautiful eyes ... personal magnetism ... loves everything modern ... goal in
life 'Happiness'...."

Robert Coles, the eminent child psychiatrist and writer, has written about
children from many different parts of our varied culture. Among his books
are the stories of the children of desegregation, the children of poverty, the
migrant children and the children of privilege. He called the children of the
wealthy, 'the entitled'. They grew up in families that gave them an outlook
on life that meant anything in the world could be theirs someday. Their
confidence and optimism knew no bounds. And these qualities would sustain

them throughout life as they met obstacles and tragedy. Adele Barbara Brawer grew up in a very large and warm family as an 'entitled' child. She gained the confidence and optimism that would help her through the dark times that lay ahead — when she was a young woman in her twenties and beyond.

Today Adele, who turned 70 on March 3, 2000, lives in Tucson with her second husband Sam, 86, and their three pottery kilns. They have a small southwestern style house on one of the ridges terraced above the city in the foothills of the Santa Catalina Mountains. To reach their level, one drives up and down a roller coaster road with warning signs posted at strategic spots, "Do Not Enter When Flooded." The dips in the road are 3 to 5 feet or more and every few years, Adele relates, during the summer, when there has been no rain for months, even the river beds become bone dry. Then, the 'monsoons' bring water cascading down the mountain and some careless driver disregards the signs and drowns.

Adele and Sam, who have been married for 32 years, share similar values and interests in life. Their home reflects the style, easy grace and authenticity she always carried from her teen years. Mesquite trees and a brick arch draped with wisteria lead the way into the low-lying house. Original ceramic pots and plates that Sam and she have created decorate the walls and table tops. Beyond the living room, glass doors open to the patio and a smashing view of the mountains framed by lemon trees. The shrubbery and the variety of trees around the house remind the visitor that the owners came from the East and brought their love of greenery with them.

Ceramic are a central interest and pursuit for them. "Over the years, Sam and I have gone to many workshops at various places in the country. Our favorite is held by the New Mexico potters association at Ghost Ranch, the same ranch where Georgia O'Keefe did much of her work and ended her days. Ghost Ranch is a rustic retreat in the most gorgeous part of northern New Mexico where many kinds of cultural events and study groups take place. When we went there we paid $35 each for room and board per day. Meals are served cafeteria style and people eat at long tables with lots of other people. Mostly homegrown food, delicious. We have gone to Horizons in Williamsburg, MA, smaller but similar and only for crafts. And Peters Valley in New Jersey."

Then she adds a comment that harks back to her childhood. "I'm not sure why Sam and I love this hippie-style life. For me maybe it's a rebellion against the 'buzzer under the dining room table'! And for Sam, it must be an extension of his innate thriftiness."

When Adele speaks of her family and her childhood, one towering figure emerges, her paternal grandfather, Arthur Brawer. "He was a tall, handsome man with a head of curly hair, bright blue eyes, a wide brow, high cheekbones and a hooked nose. He had a very warm personality and a very imposing bearing. Arthur made a strong impression on everyone who met him. I was always a little afraid of him."

He emigrated from Russia to Ireland and then to the United States around 1900. In Ireland he spent some time as a bartender or seller of whiskey and thus was assigned the name "Brawer", based on 'brewer' as an occupation. Once in this country he married Ida Kaplan, another immigrant from the area of Kurland in Latvia and they settled in Paterson, New Jersey known as the 'silk city'. Arthur Brawer was to build a family business and dynasty that stretches down to the present. His is one of many fabled immigrant success stories of that era.

Adele enjoys telling her family history. "Arthur went into the silk business in Paterson with his brothers. He was very bright and organized many businesses as well as being active in the community, non-Jewish as well as Jewish. Arthur and Ida had six sons and one daughter, who died at birth. The sons in birth order were Isaac, Sidney, Irving, Joe, Milton and Louis. They were all born within ten years between 1906 and 1916. Isaac, the oldest, was my father.

"They lived in a number of homes in Paterson, but the only one I remember was a three-story typical Victorian-style house with a porch all around and a back staircase. There were lots of oriental-type carpets on the floors, an old-fashioned black telephone on the desk and an upright piano which Arthur played by ear. He liked to sing as well and all his sons had music lessons. All the Brawer sons were encouraged to go to college. My father Isaac studied business at NYU and my uncle Sidney went to Philadelphia College of Textiles. Arthur wanted Isaac to learn Japanese in order to go to Japan to make contacts for the silk business. But Isaac couldn't satisfy his father, and around 1925 Arthur took a ship to Japan. Apparently the trip was successful, for the Brawer Brothers Silk Company prospered for many years. Arthur was the head of the firm throughout his lifetime. Everyone called him, "boss".

"Arthur employed immigrants to work in the silk mill; many were Irish people whom he had met while living there. He loved the Irish and marched every year in the St. Patrick's parade. My father worked at Brawer Brothers and I often went there with him and loved to go up and down in the hand-operated freight elevator. Being the oldest grandchild, all the relatives and the employees made a big fuss over me. However, I once spilled a bottle of ink all over a desk full of papers. My father was very upset."

Holiday times were special, shared by the large Brawer family. "Arthur and Ida had many celebrations at their house. I especially remember the Chanukah parties. During World War II, my sister Norma and I and all the cousins sat around the dining room table and Arthur gave each of us a Defense Bond. At Passover, with all the aunts and uncles and cousins, the crowd was too large for their dining room, so the Seder was held at someone else's home or at the S & Z kosher restaurant. There was always a lot of noise and excitement and singing. Arthur sang the loudest, off key."

There was also her Grandma Ida's family, the Kaplans in Red Bank, New Jersey, where there was a house large enough to hold everyone for summer vacations. Adele's father's earliest memory was when they all packed up in a big car and drove to Red Bank to play on the beach and swim. Sadly, Adele wrote in a memoir, "Grandma Ida died of cancer when I was twelve. I went to her funeral which was at their home. And after her death, Arthur sold their home in Paterson and moved in with us. My mother always had a love-hate relationship with her father-in-law. She admired Arthur but she was afraid of him too."

Adele remembers her grandfather in his later years as an inveterate traveler, flying on an early Pan-American flight to Miami and then spending winters there. However, he remained the "boss" at Brawer Brothers until spring of 1946, when he died of a a sudden heart attack at age 70. "I was 16," Adele writes, "and the funeral was at our home. People overflowed into the street. I would guess a thousand people came. He is buried next to Grandma Ida at the Brawer plot in the cemetery in Totowa." End of an era for the Brawer family, but Adele had the security and enormous warmth and love throughout her childhood from her mother's family as well.

Matilda (Tibe) Silverstein, Adele's mother, was the next-to-youngest of nine children of Fanny and Samuel Silverstein, who had also emigrated from Kurland in Latvia. He had been a harness maker there and with the advent of cars always seemed to be retired. Adele was very close to "Grandma Fanny", whom she describes as "a strong woman, bright and with a good sense of humor." Her maternal grandparents lived in Paterson and she and Norma sometimes stayed for a weekend with them when their parents were on vacation.

"Visiting Fanny on the weekend was special fun as Mother's sisters had a hilarious time together showing off clothes and talking girl-talk. Grandma Fanny used to called me a "longa luksch" ('long noodle' in Yiddish) because I was tall and skinny. The cousins were all around my age. The women and girls congregated in the kitchen; the boys and men in the living room to listen to the radio. In the summer we often went to Far Rockaway to visit the cousins there or rented a house nearby. I learned to swim at Island Beach before it became fashionable. My childhood memories are of good times with lots of cousins and relatives."

When Adele talks about her life today, there is a resonance of these early formative days. "I guess you've noticed how much I love people and love to be surrounded by them. And that requires an extra 40 hours in each day. And I am always feeling as though I'm not giving enough time to the people I love. Just about everyone."

Adele speaks of her mother as her role model in life. "Tibe was the tallest of the sisters, 5'7", with dark curly hair, high cheekbones, a big nose and expressive green eyes. Her sisters all looked up to her even though she was younger, as she had married into a wealthy family, was the most educated and had the most refined taste. Tibe was very smart and had liberal ideas before they became popular. She never forgot what it was like to be poor and so was charitable, concerned about minorities and a feminist before Betty Friedan! She admired Eleanor Roosevelt and Margaret Sanger.

"We were taught to be respectful of other races and people different from us and less fortunate. During the Depression, Mother often fed homeless men on the back porch of our house. We always had household "help", a series of Polish and Hungarian girls who came from western New Jersey and lived in. But in 1942, Bertha Hurst, a black woman, became our housekeeper. My mother was sickly at the time and Bertha came in every day about ten and stayed until after dinner. Mother took us to Bertha's church supper every year. Norma and I were the only white children there."

Her mother also introduced Adele to the world of the arts, an area of life that is of great importance to her. "She took me to exhibits of modern paintings and to concerts. She had me take piano lessons and we always had a baby grand piano in our home — a Chickering that now belongs to Bill, my middle child. There was also elocution and dramatics and music theory to study. When I was fifteen, she encouraged me to take modern dance at Martha Graham's school in New York."

In Adele and Sam's home today, embroidered wall hangings and the needlepoint covers on two Chippendale armchairs were stitched by her mother, a woman of many talents. Tibe also sewed clothes for both daughters on a Singer pedal machine. "She decorated our house in an eclectic style, starting with some old stuff she found downtown in Grandpa Arthur's warehouse, objects that were interesting but not valuable antiques. He had received them from a debtor and Tibe called them "collectibles" and said that all beautiful things went together. They didn't have to be of one style."

Adele's Tucson home, with the mix of furniture and design, is a reflection of her mother's aesthetic tastes. And at the brunch she and Sam hosted for friends one Sunday morning, Adele was completely at ease, wearing a long dark flowered skirt, creme blouse and a sparkling hot pink scarf at her neck. Her feet were bare on the clay tiled floor. The guests were varied and interesting. A maritime lawyer. A man who had been a British Navy pilot in WWII. A woman who lives part of the year in Jerusalem. A former Dean at Northeastern University. A tiny Asian woman with a handicap of 3 on the golf links. Conversation flowed on many topics. Food was delicious and plentiful. Adele had poached a salmon that morning; Mexican dishes added spice. And desserts were beyond sinful.

Again the echo of her mother. "Our home usually had company in the evenings when friends or family just dropped in to visit. My father often played the piano, especially when there were guests, and everyone sang a lot. Then there was much conversation, more of a personal nature than intellectual, and men and women played cards; mah jong, bridge and gin rummy. My parents had many friends who shared joyful times and sad ones. I do think that Tibe was intellectually frustrated and would have enjoyed teaching or some other career. But most women of her time did not do that. And my father didn't approve of women working."

Looking back at her childhood, Adele also observes, "Most of my first cousins (Brawers) who lived in Paterson and many of my second cousins too were boys. You can imagine the male chauvinistic atmosphere. The girls were treated like sweet little pets, to be admired but not considered very useful. Thank goodness my mother was an early feminist and realized that girls could do things. My aunt Selma, Isabel's mother, felt the same way."

When Adele speaks of her father, Isaac, it is with mixed emotions. "I attribute to him my love for music and my enjoyment of travel and ability to read maps, which he taught me at an early age. Unfortunately, he always looked worried — as though he expected the worst. Isaac was not a good businessman. He had narrow vision and did not change with the times. An independent venture failed and he worked as a salaried employee for his brothers. He also was passive in his relationships and preferred to let others make decisions, especially my mother, whose judgement was clouded by her feelings toward him. Loving him, she didn't realize his inadequacies. He was dependent on her in every way."

As a child, Adele received much attention as the oldest grandchild and was dubbed "precocious". "I went to P.S. 20, where I was one of the youngest, one of the smartest and one of the naughtiest in my class. I often got caught talking, passing notes and fooling around and had to stay after school. On my report cards, I usually had all 100s but failure in 'Conduct'.

I don't really remember much concern on my parents' part. I was popular with my peers and we walked to and from school together, about eight blocks, and played after school."

"One of our favorite activities was writing plays and acting them, using the garage as a stage. The audience (neighbors and parents) sat on chairs in the driveway. We sold tickets and gave the money to 'poor children'. Since those were Depression days, there were plenty of 'poor children' all over. I was also occupied with all the lessons mother arranged for me to take. And I loved to read and devoured books. Norma and I played dress-up and sometimes played tricks on the maid. One girl left after we did a ghost act and scared her to death! But Mother punished us for that. Of course, we listened to the radio. But we were never expected to help around the house. I think Mother expected us to always have household help and I knew nothing about housekeeping. When I married, I couldn't cook, clean or pick out a ripe tomato!"

Adele's childhood mirrors the lives of the "entitled" children in Robert Coles' book. In the summers there were family vacations, auto trips to New England, Pennsylvania and Washington DC. Her father always stopped at state capitols, where Adele and Norma had to read information on the historic markers aloud. They each had a Brownie box camera to take pictures. When they were ten and eight respectively, they went to sleepover camp for eight weeks, and from age twelve to fifteen, Adele went to summer camps in New Hampshire and Maine. Her memories are happy ones. "I loved swimming and tennis, and also was in theatrical productions where I sang, danced and/or played the piano. All those lessons paid off!"

The junior and senior high school years had somewhat of a rocky start. "When I was finishing sixth grade, I took a competitive exam for entry into Montclair College High School, which I passed. I went there for seventh and eighth grades and hated it! I loved the intellectual challenge but felt like a social misfit. Everyone had friends except me. I was not used to the atmosphere. Some of the students came from restricted (i.e. Jews excluded) towns and their lifestyles were unusual to me. Instead of discussing this with someone, I started getting stomach aches and by the end of eighth grade, my mother had figured it out. I was very unhappy and she let me change back to the public schools, where I felt more accepted."

All the Brawers belonged to Temple Emanuel, a large Conservative synagogue and Adele began her religious schooling there at the age of six. Then during the year, she refused to go because my teacher did not include her in a class play! "My parents chose to send me to the Reform Barnert Temple instead where I continued my Hebrew studies and was confirmed in

June 1943, when I was thirteen years old. I don't consider myself religious in the traditional sense at this time in my life."

At Eastside High School Adele took the Classical or College-Prep program and was graduated 9th in a class of about 400 students. She was given the Francis R. North award for "All- around Best Student". She was active in athletics, especially basketball and tennis, and was also a reporter for the school paper. "My biggest interview was with Bess Myerson, Miss America of 1945 who spoke at the school. And twice a week I took the train and bus to New York, caught the subway to Greenwich Village and took dance lessons at the Martha Graham School and then returned home after dark. It felt very adventurous. My lessons were with a group of five other teenagers taught usually by Erick Hawkins."

Adele had a close set of friends during high school. "And there were several boys a few years older. We four girls had great crushes on them and chased around the halls hoping they would notice us! They never did." As for dating, she notes, "I seldom had dates in high school until I met an older man of 23, a WWII veteran, during my senior year. I fell madly in love but I guess he found me too immature, for he dropped me after four or five dates. I was afraid I wouldn't even have a date for the Senior Prom but at the last minute one of the seniors asked me. We went to a New York nightclub after the prom! I don't think I ever saw him again after graduation."

Adele's father taught her to drive since this was not taught in school. And he made her learn to change a tire before she could go for her license. "He was a good teacher. He had money in the '40s and bought me a red convertible in my senior year. I promptly dented a fender but generally I was a good driver. Of course, in a convertible without seat belts in those days, I was lucky to have survived." Adele was bound for Smith College after graduation in June, 1947. She had applied to Smith, Wellesley and Bennington and was accepted by all three. She did not want to attend a co-ed school as did her closest friends.

Despite her choice of an all-women's college, Adele says with a laugh, "In the summer of 1947, I was ready for a big love affair. Our family had gone to Daytona Beach for the hay-fever season (August and September), and I met Simon Dingfelder there. He was 18, entering Cornell University and gorgeous! Simon and I dated and went together for the rest of the month and were in love — or at least strongly attracted to each other. We were to see each other and talk on the telephone many times during the next two years. I was 17 when I entered Smith and felt very young and unsophisticated compared to many of my classmates, who came from well-known prep schools, played bridge and were second- and third-generation 'Smithies'."

"However, I was very excited by the college atmosphere and loved researching and writing papers. I took Liberal Arts courses and Modern Dance. Our social life was very restricted; we were seldom allowed off campus, only three weekends a year. And there were no boys around unless you were fixed up on a blind date. Sadly, though we had every intellectual advantage, all we thought about was boys and marriage. That was also the emphasis from our families."

At the end of her sophomore year, Adele went to Europe with a friend, Laura, on a 'student ship', an unconverted WWII troop ship, the Volendam. It took ten days to cross the Atlantic. They landed in Holland and traveled to France, Switzerland, Italy and England. They hitch-hiked much of the time and also took buses and trains. She relates that the whole trip cost $1500. And was "wonderful!" It was the summer of 1949 and she was 19 years old.

That September, Adele transferred to Wells College to be nearer to Simon at Cornell, as their relationship had deepened and grown very serious. During that year, they were married and did not reveal this to their parents until Summer of 1950. At that time, they took an apartment in Ithaca and on February 7, 1951, their daughter Jan was born. Their parents paid the bills in order for Simon to finish college. Simon was Commanding Officer of the ROTC during his senior year and so received a regular Army commission as a second lieutenant, comparable to the West Point commissions. He was signed up in the Army for three years.

After Jan was born, Adele says, "As with all things domestic, I knew nothing about babies; so we hired a baby nurse to help out for a month. She was wonderful and taught me a lot that I put to use when Bill and John were born. After Simon graduated, we were assigned to Fort Sill, Oklahoma, where we lived in a 26-foot trailer during a very long hot summer. In October, we moved to Fort Bragg, North Carolina, still living in the trailer which we had bought with our wedding present money for $5000. This was during the Korean War and Simon's 756th Field Artillery Battalion was sent to Baumnolder, Germany. I was pregnant and went home to Paterson with Jan, waiting to hear when housing would be available in Germany."

"In June we went over but the dependents' housing wasn't quite ready. We lived in town over a tavern for a few weeks and then moved into a beautiful apartment on the base, all furnished, the 4th floor of a walk-up. We had a German maid, Hildegarde Stein, who spoke only German. I managed to communicate with my one year of German from Wells, and Simon had heard his grandparents speak German at home. Jan was only one, but she too learned a little German."

In October, Bill Dingfelder was born at the U.S. Hospital an hour from the base. Adele remembers vividly that Bill was born within one hour of their arrival at the hospital. Babies roomed in with their mothers in Army hospitals and maternity cases spent ten days. Mothers were expected to wash their baby's clothes as well as their own by hand in the bathroom sink. Adele nursed Bill for several months and recalls, "Bill was an exceptionally good baby. He seldom cried and had a sweet disposition."

Simon and Adele were transferred back and forth in Germany and Simon's work kept him away from home often. Adele has an unsparing view of her reaction to this period in her life. "I complained a lot instead of taking advantage of the opportunities of being in Europe. Too immature, I guess. With two small children, I wasn't up to venturing too far away on my own except locally to some nearby towns. My mother and dad came to visit in the Spring of 1953. Then in November of 1953, I took the children to New Jersey to visit."

What Adele recounts next was the beginning of a terrible and profound time in her life. "We went on an Army transport plane that took 24 hours from start to finish. When we arrived, I was exhausted and never felt well for days. I awoke on November 14, dizzy and unable to speak clearly. Our family doctor came right over with a neurologist who did a spinal tap and diagnosed spinal-bulbar polio. I was taken by ambulance to the Sister Kenny Clinic at the Jersey City Medical Center. My sister, Norma, rode with me in the ambulance. I was 23 years old."

"When I got there, I was put in isolation and given vitamin C shots that were extremely painful. Jan and Bill and everyone who had been near me were given gamma globulin shots. Fortunately, no one I knew ever caught polio from me. Simon was still in Germany and didn't come home until almost a month later. My parents hired a nurse to care for the children. Miraculously, I recovered from the respiratory (bulbar) symptoms and was never in an Iron Lung. But just a day before I was to leave the hospital, my right leg collapsed, which meant the spinal-polio was active. I stayed in the hospital for another six weeks, where I was treated with hot steam packs, hot wax treatments and physical therapy."

During this entire ordeal, Adele's spirits did not falter. "When I had polio, I was completely optimistic. I never felt very sick and I hated being there with very sick patients. After the first acute phase of ten days, I was moved to a ward with about sixteen other women. At the time, I was probably in denial to an extent, but also my case was so much less crippling than most women who were in the hospital with me. Around February 1, I went home in a wheelchair and about two months later graduated to crutches, which I used for about two years. I could manage my life on the crutches. Then a leg brace. Then a cane. And finally, I walked independently. I was very cheerful and optimistic and not at all in touch with the frightened and sad feelings which caught up with me later."

Adele's account of her recuperation reveals undercurrents of her feelings toward Simon and the effects upon her parents as well. "I was told to continue with physical therapy but at that time, in the spring of 1954, there were no therapists in Paterson so my mother tried doing it with me. And not very successfully, as it was too strenuous for her. There were no Nautilus machines, health spas or hot tubs in those days. Simon was transferred to Fort Dix, over an hour away and may have felt helpless. He was only 24 years old himself. I spent my days reading and watching the McCarthy hearings on television. I realize now that I regressed to a child-like role, letting everyone take care of me and my children. My mother was very upset. And my father was upset about my mother! I think I became somewhat more spoiled and demanding than I had been and that led eventually to marital problems. I was happy to give the responsibility for the children to my mother for the two months and even later."

In April, 1954 Adele flew with her children to Daytona Beach, hoping that the swimming and warm air would help. Her mother was also hoping that Simon's family would help, since she was exhausted. "It was a bad time for me. I could barely take care of the children and was feeling desperate until Simon got discharged from the Army." In June after serving three years, he was released and they moved to Sanford where he started a job search. It took the entire summer until he got a sales job with a citrus outfit and then they moved to Tampa. Simon changed jobs a year later and became a food broker. They then bought a house with a down payment from Adele's parents. As they settled in, they also joined a Reform Temple.

John, their second son, was born in December of 1956. He was an easy delivery and she nursed him for two months. At about the same time in Paterson, the younger Brawer daughter, Norma, was diagnosed with Hodgkins Disease. She was 23 years old and had been married three years earlier in June of 1953. Norma was treated for the illness, a form of cancer, and she and her husband had a child, Richard, in 1957. Her baby was one year old when Norma was hospitalized for the last time.

"My sister Norma died on February 2, 1959 at the age of 26. She had been sick for three years. This was a terrible blow, which affected all of us very badly. I felt I had hardly known her as an adult. I had been away from Paterson since age seventeen and have always felt the deep loss. Fortunately, and by chance, I was visiting in Paterson the week she was in the hospital when she died. I was able to spend some time with her. We were able to talk

103

together and be close. When Norma died, as with the polio, I had a lot of denial. I was very angry and not supportive of my parents and still in my narcissistic mode. That is something I have always regretted. A year after Norma's death, my mother suffered a severe heart attack. She was ill with heart disease and attacks for the last ten years of her life."

Over the years, Adele has drawn upon psychotherapy to help her through the hardest times in her life. This is reflected in her comments about her struggle with polio and the impact of Norma's death upon her personality and her marriage. "My anger about Norma's death affected my relationship with Si because it was non-directive, just all over the place. I'm sure for the following years I was not very pleasant to live with. I wish I had been mature enough to help my mom, but I was just all into myself and Si was not very supportive of me. During the '60s, I was unhappy with my life and my marriage and complained a lot, which only made things worse. I had never finished college, so I went to the University of Tampa to receive a B.A. degree. I went part-time for three years. And after graduation, I got a part-time job as the Director of the Tampa Art Institute. However, Simon and I were getting very angry with each other and had little love left. Finally, he walked out one day and about a year later, 1965, served me with divorce papers."

Adele reflects on how she felt at the time of the divorce and now. "It's still hard for me to sort out what led to the divorce. I was quite egocentric and not at all tuned into my husband's feelings. So, I was surprised and very angry when he left me for another woman. It never occurred to me that he might do that. I would say anger is the feeling that I had for a long time, and I am still angry with him that he broke up our family. Even though I personally was able to marry and be happy, I know my children always suffered from the loss of their father. And he was a pretty good father. For many years, we had a good family life. Sam is a wonderful husband, but for the children, a step parent is never the same, especially when they have good memories of their own father."

She adds that the children stayed in close contact with their father over the years. She also observes that there was a good part to the divorce since it started her on therapy. She credits psychotherapy with her becoming more sensitive to the feelings of others and becoming less narcissistic. She believes this as beneficial for her second marriage and for the children as well. When Simon left in 1964, Jan was thirteen, Bill was eleven and John was seven. They were divorced a year later.

During the next year, Adele describes herself as "so upset I couldn't work for a while." She also felt she should stay home with the children who were also upset. She did enroll in a counseling course at the University of South Florida and drove back and forth with a woman who was to become a lifelong friend, Marysol Johns. And she decided to go to secretarial school to brush up on typing and learn shorthand as she was not prepared to earn a living. Simon was paying $200 a month child support and $200 a month alimony. The divorce, settled out of court, was final in 1965.

The next year was to prove very significant for Adele. "I was 35 at that time and wanted to have dates and a social life. That didn't happen in Tampa. So, in June of 1966, I sold the house and moved back to New Jersey into one of the new high rise apartments near the George Washington Bridge. Fort Lee was not too far from my parents, who were as always helpful to me in every way. They gave me an extra $100 a week and I found a secretarial job in New York. I was able to manage fairly well. And I had money in the bank from the sale of the house. I loved working in New York for a large corporation at 3rd Avenue and 47th Street. The first time I ever had a real job! It felt very glamorous, and my good mood got me through that year."

Socially, Adele was to find that the move to New Jersey changed her life. "We always joke about it. Mother alerted every eligible male within fifty miles that Adele was coming! I had lots of dates and my parents took care of the kids. And Mother let me go to the store and charge clothes on her account so I looked decent. I had a gorgeous apartment which made me look prosperous. I do think that most men are not interested in women with three children who look down and out."

Adele arrived on July 1 and later in the month her parents took her with them to a wedding of friends. She wore a "silver gossamer evening dress" that her mother had borrowed and she was introduced to Sam Baydin. The rest is family history. "At the wedding, Sam and I danced all night. We were very compatible from the beginning. He's a wonderful dancer. And he always liked tall women. Sam took me home after the wedding. As we left, the doorman said to me, 'Your husband is the best dancer here.' I just smiled and replied, 'Oh, but we've just met!'"

Sam was sixteen years older than Adele; a widower of six months with two sons, Jeffrey and Richard. He owned a jewelry business in New York City. His personal characteristics were very attractive to Adele. "His tremendous energy. His good sense of humor. He is lots of fun. And very sweet. A solid citizen. He had made his way with a great deal of common sense. I wanted a nice, normal person."

Their relationship grew and deepened during the next year. Adele says that Sam hesitated about marriage because he wasn't sure he could manage a family with young children. She did not see the age difference between

105

them as a barrier. They were married at her parents' home on September 17, 1967. "A beautiful wedding that my mom planned from her bed because she was seriously ill with heart disease. It was really elegant. Thirty-five guests at a luncheon prepared by Jackie Kennedy's caterer, whom Mother read about in *The New York Times*. Gorgeous flowers! Our five children and other relatives. A few close family friends. Somewhere I have a photo album." Their honeymoon was spent at the Nevele Hotel in the Catskills.

They found their first home accidentally. "I loved living in an apartment, but Sam wanted a house as he had never had one, preferably one with land and fruit trees. Mom and I were driving around Fair Lawn in July before the wedding when we saw a man hammering a For Sale sign on a tree in front of an adorable Cape Cod shingle house. He sold us the house for $37,500; Sam and I each put $5000 for the down payment. We had half an acre of land and thirteen fruit trees. Sam and I were to live there for twelve years until the children were grown and some were married."

In 1969, just a year after Adele and Sam were married, her mother died after fighting heart disease for ten years. "As my children had spent so much time with Tibe, they were very attached to her. But I didn't realize how bad the loss was for them, especially for Jan. I've always felt I was not in tune with her unhappiness. It was similar to the time after Norma's death when I didn't give enough to my parents and their loss. Too bad I didn't have the psychotherapy earlier in my life instead of later at 41."

Adele found the inner strength to come through the darkest years of her life; the years that brought polio, Norma's death, her divorce from Simon, and then her mother's death a year after marrying Sam. She does not think of herself as a spiritual person. "I'm more of a pragmatic person, dealing with what I have to deal with. Sam's son Richard left college after his first year and we had four children at home for while. Then, when Jan was nineteen, she took off from college and traveled for about a year and a half. Those were stressful years for us. But Sam and I knew we were going to stick with it. So whatever happened, we just kind of stuck with it. Together. My husband is a very good person. And he was wonderful to my children."

In 1971, Adele began psychotherapy that extended over a period of five years. She took part in a group as well as individual sessions that she felt helped her enormously. She credits this experience as widening her understanding of others as well as of herself. Today, Adele is an outgoing empathetic woman who touches other people with warmth and sincerity. She exudes vitality and energy. One of her favorite sayings, which she says began with her grandfather, Arthur Brawer, is "What we lack in finesse, we make up for in enthusiasm!"

When asked how she feels about turning 70, she laughs. "It's great! So long as my mind and body are holding up. I think I'm in a better mood than ten years ago. Mostly, because of knowing that my children and grandchildren will carry on independently and well. In retrospect, it was a good thing to have them when I was young as insurance for my old age. Surely, someone out of that bunch will look after me!" That 'bunch' means Jan in Denver and her daughter, Lisa; Bill and Laura in Philadelphia and children Kate, Hilary and Daniel; John and Lynn in Tampa and children Sadie and Saul; Sam's children, Richard in Boston; Jeffrey and Lynda in Morristown and children Mara and Alexander, and his stepson, Christopher Humphreys. "We all visit back and forth and keep in touch by phone, letters and e-mail. It's sad that I don't have the siblings my mother and father had. I guess I look to my children to give me that family feeling my mother had with her sisters and I had with my cousins. They're all in the East now and I miss them. But I do keep in touch with them; Isabel in Fort Lee, Anne and Bernie in Tampa and Lil and Arnold in Boston." Adele and Jan also take trips together; their first was to England one winter when "we froze to death and had a great time!"

And then she adds, "I never had any definite expectations of what life would bring. So I have been pleasantly surprised that it's been going along pretty well. I've not been ill since I had polio at 23. No surgeries. One overnight stay in the hospital. I've been lucky in that respect. Ever since Norma died and Mother had her heart attack, I have observed and truly felt for a long time that when something very serious happens in life, it goes into the body. And I have just resolved that I was not going to let that happen to me. I feel that mental attitude has a lot to do with one's physical being. I stay very, very active physically, socially and mentally. And I feel well."

Adele describes some of the best times in her 33 years with Sam. "The travel was special. We traveled a lot even when the children were in high school. We would take two-week trips to South America, Europe, Israel. Not on tours. We would rent a car and go on our own. Just the two of us. My parents took trips to Europe and it sounded so wonderful when my mother would describe it. Sam and I spent the past two summers in France, renting small place, and I think, *I wish my mother could see me now.*

But I think the most fun for us was when we lived in New York. In 1977, we rented an apartment right near Sam's jewelry store and went home to Fair Lawn on weekends. I loved being in New York, living in an apartment. It was nice and compact and I couldn't accumulate too much stuff. That's a very bad habit of mine. And I also loved seeing all the people coming and going. We were right in the financial district and I loved going out for lunch, even if by myself. We were only one block from Wall Street and there was so much action going on. And I loved it because I worked with Sam in the store for seven years. I did everything; selling, cleaning the cases, sweeping the sidewalk, running errands to the 47th Street jewelry district. I loved the New York scene."

Adele held different full time jobs during the '60s and '70s. She worked at Medical Economics magazine for over four years, first as a secretary and then in the editorial department. She laughs disparagingly about being "a terrible secretary" and was much happier working on the editing side of the magazine. She also went to NYU to earn an MA in Counseling and then became part of a five-person team at the mental health center in Paramus. "A wonderful job." However, when they rented the apartment in New York for Sam to avoid commuting, she left the Day Treatment Center and began to work with Sam in the jewelry store. At the same time, she began taking courses at the Greenwich House Pottery. These years show Adele as a woman of great resilience with multiple talents and interests as well.

In 1979, they sold the Fair Lawn house and bought "another dream house", on a mountain-top in Denville, New Jersey. She describes it as smaller, high above the tree tops. There was a lake close by with swimming privileges and they spent weekends there until Sam retired. They began going to Tucson in the winters during the early '80s. By 1985, when Sam retired, they knew they wanted to relocate to Arizona. The beauty and ease of the desert life were most agreeable. They sold Denville and bought their home on Grey Mountain Trail at the foothills of the Santa Catalina Mountains.

During her years in Tucson, Adele has pursued many interests. And she credits Sam as always being completely supportive and encouraging. "I couldn't do all these things if he weren't. And this has made me feel that a supportive spouse is one of the most important requirements for a happy marriage. At least, it is for me. I try to be supportive of his interests and activities too." She became active on the local ACLU board and originated a talk show on the local TV station. "I feel strongly that everyone should be treated fairly and the ACLU seemed the right agency for my energy." The TV show went well for about a year, with Adele serving as the host, but then closed when other volunteers were not available to help with the work. She was then elected to the Arizona state board and served for five years. During that time, she was awarded volunteer of the year for the Tucson TV program.

There are many passions in Adele's life. "The environment. What we are doing to the earth, the air and the water. I belong, of course, to the Sierra Club, and concerns about these issues affect my voting and political persuasion. I guess I'm pretty left, very liberal in my thinking and my positions. I learned from my mother and my Uncle Irving, my other role model, about caring, sharing and being generous. Not to keep everything for oneself. And I am strongly pro-choice and favor birth control all over the world."

Her love for the Arts has grown ever stronger over the years. "I love all kinds of music: concerts by our local excellent orchestra, our local wonderful chamber concert series, jazz groups, country, rock — just about everything. My all time favorites are the Beatles! Though I took piano lessons for years until age fifteen, I never became proficient. And I took cello lessons for eight years (1991-1999) and gave that up because I couldn't master the thing! I should have started sooner. Playing a stringed instrument is one of my unfulfilled ambitions. I thought it would be so much fun to play with my grandchildren, Sadie and Saul, who are violinists, and with Bill, who can play anything."

"In 1998, I actually danced on the stage at the University with a group led by Stuart Pimsler, an exceptional modern dancer who used local non-dancers of all ages and abilities in his performance. That was the first time I'd done modern dance since college. I love it. Stuart was an inspiration, very patient and helpful and creative, using choreography suggested by the twenty members of the group. The Arts have contributed a great deal to my enjoyment of life, to be able to appreciate music, to go into an art gallery and really enjoy the art and architecture wherever I am. I am very grateful that my horizons were broadened at a young age."

She is more interested in the artistic aspect of clothing and jewelry rather than "making a fashion statement". She doesn't shop for her outfits, rather picks up "little bits of things to put together, a blouse, a belt, a pair of slacks." The net result is a classic individual style using natural fabrics and colors that enhance her 5'7" figure. Not everyone can match up jeans, a shirt, drop earrings and a minimum of makeup and look as good as she does. She compares her clothing to her cooking. "I love to take leftovers and create imaginative dishes. All those things in the refrigerator; I take them and make a casserole. Twenty ways to use up a Thanksgiving turkey! And pasta, my favorite stuff. All kinds. But not baking. Never did that."

Since she has moved so many times in her life, forming friendships has been difficult. "I have a good friend in each place we lived, Tampa, Denville. But it takes a while." One of her dearest friends, Marysol Johns, whom she met in the '60s, died of cancer in 1996. "A great loss for everyone who knew her as she was such an exceptional person." Adele belongs to three women's groups; a book club for six years, an investment club for three years and the ongoing association with the Smith College alumnae. "I love learning and I feel very good with women friends. The book club has helped me read some books that I might otherwise have missed. I seldom choose the book. In this group I'm a follower, as there are members who are more literate than I. My reading is mostly newspapers, magazines, book reviews and all the info one has to read to keep up with politics, finances and local events. Some of my favorite books are: *No Ordinary Time* by Doris Kearns Goodwin, *Undaunted Courage* by Stephen Ambrose and everything by Barbara Kingsolver. As for the investment club members, they are mostly young working women who bring a whole different viewpoint to my life. And they are way ahead of me in math and economics. I'm learning a lot."

When the serious questions of concerns about illness and death are raised, Adele answers in a way that combines her practical view of life and her sense of humor as well. "I do think about that. I do. I am covered with a policy for long-term care. And we have financial trusts in place: 'His' and 'Hers'.I would love to be buried with my ancestors in Paterson." And now she laughs heartily. "But on the other hand, my pragmatism tells me that it would cost a fortune to ship my body from here to New Jersey. And maybe the kids can find a better way to use the money. I used to be kind of nervous about death. But now that the children seem to be quite independent and able to get along without me, it doesn't bother me as much." And again, she laughs. "I feel like, well — I can leave."

As for the future, she comments further, "Of course, we don't know what's coming up in the future. And I'm glad I won't be around too far into the millennium, as I feel very pessimistic about the condition of the world. I do worry about my descendants' life here on earth. I think we're probably living during the height of good times. I can't imagine things could be this good again."

Adele has embarked on several new endeavors — bridge lessons, studying Yoga and taking a course at the University of Arizona, "Questioning Genesis." She plans to attend a series of concerts with her women friends and is looking ahead to the summer with a possible return to New England. "Probably the most outstanding aspect of my personality is that I want to do twenty things at once. I usually overschedule. I just have too many interests." Her enthusiasm for new ideas and experiences and her zest for living every minute to the fullest are salient characteristics of Adele Baydin.

In her living room, the sun is low in the sky and the mountains are taking on deeper hues of sienna and purple in the changing light of the late afternoon. She is at home on Grey Mountain Trail. But then, Adele would be at home anywhere in the world. Her open approach to life and her inner confidence were nurtured by the years of approval and the security of her

110

'entitled' childhood. She has found the courage and optimism to come through the dark times in her life. And to meet the challenges she faced. Each day, Adele continues to make the most of all life has to offer.

CHAPTER VI

LILLIAN'S STORY

"And still I rise...."
— Maya Angelou

Lillian Vaughan brings drama with her when she enters a room. She dresses with flair and vivid color, wears numerous rings, bracelets and necklaces, and flashes a klieg-light smile as she tosses a mane of long blond dreadlocks about her shoulders. Her eyes sparkle as she speaks, conveying a wealth of energy and warmth. Her voice has a certain timbre and almost casts a spell upon the listener. She is an African-American woman of seventy who looks at least ten years younger. And she is more than ready for the next adventure in life.

Lillian begins her story with memories of her early childhood. "I was born in Brooklyn and my mother died when I was five years old. My father, who was fifty-one when I was born, had the option to have other relatives bring me up. But he chose not to do that. And I feel I am very blessed because my father was a wonderful person. He did everything for me." She describes how her father washed and ironed her clothes. And cooked. He took her every Saturday to the movies. The one thing he could not do was braid her hair. But he found someone close by to help. Robert Lewis had been married before and Lillian was his thirteenth child. She was the only child her mother, Gertrude Lewis, ever had.

"My father said I was the lucky one in his life. The other twelve lived in Boston and were much, much older than I. By the time I became aware of them, there were only two left. It wasn't really spoken of. He was an extremely protective father. When I first met them, and his first wife was still alive, they made my father cry. As a child, I only knew that I didn't want anyone making my father unhappy. Especially when he had been so good to me."

About her mother, Lillian remembers very little. "It's so hard. I remember

113

her taking me to Macy's and buying me a doll. I remember walking down the street with her. And I remember a pin on her dress and the rise as she breathed. I don't know why that just stayed with me." Her mother was forty when Lillian was born, considered late in those days. She recalls that her father was more affectionate, reading the Sunday "funnies", while her mother lacked patience at times. Lillian also explains that her mother was extremely fair skinned and when she first came to New York, she passed for white. "Later, she came back in." Her mother was also the disciplinarian. There was no waiting "until my father came home." Her mother took Lillian to the circus in the winter and caught a cold that turned into pneumonia. By the time she was taken to the hospital, it was snowing and "she was left on the sidewalk for a while." She developed double pneumonia and died in the hospital. The year was 1935, before penicillin and sulfa drugs were created.

Lillian's father worked in a drugstore and arranged for someone else to give her lunch. He always cooked dinner and fried chicken was special. He had served in the Navy in the Mess, where he had developed his skills as a cook. He loved the movies and Lillian came to love them as well. There were two movies plus the news and the cartoons. She recalls the trips to Rockaway Beach in the summers and the times they went to the World's Fair in 1939. "I was in public school and I remember the boy who kept bothering me. He would throw stones at me. My father came to school. He was always there for me. He was my protector." Lillian describes herself as a good student and a "good girl" in school." She also makes a point of saying, "My father never put his hand on me. He believed that no man should put his hand on a female!" Rather, he discussed at great length all the problems and growing-up issues that arose. She laughs ruefully and comments, "He talked and talked and talked. Sometimes, I'd rather he whipped me instead of all that talking!"

Lillian and her father moved to Boston, where she found herself put back a grade in school. "They looked down on the New York schools." When she was twelve and getting ready to enter high school, she was stricken with nephritis, a severe kidney disease. She was hospitalized and treated with the methods of the day, complete bed rest and drinking water constantly. There were no medicines. Lillian believes that "God has been good to me. But I had to be flat on my back for over a year. When I was in the hospital, I had turned thirteen and I was in the adult ward. And it was colorful there with pretty curtains. I became very close with the other women who were seriously ill." She was not in pain except for the dreaded monthly examinations. "They would insert a rod up into my vagina so that they could see my kidney. It was extemely painful. I would turn white just thinking about it."

114

During that year, her father had moved back to New York. Lillian lost an entire year of school while she recovered at home. But she does not speak of her illness with bitterness or regret. "I was used to being alone so I managed to get though those long months." They lived in Brooklyn and when she was well, Lillian attended Girls High, where she formed new friendships. She spent every summer in Washington with relatives on her mother's side of the family. She called one of her cousins ,'Aunt' since she was so much older. "They were educated middle-class people. Some were teachers; others worked in government positions. And they had their own houses and neighborhood. I had so many friends there. I loved going there, even though there was segregation."

Lillian recalls her experiences with segregation. She describes sitting in separate sections in the movie theaters. "And one time, we were about a stone's throw from the White House. We were in a drugstore and went up to the counter to get a soda. And we weren't allowed to sit at the counter and they put the soda in a paper container. That left a big impression on me. I could see the White House! And I could never get over that." She was in high school at the time. When she returned to New York after that summer, she spoke about what had happened to her friends. And she remembers until today how she felt.

Lillian speaks of her father with deep love and respect. Although she spent summers with her mother's family, she gives her father full credit for her upbringing. "No one brought me up but my father! I don't want anyone taking that away from him. Often, African American men are criticized for what they do or don't do with their children. But I've never criticized my father because of what he was to me." Robert Lewis lived to be 84 years old. Lillian was married by that time and pregnant. She regrets that he did not live to see her children. "He had a very strong sense of who he was. I got that from him. If anyone pushed him — even when he was in his 70s and 80s — he was ready to defend himself."

She talks about the friends with whom she grew up and how important they still are in her life. "I have such good friends. My friends are very important to me. I have one friend from when I was ten and we moved to Boston. And we are still close. Then, there was the time when I was fifteen and my father contracted pneumonia, followed by tuberculosis. I moved in with my friend Iris, who lived up the street. Her family took me in." Lillian says of another friend in New York, "She and I are like sisters. She was nine when I was seventeen. Her children are my 'nephews'. They call me, 'Aunt Lillian'." She admits that there have been differences in politics and disagreements at times with her friends, but not enough to sever the relationships. Her friendships have held because she has wanted them to hold.

Boys and dating played a part during her high school years. "There were brownstones in Brooklyn with stoops and front gates. And my father was always waiting on the stoop or at the gate for me to come in. He would ask, 'What are you doing out there so long?' There was no privacy. Certainly not for goodnight kisses." Lillian belonged to a social organization at the church, where she and Iris found other teenagers to mix with. They would all go up to the Bronx, where they felt very out of place. "It seemed as if we had signs that said, 'We're from Brooklyn'. Everybody looked at us. It was so strange. We felt like a fish out of water." The group was a social center for Lillian. She did not attend church on a regular basis, nor did her father.

During her summers in Washington, she took part in church services. Her relatives were of different denominations, Baptist, Methodist and Catholic. "The aunt that I stayed with, that I was named for, I looked up to her so much. Lillian Harper. She was very intelligent. She was a supervisor in the Pentagon. She was a marvelous cook. And she loved to travel. She was a role model for me." Lillian adds sadly that there was a falling out with her Washington relatives as she grew older. She recalls in the '60s when they did not approve of her 'natural' hairstyle. And more significant, when the riots occurred after Martin Luther King's assassination in 1968.

"They would sit and talk about 'What do those people want?' I would ask, 'What people? Whom are you talking about?' I was from Brooklyn where we had pride before 'Black Pride' came along. I got that from my father." Lillian describes Washington as a place where skin color and hair texture mattered more than in New York. And she sees much truth in Spike Lee movies which explore this subject today.

After her graduation from high school, Lillian had planned to go to college. But she recalls clearly that the guidance counselors, even in New York, did not push the black students in the direction of college. "I can remember sitting in the counselor's office and hearing her say to someone else about me, 'I don't think she's college material. Do you?' I felt very badly. It hurt my feelings and I didn't have the chutzpah, as I would have today, to come back at her. I don't mean violently, but even verbally I would have been thrown out of school!" Lillian did not tell her father about the incident. She had good grades in all subjects except the commercial areas and was graduated with an academic Regents diploma. At first, she wanted to be a medical technician but soon transferred to Brooklyn College which was tuition free. With the encouragement of her father and her aunt in Washington, she enrolled in Liberal Arts courses. Then, Lillian adds, "After

116

a year and a half, I met someone."

During the summer, she took certain courses at night school to make up subjects that had been omitted in her highs chool preparation. She had taken accounting instead of algebra. It was during night school that she met Terry Vaughan. "I met this young man, who I thought was very, very nice. He was raised by nice parents and always a lot of fun to be with. And he was handsome and had a good build. He was into sports, football and track. I had always thought that Washington men had more panache. But I met Terry and that was it!" Lillian laughs as she tells me about him and how they started going together. "My father liked Terry. That was important to me. I was twenty and he was nineteen. And he wanted to join the Army and become a paratrooper." The year was 1950.

When Terry enlisted, they separated for a while, but then decided to marry. Since New York required the couple to be 21, they needed their parents' permission to marry. Both sets of parents were in favor of the marriage and gave their approval. Terry came home on leave and they went to the judge to waive the three-day waiting period. "I remember the judge asking him if he was sure he wanted to do this. He said, 'Yes'." They didn't have a big wedding. They were married in the home of the minister from his parents' church. And after a small reception, they went to the Statler Hotel for a two-day honeymoon. "We walked around the city and went to the movies. And we had a favorite place we liked to go to eat Italian food. We had a wonderful two days."

After their honeymoon, Terry was sent to Fort Bragg in North Carolina. Lillian's father came down with tuberculosis and she moved in with her in-laws. Lillian says that her mother-in-law resented her at first. Terry was the only son and the oldest child. She credits her father-in-law with clearing the air once and for all. "In those days, the father ruled the roost. He said to her, 'Margie, I don't want any foolishness going on in this family! You accept.' And that was the end of that." From that conversation on, Lillian had a good relationship with her mother-in-law. She then made a decision that would affect her life in the years to come. She dropped out of college and went to work. "I'm not sure what I was thinking. Probably that I was married and didn't need college. And I was very headstrong. Even if my father or any of the relatives had tried to dissuade me, I probably wouldn't have listened. I just did it."

Lillian worked as a receptionist for a dentist in Manhattan. Then Terry sent for her to join him and she traveled down south in a segregated railroad car. They lived in Fayetteville, which had a slave mart in the middle of town. They didn't know that they weren't allowed to walk through it and once did

117

so by mistake. People had tried to bomb it and it was off limits. She says, "We were walking down the street at times and people driving by would yell out, 'Niggers'." If they did go into town to the movies, they sat in the separate section for 'Coloreds'. Lillian says that she spent most of her time reading and did not go into Fayetteville alone. Terry bought her a puppy to keep her company. After five months, when he was shipped out to Camp Stewart in Georgia, she packed up to move back to New York.

She relates what happened next. "I got ready to board the train. I just jumped on with the puppy in my arms. But the conductor said, 'The puppy will have to stay in the baggage car.' He took me to the baggage car, where he also gave some food for the dog. Then he let me sit in the 'white' car because it was nearest to the baggage car. I still remember how human he was. He was white. All the people who came in and walked through the car just looked at me. But he had told me to sit there. And I did." Lillian returned to New York to care for her father, who was recovering from tuberculosis, and to find work.

Lillian entered the Civil Service, taking the exam and doing clerical work in the New York State Insurance Fund office. "I met a most wonderful woman there. Helen Wiley. I didn't know what she was. I thought she was white, but she wasn't. She was black. We became the closest friends. And talk about a role model! She's in her nineties now, lives by herself in a co-op and still goes out every day. She's been wonderful to me and my children. Like family." Lillian describes the work she did as very boring and routine. But she needed the income and the salary was steady. She saw the job as a means to an end.

The era of the mid-'50s was the time of focus on the Civil Rights movement in the country. The historic desegregation of the schools meant that "separate was inherently unequal." Changes were taking place in many areas of life. Lillian became interested in the political campaign of Shirley Chisholm, who ran for a seat in the New York State Legislature. "My father always was involved in Democratic politics and my values were very similar to his. I worked on her campaign. She was a firebrand. And she won. Later she ran for a seat in the United States House of Representatives. She became the first black woman to enter Congress."

During this time period, Terry had been transferred to Fort Bliss in Texas. He earned promotion to the rank of Sergeant and was sent to Fort Slocum in New York. There he served as a Training and Information officer. His next transfer was to California and Lillian decided to go with him. She left her job and they took the train cross-country, a trip that she describes as a second honeymoon. "We left from Grand Central. We had a little compartment. We were the only young black couple on the train. He was in uniform. He was a good-looking guy. The steward in the dining car was black and we got such service!" The trip lasted four nights and five days with a stop-over in Chicago. Lillian remembers it as a very sweet time of being together.

Once in California, they stayed with friends until they found a place to live. Terry was stationed at Fort Mac Arthur in San Pedro, south of Los Angeles. Lillian still has reservations about California. She describes the people as 'plastic' , especially compared to New Yorkers. "I was never too particular about California. I didn't know whether it was because of Hollywood. Of course, the only people we became friendly with were in the service. We lived close to the base. It's a very pretty place with flowers growing up around telephone poles. But the people were very shallow."

An incident occurred that cemented Lillian's negative feelings about California. She went into San Pedro, following up an advertisement in the newspaper for a clerical position. She felt her Civil Service experience in New York more than qualified her for the job. She took the trolley into Los Angeles and found the employment agency. "As soon as I stepped off the elevator, a woman stood up and came over to meet me. We were walking toward her desk, when she said, 'Oh, my dear, we do business with southern oil companies. And they won't hire little colored girls.' To tell you the truth — to this day, I feel it. She had an open inkwell on her desk and I saw colors. I saw all kind of colors! And I guess God stayed my hand, because I wanted to pick up that inkwell and fling it!" Lillian never went out looking for a job there again. Terry was angry and disgusted when she told him what had happened. The ads at the time openly called for 'white' or 'Caucasian' applicants. Her crushing experience in California has stayed with her for almost fifty years. Her voice conveys the outrage she still feels when she talks about it.

When Terry was discharged, the couple relocated to New York. Terry worked at the Brooklyn Public Library and Lillian was at The Department of Labor, within the Civil Service. She liked the position, working on unemployment insurance. They lived in an apartment in Brooklyn, in Crown Heights. "It was a nice neighborhood. Near the Brooklyn Children's Museum. Big old apartment houses. We lived there for twenty-two years." They wanted to start a family, but it took seven years until they were successful. Lillian had been told that she could never have children because of her girlhood year-long bout with nephritis. She went to the Margaret Sanger Fertility Clinic, where she met a doctor who was to take care of her during her pregnancy. "He became my father figure. Dr. Leonard Steiner. A very bright man who used to donate time to the Clinic."

119

Lillian speaks with great happiness about this time in her life. "My husband and I were filled with joy when I became pregnant. My father-in-law was ecstatic! My mother-in-law too." Terry Robert, named for his father and grandfather, was born on May 10th. Lillian had gained over forty pounds, despite the warning to avoid salt and water retention. Her kidneys were burdened but she was able to complete a full-term pregnancy. "The doctor kept telling me, 'It's all water.'" She kept working until January. "I left to avoid climbing the stairs." When she went into a long, protracted labor, the doctor felt a Caesarean section was needed. The baby boy weighed 8 pounds, 12 ounces, and was healthy in every way. And Lillian found out that the weight she had gained was not all water!

Lillian says that she was not a confident new mother. "I had a most wonderful pediatrician, Dr. Rosenberg. In those days, doctors made house calls. And you could call him at a quarter to eight in the morning and three in the afternoon with questions. When he didn't hear from me in two days, he would say, 'Congratulations, Mrs. Vaughan, I haven't heard from you in two days!'" Dr. Spock was the popular baby book at the time and Lillian read it with a passion. She worried if Terry cried and if Terry did not cry. If he threw up, was that projectile vomiting? Unfortunately, the baby did have colic with ongoing crying and screaming. Lillian's aunt came to help her for the first weeks. "I was terrible. I hadn't been around children. I didn't know a thing about children." As with so many other new mothers, Lillian survived her on-the-job training, Terry outgrew his colic and she settled into full-time motherhood. She never nursed him, since mothers were discouraged at that time. Today, she is aware of the theory that the pills that stopped milk formation may be linked to breast cancer in later years.

As the baby developed, Lillian spoke about going back to work. But that was not what Terry wanted for his family. "My husband was very emphatic about my not working. He told me that my life was at home bringing up our child. That was my life. He had been brought up that way and he was adamant about it." Lillian agreed to follow his wishes. She cared for her son, took walks to the park and joined the League for Parent Education. This group met once a month and had visiting child experts and psychologists speak. The heart of each session was a discussion where the mothers shared their experiences with their children. Today, this group would be called a 'support' group. Lillian says, "It was wonderful! It wasn't for parents with problem children. Just to share."

Lillian did resent Terry's insistence that she remain at home. When their son was two, she tried to go back to work. "But my son was very attached to me. I was his security blanket. He didn't want anyone else taking care of him." She tried to take him to a church where there was day care, but every day he would complain of severe stomach aches. Her pediatrician advised that he was not ready for her to be away. Then he came down with a series of ear infections and the need for a tonsillectomy. Lillian became discouraged and gave up the idea of going back to work. And she did want to have other children. Five years later, Vanessa was born. She was delivered by Caesarean section as Terry had been. "I used to worry because I loved Terry so much. And I wondered how was I going to have enough love for another child. But the minute you see that baby, your heart opens up." During Vanessa's delivery, Lillian was awake. She remembers saying the Lord's Prayer in thankfulness.

When Vanessa was born, Terry was in pre-school. Lillian found that with the new baby at home, Terry became independent. "He was very bright and moved right into first grade." She also found that Vanessa was much easier to care for. "I guess I was so much better!" But the new baby did have a serious physical problem. Her feet turned in and every two weeks, Lillian took her to the hospital, where they tried to straighten her feet manually. "She would scream and turn her little head and look at me. It was terrible!" Then they put casts on, from her feet to her knees. This lasted for three months. The method worked and she was able to progress to special shoes when she was old enough to stand and walk. Then to regular shoes when the problem was eliminated.

When Vanessa was three, Lillian says, "Things fell apart." Terry was a member of the police force. He had made the career switch before their son was born. And Lillian felt that he changed as a person when he left the Library to become a police officer. "To me, he was a gentle man. He could write poetry. It's like taking someone and throwing him into what was the opposite of what he was all about. He became hardened being out on the streets. He was in East New York and he saw so much. His whole manner of looking at life changed and we were definitely on opposite sides. And things fell apart in our marriage. I didn't want to live that way." Terry's father was very ill with cancer and his death affected him deeply as well. Lillian describes their discordant marital life. "We were forever arguing. The children would be there. Vanessa would just sit and sob. And I felt there was another woman out there. I decided one New Year's Day that I wasn't going to live like that anymore. I told him to get out!"

Lillian had met with a psychotherapist before the breakup, trying to understand why she felt that she had failed at marriage. Terry only came once to these sessions. When he talked, he would bring up incidents that Lillian couldn't even remember. "I said, looking at him, 'I don't know this man!' He got up and left the room. He didn't like to talk. And by that time I was able to express myself." Lillian says she always felt marriage would be like Hollywood — living happily ever after. The psychotherapist told her, "You act as if it's all your fault." The separation was a shock to her and she went into a decline. She couldn't eat, lost weight and became very thin. She never told anyone at work what had happened. She explained the weight loss by saying she had low blood pressure. Since the job was only a temporary position, she did not want to jeopardize it in any way.

Lillian had friends who were her confidants. But she adds, "A lot of women at that time felt, if he's paying the rent, what's the big deal?" She did not feel that way. Her aunt and uncle also came to advise and help her. Terry would come to visit the children, but Lillian did not consider allowing him to come back. The differences between them were too great. She does emphasize that he was a good father to their two children. He was working in the schools as a policeman. He bought food and paid the rent. "He was raised that way. I give him credit for that." Lillian says with sadness that the separation deeply affected the children. "Oh, my son. He went out one day and took too long to come back. I was so worried. He was eight and we always talked , one on one. I explained to him that he had a good father and he would see him. I went to school and told the teachers. And he seemed to handle it. But with Vanessa, she was more introverted. She was only three when we separated. Later I learned that she always felt that we would get back together." Lillian thinks Vanessa felt, as children often do when a divorce occurs, that it was her fault. She regrets now that she didn't have the time to spend with her as she had spent with her son. She had to work and was "torn up myself inside."

Lillian sees this very hard period in her life as a turning point. This was also the time when her father-in-law had become ill and died a very painful death. Lillian describes the significance of his death to her. "My own father was much older when he died. In his eighties. This man was in his fifties when he died. A very hard death. I found out from him that you'd better enjoy life while you're here! And if I couldn't speak to Terry and get along, it was no good. I don't believe in staying together if the marriage is a farce!" She does not believe that it is better to stay together for the sake of the children. "Children are not stupid. They know what is going on!"

Lillian feels she is very spiritual, believing in prayer and God. She shares a very important event that occurred after she had been separated only a short while. She was trying to find her way and felt burdened by the shock and the changes she was going through in her life. "The kids had gone off to school and I lay back down to rest. I was very unhappy. All of a sudden, I felt a presence in the room. I tried to turn and look. And suddenly, the weight that had been on me was lifted from me. So help me, God! From that day, I said, 'I'm going forward. I'm going to be all right. I felt the presence was God." She believed that she could do whatever she had to do. Terry told her that she would be like a 'sheep thrown to the wolves' if she persisted in the separation. But Lillian was determined that she would make it.

The divorce took years before it became final. During that time, Lillian took temporary jobs until the children were older. She worked at the Motor Vehicle Bureau in Brooklyn for two months. "A nightmare job. It was horrible! Those were angry people. Not like the people at the unemployment office." She worked at several other jobs, one with Union Carbide. Everything was still in Terry's name and Lillian wanted her own charge card and bank account. The bank officer at Manufacturer's Hanover was receptive. "He said, 'You impress me.' And he gave me a loan of $500 and told me to go out and buy something in order to establish a line of credit." She went to Saks furniture and bought a coffee table. Lillian was now financially independent. Her next job was as a counselor for Manpower, a private placement agency. "You didn't need a degree in those days. I was very good at talking to people and drawing them out. I had to find out what their assets were. And test them. Then I had to talk to employers as well. To mesh the two together. I always enjoyed talking to people."

After a few years, she moved to the Ford Foundation, where she did clerical work in different departments. She started in the library, then as an assistant in the mail room and finally into systems, which she did not like. She had no training for the technical work required and also found that the man she reported to was a very difficult boss. She has only the highest compliments for the Ford Foundation itself. "They were really on top of things. Ford was ahead of the curve. Whatever you wanted to know, they had the information — like that!" But Lillian found working with her boss to be very stressful. "I had always been able to work with people before. It just got to the point where it was all too much. I had the children, of course. And my stomach would get in a knot when I walked in the door at work." She couldn't go back to her old position unless she stayed where she was for six months. And this she felt she could not do. Instead, she went to the bank, took out a loan and gave them two weeks notice.

Her boss, who had turned down her request for a salary increase, said, "I didn't know you were looking for a job."

And Lillian said, "I haven't been."

He replied, "You have two children. How can you do this?"

She told him, "I'm not worried about it and I don't think you should be."

Lillian did consider going back to college. She tried to do that while she had been working at the Ford Foundation. "I met a young man, a bright guy. He was a detective in the police department. He was a law student and he encouraged me to go back and finish my degree. He gave me that incentive and I started back at NYU." She took classes at night after work in a program for returning students. The homework load was very heavy with library assignments and extensive reading on the weekends. "Vanessa was very young. And I started to see a change in her behavior. I said, 'It's not fair to her.' I spoke to one of the teachers and she said, 'Bring her to school with you.' But how could I do that? At night! So I just stopped." Lillian felt that if she hadn't gone back in the seven years before she had children, then it was not fair for her to do it when they were still young. She adds somewhat wistfully, "I didn't go back. After they were grown, I guess I could have. But I didn't."

After an interim return to Manpower, a friend gave her a recommendation to The New York Stock Exchange. She took a position as a customer service representative. The salary was less at the beginning, but she quickly earned promotions in seniority with appropriate increases. The benefits were exceptional, as they had been at the Ford Foundation. "At the Stock Exchange, you were dealing with people all around the world. I was in market data. You had to be approved to handle privileged information. And I was approved." Lillian describes the Stock Exchange as 'a little private club'. The pay rose within a year. And eligibility for the 401K program took place after a year as well. Two weeks vacation was a most attractive part of the benefits program to Lillian. Overall, she says that she liked the people she was working with more than the work itself, which entailed handling numbers and data. She held her position there for nineteen years.

During these years, both children were advancing through the parochial school system. Terry entered Phillips Academy on a scholarship. He had qualified for the ABC(A Better Chance) program sponsored by Dartmouth. Vanessa went on to Brooklyn Tech, from which she was graduated. Lillian comments, "Parochial school is good for the formative years. The discipline. But after a while, you have to get out and see what the world is all about." Lillian felt the same way herself and during the summers, she arranged for someone to stay with the children for two weeks so she could travel. "I had to have something to hold me together. I had to take care of me. I had to be happy about me. And I started traveling in 1969 and I've been out of the country every year since. I love it! I love different cultures. I love different people. I just can't stop!" Lillian first visited the Bahamas, then traveled to Madrid, Seville, Morocco, London, Jordan, Belgium and many times to the

Caribbean Islands for "total relaxation". Her six trips to Africa have been of great importance to her.

The '60s were the era of the Civil Rights Movement. Lillian comments, "I was not active. The children were still young. But we would watch what was happening on television and I would be very angry! The day of the March on Washington in 1963, I was in the hospital with a miscarriage. Vanessa was just three months old. I don't know how that happened!" Lillian describes herself as very militant. "I had always said I would be in the Black Panther party if I didn't have children." She wanted to be on jury duty since so many black people were being brought into the courts. When she signed up, she was immediately chosen for the Grand Jury. She found the cases very interesting. "I saw so many things that came through that were not in the papers. A lot of times, I had to wear sunglasses especially when children were involved. I found some of the assistant district attorneys to be prejudiced." Lillian questioned the repeated reference to a Hispanic woman as a 'common-law wife'. She asked what that had to do with the charge. "I was very outspoken."

She left the Grand Jury for service on the Petit Jury. She used to carry books that were very militant, like Eldredge Cleaver's, *Soul on Ice*. One of her friends warned her, "Lillian, you don't go into court carrying books like that!" She met a white man in the jury pool who wore a huge Huey Newton button. He called himself a 'White Panther'. Every time they called him up to be considered for a panel, he was disqualified. "We would have lunch together. And I had this big Afro. The two of us! They would look at us, each with our way of rebelling." She also became active against apartheid in South Africa while she had been at the Ford Foundation. She took part in marches outside the South African Embassy, carrying coffins and placards. And she belonged to an organization, 'Sisters Against South African Apartheid'. They raised funds, and urged pulling money out of banks. Lillian stresses, "This was very important to me!" She does note that one of the managers at Ford saw her one day and cautioned that she should not be taking part in protests during her lunch hour.

Lillian becomes very animated as she says, "I have always been for the underdog. Always! No matter whom or why." She feels this came from her father and his beliefs. And from living in Crown Heights, where most of the people were Jewish. "I remember a little boy who was Orthodox Jewish moving next store. I saw a group of older black boys picking on him and I ran over and made them stop." She shares that she is a Libra, the sign with the scales. "You just don't like to see injustice. And it gives me a good insight into people."

When Lillian is posed the question, "What is it you are most passionate about?", her answer is complex. It seems to escalate as she speaks. "There are many things that are important to me. My children, of course. I want to see them succeed and have really good lives. And I'm passionate about politics. And Africa! I'm very passionate about Africa! I'm passionate about different cultures. I'm passionate about reading. I am a passionate person! Sometimes too much so." She cites the song from *Funny Girl* that Barbara Streisand made famous — "People". Although she describes herself basically as a loner, liking to come into her place and shut the door, she also wants to have her friends to go out with and have a good time. "I feel I have a good intuitiveness into people. The people who want to be a part of my life turn out to be the right people. I'm polite to everyone. But I know when I really want to be bothered with someone, male or female."

Lillian was 64 and working at The Stock Exchange when she encountered the physical illness that American women say they fear more than any other — breast cancer. "I always went for a mammography and as I was showering one evening, I felt a lump. I felt false safety because of having the mammography. I called my doctor the next morning, who referred me to the radiologist. He was a great doctor. After the biopsy, he called me the same day and told me that it was malignant." At first, Lillian says she was very frightened. But she credits the surgeon with a combination of skill and compassion as setting her on the right course. He assured me, "This is not going to be the end of your life." Because of the size of the growth, Lillian had a modified-radical mastectomy followed by six months of chemotherapy. The lymph nodes were found to be free of cancer cells. "I was fine, because I had faith. If I didn't have faith, I don't think I would have gone through this as well as I did. I was fine in the hospital. I was there ten days. Today, they throw you out! Same-day breast surgery. That's ridiculous! I am so angry about that for women today."

Her son brought her home from the hospital and sought to reassure her that she would be fine. Her daughter had bought Lillian a beautiful set of silk pajamas to welcome her home. When she undressed, she was shocked as she saw the scar for the first time. "That threw me and I started crying." She says her son was sympathetic but not too much so. He stressed that she would survive and make a good recovery. Lillian did not find the months of chemotherapy to be an ordeal. At first, she was tired and encountered some nausea. Her regimen was two weeks on and two weeks off. Her doctor prescribed a pill that controlled the nausea and she also escaped losing her hair. She feels very lucky not to have had the side effects that so many women have to endure during chemotherapy. "I had wonderful doctors. All my life, I have had wonderful doctors. God has been good to me. I have been very lucky!" During the months of her recovery, Vanessa was married. And Lillian danced at her wedding.

Lillian urges young women to do monthly self examinations as well as the periodic mammography. "I lost two friends to breast cancer. And it is something that can be stopped if it is caught in time. One friend waited until the thirteenth hour, when it was too late." She feels some women are afraid or in denial. She stresses how important it is to have good doctors. And to have a second opinion. Another important help for her was the support group she was a part of. She had an 800 number to call in Chicago, 'Why me?' Lillian comments that the name of the group didn't make sense to her. "Why not me?" But she found their answers to her questions very helpful and reassuring. "I had been in a longtime relationship. And you begin to wonder about your femininity. Breasts in this country are the epitome of sex. And here you are without one! I just wondered who would want me in a relationship." Lillian confides that her fears were unfounded. It was not to be important in her relationships with men she became very close to in the years that followed.

Lillian, who now lives in Alexandria Virginia, belongs to a group called, 'Rise Sister Rise'. The members are all African American women who have had breast cancer. A well-known jazz musician, who lost a close relative to breast cancer, has publicized their group with a picture of the women on the cover of his CD and on the inside of the jacket. Lillian stresses that it was her faith that kept her together during her recovery and continues to give her inner strength today. "It was a challenge. I was very involved in my church at that time. The people were there for me. I would go to chemotherapy by myself. I just lived." Lillian planned to travel to India and Jordan when she completed chemotherapy. But a close friend who was a nurse cautioned her to take a less arduous trip. She went instead to the island of St. Lucia, where she relaxed and rested for two weeks.

Lillian did not return to The Stock Exchange after the six months spent in chemotherapy. She found that she needed to evaluate her life's direction. She had lived in the same co-op apartment for 22 years in Brooklyn. "I had the corner apartment on the 13th floor. It overlooked the Manhattan skyline. I could see all three bridges, the Empire State Building and the Chrysler Building. It was a beautiful apartment! When I would walk through at night, I would be drawn to the windows and the view. I love New York! I always will!" Despite her deep feelings about living in New York, and her ties to the home where she had raised her two children, Lillian made the major decision to move to Alexandria, Virginia to live nearer to Vanessa and her family. Her doctors asked her, "What are you going to do down there in Virginia?" Lillian calls herself 'a New Yorker in Diaspora'. Her closeness to Vanessa was the driving force in her decision.

She sold her co-op and rented an apartment in Alexandria. But she never cut her ties to New York. She often travels by train to spend the day with friends and soak up the atmosphere once more. Lillian has found that Washington DC became the center of her interests rather than Virginia. "I like Alexandria because it is so close to Washington. It's like going from Brooklyn to Manhattan, four stops away. I don't do anything in Virginia. My father was born in Virginia, but he left home when he was seventeen. He knew." She describes the people as 'nice' but not 'worldly'. She goes to church and shops in Washington. The only drawback to her move is that Lillian never learned how to drive. Her voice becomes wistful as she talks about this. "Isn't that sad. In New York, I didn't need to. And I never wanted to. And now, I feel it is too late to learn. And the traffic down here in Virginia and Washington is terrible. They planned the city that way so that the enemy would be confused!" She agrees that this is an exception to her overall pride in being independent. However, she stresses that she uses different means of mass transportation to get anywhere she wants to. She feels that not driving does not hold her back. "I have been to places that people with cars have not been!"

Lillian feels good about herself. "I like me. Basically I am a good person. I don't begrudge anyone. I try to be good to other people before I can sleep at night. There is no one I hate. There is no group of people that I dislike. I feel good about myself." She also talks about whether she feels fulfilled as a person, emotionally, intellectually and sexually. "I feel fulfilled, up to a point. Recently, I have not had a relationship and that is important to me." And then she laughs and says, "You come to a point in life when one can live without sex. God knew what he was doing when he aged us. And it is the companionship that is more important. Going to museums, taking walks together, sharing all the experiences with someone else." She is thankful for her friends and finds fulfillment in being with them.

The move from New York to Alexandria also brought a second important change in Lillian's life. She converted to Catholicism, something she had never expected to do. She says, "I think back to my father, who was doing housework for an Irish Catholic family. They would always send me those religious medals. And on my way to school, I would pass this Catholic church. When I got older and had something on my mind, I would go in and sit down and pray. I didn't know which saint was who. It didn't matter to me. And later I would go to St. Patrick's Cathedral all the time." She belonged to the Baptist church in Brooklyn as an adult and joined again when she moved to Alexandria. Then, Lillian met someone who asked her to come to her Catholic church in Washington. She returned many times to be part of the charismatic service. She found the church to be full of "warmth and love." "They sing Gospel, praise the Lord — full of love."

Lillian describes the church as a mixed congregation with different groups of people. After three years, she began the conversion process. She took classes and was confirmed. She is able to take Communion. "It was a very interesting ceremony because it was Easter Saturday. And a man sat on the altar and said, 'Why is this night different from any other night?' It was very interesting to me that the Catholic church would take that from the Passover Seder in Judaism." The priest on Sundays was young and a fiery iconoclast. He believed the Catholic Church needed to be changed. He said it was "full of cheap incense and there should be women in the pulpit." He shocked some of the congregation when he said, "Don't let an old man in Rome take your joy from you and tell you what you should and should not do! Because he puts his pants on one leg at a time, just as you do." Lillian adds, "He is not there anymore. But he is still a priest. Now, we have a young seminarian who tells us to 'Loosen up!'"

Her inner belief is that God is a forgiving God. "Anything I want to ask him to forgive me for, I am entitled to do. There's just one God, no matter what faith we have." She takes many people to the church, who are not Catholic, to see the service with the singing and participation. "I feel a sense of belonging to this church. If you come Sunday, you would feel it too." And she has shocked some people who say when they hear of her conversion, "What! You're going over to the dark side! You pray to saints!" She was not aware of prejudices against Catholics until she made her conversion. Lillian is amazed that other people would make such judgmental statements about another person's religion.

From the subject of inner faith, Lillian segues to the aging process and the effects on our bodies and our faces. "Age has never been important to me. I never put a number on people. It's just lately. I'm seventy. And I can't for the life of me believe that I'm there!" She and her friends joke about it. "Whoa! When I get up in the morning, I don't move as fast as I used to. This is not as much fun as I thought it was going to be." In a serious vein, Lillian is thankful that she is here. "I don't mean just the breast cancer. I get up in the morning and I can go and do. I have a fair amount of my faculties. I feel I am blest. I don't feel old. I still feel vibrant and able to do." She accepts that changes are taking place and there are things she no longer can do. The bone density test showed a certain amount of loss and she takes calcium and drinks milk to counteract this. She walks and is planning to work with weights to build muscle strength. She tries to eat healthy foods but finds the 'eating-out' temptations an ongoing challenge. She confides that she is not happy with her weight and needs to get in a regular exercise program. And she admits, "I am a procrastinator!"

As for physical beauty and aging, she adds, "My hair started turning gray when I was very young, twenty-seven. I've always colored my hair. My mother was completely grey at forty. I look at women, rich women who have had plastic surgery on their faces. Oh, not for me! Never!" Lillian did not opt for plastic surgery when she had breast cancer. The doctor told her she was an excellent candidate for reconstruction. "I said, 'No, that is not for me. It's gone. I've gotten beyond that. This is a part of me for seven years." She shares these intimate feelings with ease and warmth. She also speaks of many women she has met who have survived breast cancer and how well they look. And she feels grateful that the disease did not come earlier in her life.

Lillian met another physical problem during the past year. She relates the unusual story of how she had her gall bladder removed, almost by accident! She was having a follow-up sonogram to her breast surgery in New York. "And then, by mistake, they went down too far taking the picture. The medical technician said, 'She has a diseased gall bladder.' I said, 'I do?'" Her doctor wanted her to have it out immediately to avert it becoming cancerous. She returned to Washington, where it was removed with just an overnight hospital stay. "They make those dots and inject gas to raise the abdomen. And then they just remove the gall bladder!" Hundreds of tiny stones were found in her gall bladder. Yet Lillian had not suffered with any of the symptoms or attacks that are common to patients with this disease. She feels again that "God was watching over me" in the serendipitous way in which the discovery was made. She caps her account with what was on her breakfast tray the following morning. "There was sausage and grits and biscuits. I asked the nurse, 'Are you sure I can have this?' And she said, 'Yes, you can.' So, I ate the whole plate! It was delicious."

Her gall bladder surgery was the second time Lillian discovered by accident that she had a serious medical problem. In 1975, she had taken her children to the ophthalmologist to have their eyes checked. Since she had misplaced her own glasses, she decided to have her eyes checked as well for a new prescription. "He said, 'Let me examine your eyes.' Then, he became very excited. He was measuring the pressure in my eyes and found that I had glaucoma." Again, Lillian feels, "God was watching over me." The condition was controlled successfully for years by using drops. In recent years, she has undergone two different types of laser surgery to drain the fluid and the

130

pressure remains stabilized.

From health, she switches to a completely different area of life for women: fashion and clothes. Lillian lights up as she speaks. "I appreciate the arts and I think there's an artistic flair about me. I like to look different. I love color. Clothes don't have to be fancy. I like to match things from different styles." She enjoys finding clothes and jewelry that she can afford and putting them together in an interesting way. She does not admire fur coats or 'status stuff'. The stone necklace and earrings she is wearing were made by a friend in an African design as a birthday gift. In discussing the jewelry, Lillian relates some of her experiences during her visits to Africa.

"When I first went to West and East Africa, it did something very important for me. It took me a while to go to Africa. I went to the places where the slaves were kept before they were put on the ships for the terrible Middle Passage to America. And I saw the cells where they were held. It was very emotional to be there. I felt a great sadness. Then in West Africa, you see people who look like you. And I thought, *This is where I come from.*" In East Africa, Lillian asked their driver, "Where do you think I come from?" She recounts with deep feeling the fact that African-Americans are a mixture of peoples through the years of slavery and the rapes that women suffered by white overseers and plantation owners. "And my father's grandmother was Cherokee. My mother's grandmother was supposedly Cherokee. All these different blends. I ask, 'Who am I?'" She has a naïve Italian friend who asked her why she wanted to go to Africa. When Lillian responded by asking her if she wanted to visit Italy, her friend said, "Do you mean to tell me that all black people come from Africa?" Lillian quotes President Clinton, when he visited Africa, as saying, "All civilization started in Africa!"

Lillian recalls a highlight of her trips to Africa, the visit to Mount Kenya Safari Club. On her first time in East Africa, she stayed with a friend in Nairobi. The following morning, she joined five others to fly in a private plane to their destination. "We flew low so you could see the animals scurrying in the bush. And when we arrived at the airport, there were two Mercedes chauffeur-driven cars waiting for us. They drove us to the Club and I could then see what Europeans had benefitted from all the years before." Everything was very luxurious. Peacocks were walking around the manicured grounds. Lillian notes that there were no other guests who were people of color. "When the maître'd, who was African, came to take us into a private dining room, he held up his hand to stop some other people who were European. He said, 'I'm sorry. This is for members only.' I can't tell you what that meant to me. I had finally come to a place where I was not the minority! Of course, I was with someone who was a member. But it also meant that I belonged there."

On the second day, when a group of African dancers performed, Lillian felt overcome with the realization that she was actually there in Africa. The power of their dancing had a strong effect upon her and her emotions. She was filled with joy! She went out on safari twice and loved seeing the animals in the bush. They visited Masai country, where she was overwhelmed with the beauty of the people. "They are tall and very graceful with a walk almost like a giraffe. They would look up when we went by in the Land Rover and smile broadly when they saw us. I don't think they were used to seeing people of color inside the cars!" She spoke to one little boy and was very impressed with his knowledge of the United States. He knew the President, who was George Bush at the time. He knew the capital. She found the people to be very warm and welcoming. Lillian, at this point, makes a comparison to the American Indians, who were open and then taken advantage of by others who came into their country.

The beauty of Africa entrances Lillian. "I love West Africa. But in the East, the soil is so rich, it is as if you could take a stick and put it in the soil and it would sprout! The flowers! The jacaranda trees. The sunsets at night! In the distance, you can see Mount Kenya. And Mount Kilimanjaro, the highest mountain in Africa!" She tells what it is like to see the elephant herds going by from the Land Rover. One time, they were there when the annual migration was taking place in late October and November. "You just see the animals going by for miles and miles. They are going to the water. It is an unbelievable sight!" Lillian stays for at least three weeks when she travels to Africa. She has also visited a factory in Kenya where sisal mats are manufactured. She was impressed by the cleanliness of the plant. "You could have eaten off the floor. It was so clean! So organized."

When Lillian visits Africa, she does not meet or mix with other Americans. She wants to immerse herself in the culture of the people there. She is fortunate to have friends who live there and invite her into private homes and businesses as well. She differentiates between the cultures and peoples of West and East Africa. "East Africa was my first real inroad into Africa. I found the people in East Africa to be more restrained. Their sense of dress and decor is somewhat conservative. They are beautiful people and I found them to be wonderful. But when I stayed a length of time in West Africa, I saw a big difference between the result of French rule in the West and British rule in the East. In the West, the colors are vibrant. Reds! Yellows! Greens! And they wear them with such pride. The decor in their houses is also more vivid. And they are more gregarious and open when you go to their homes." She enjoys African food and has found it to be closely connected to West Indian foods. "I grew up in Brooklyn, which is a stronghold of West Indian culture. The rice dishes. The bean dishes. Okra. The way they use tomatoes and fish. All came directly from West Africa to the Indies."

The most powerful times for Lillian in Africa have been her visits to Goree Island in Senegal, where the Africans were kept before being taken on the long voyage to America. "Goree Island is the most infamous of the holding places! The cells were right downstairs under the dining room where the French officers ate. All the Africans piled on top of each other like cords of wood! We saw the chains." We talk about the two ways the slaves were jammed into the holds of the ships, 'tight packing' versus 'loose packing'. Over the years, the Dutch and British ship captains decided that the former method produced a net gain, even though more of the slaves perished during the voyage from the horrendous physical conditions. Lillian speaks with great emotion of Goree Island. One time, she met a curator there. He was French, and through an interpreter he said to her, "They took you away from us. But you are back."

There are ties to Africa in the community work that Lillian has done since she made the move to Alexandria. When she first relocated, she volunteered at MESAB, Medical Education for South African Blacks. The organization, at the time of apartheid, gave scholarships to enable the recipients to go to medical and dental schools. "It was an extremely worthwhile group and I went there once a week. The doctors and dentists were needed! I still try to help them whenever I can." MESAB has since moved its headquarters to New Jersey and Lillian has shifted her community efforts to the African Arts Museum. She works in the extensive research library and helps prepare files by organizing and typing information. "I get a sense of satisfaction. First of all, I love art. Of all kinds. Music. Dance. All the performing arts." Being in the African Museum, Lillian also meets the artists who visit. She particularly enjoys these firsthand experiences. "I met a young Ethiopian painter, just thirty. He impressed me so much. To be so young and yet so deep. He did self portraits, merely a shadow of himself. You could almost see through it!"

Lillian's interests cover a wide range in the Arts. "I like classical music, modern music, jazz and opera. The ones I am familiar with like *Carmen* and *Aida*. Something I know the story of and I can follow. But not Rap music. I'm not a Rap person!" She loves movies and the theater. The years she lived in New York, she took advantage of seeing as many shows as she could. She speaks very positively of the cultural scene in Washington. "You have the Kennedy Center, the Arena Stage, Studio Theater. The performing arts are strong here now." Lillian values the two original paintings she owns. One by a friend in Trinidad who is also a painter and the other by a Congolese painter. "They may not be very valuable, but they are important to me."

Lillian reflects on when she is happiest. She flashes her brightest smile as she shares, "I'm happiest when I am with my family. With Vanessa and her family and when I go out to visit Terry in Chicago. And being with my friends too. Of course, when I go up to New York, I'm really happy because I miss it so. And I'm happy when I'm getting ready for a trip, when I'm on a plane. There is a feeling of anticipation and excitement when we are taking off. I feel wonderful!"

When she considers the people she most admires, her initial answer takes her back to Africa. "I do admire Mandela. He comes to mind first because of what he endured. And how he came out of it. He is some kind of royalty as far as I am concerned." She next cites Maya Angelou, for the way she talks and the way she writes. Then, she shares her admiration for Hillary Clinton and her belief that Clinton will be a formidable senator. "I think she has the right stuff!" She closes with her memories of Eleanor Roosevelt and how she looked up to her for all her accomplishments, as the First Lady and afterwards as Ambassador to The United Nations. Most of all, as a woman ahead of her time.

On the difficult subject of regrets, Lillian is both serious and pensive as she replies. "I don't really regret separating or divorcing. If things had been different, but they were not, I wish I had been in a marriage that had worked. That the children would have had two parents to come to. But I don't think about it too often." Lillian adds that she has grown since she separated. She doesn't feel she would have done the things she has done and accomplished what she has in the work world. "And I know I would never have been able to travel to the marvelous places I have gone. I know that." Her only regret is that she does not drive. But she explains that the traffic in the area is too forbidding. And she never loved the idea of driving as a younger woman. She says forcefully that she will not do anything about it at this time.

Lillian speaks firmly about whether she has thoughts or fears of death. "Not now. I remember when I was young and I would think about death. Oh, how terrible to die! That's the end! I don't feel that way anymore. I'm not saying that it is not the end. I don't know if I believe in reincarnation or not. I do believe that there are spirits out there. That the spirit lives on." She then relates an incident that happened to her on a plane flying to London about eight years ago. She has allergies to certain foods. When she took a small taste of the rice mixture, she felt her throat constricting and her mouth swelling. Her eyes also began to puff. Her breathing became more and more difficult. The stewardess gave her oxygen and called for a doctor. "I couldn't breathe! I thought, *This is it.* I didn't panic. I thought, *This is the way I should go."* She thought it would be ironic that she would die on a plane traveling somewhere. She made it to London, where she was hospitalized and recovered rapidly. The next year, she returned to London on the same carrier and had the same reaction from a small taste of food. By that time, she had an anti-histamine to take as a preventative and the reaction was not as severe. Lillian says she does not eat on airplanes anymore! And she takes her own food with her when she flies.

She sums up her feelings about her life in a powerful way. "I feel very blessed. God has brought me through so many things — the mastectomy, the glaucoma. I feel productive. I get up in the morning and do what I want to do. I don't like 'pity parties'. I don't like cancer support groups where you sit around and bemoan things. I want knowledge. But I don't want to feel that God has done this to me. Or why has he done this to me?" Lillian emphasizes that she looks at the glass being half full as opposed to half empty. And she quotes Maya Angelou as her role model in life. "The line she wrote that I always think of is — 'And still I rise....' That wonderful statement is a guide for me in my life."

CHAPTER VII

SHERRY'S STORY

"What I most regretted were my silences. Of what had I ever been afraid? If I was going to die, if not sooner than later, whether or not I had ever spoken myself. My silences had not protected me. Your silence will not protect you ... it is not difference which immobilizes, but silence. And there are so many silences to be broken."
— Audre Lorde: *Sister Outsider*

Sherry Ruth Anderson, the co-author of *The Feminine Face of God*, is a study in contrasts. Spiritual and sensual. Intense and serene. Nearing sixty, Sherry is brilliant, beautiful and complex. She is tall with erect carriage and a body toned by miles of running each day. Her black curly hair is flecked with grey at the temples. She has what can be best termed as a movie-star smile. During our first meeting, she is wearing a purple velvet shirt over a long black cut velvet skirt, Four inch beaded drop earrings sway as she speaks. She looks directly into my eyes and the tone of her voice is soft, with each word clearly and slowly paced for emphasis. Sherry lives near San Francisco and is in the East on a business and pleasure visit. Completely open to all questions, Sherry tells an intriguing story.

"The first memory that comes up for me is when we moved from Philadelphia to Atlantic City. I was four years old and I remember being with my little brother Howard, who was only two, and taking care of him. When I look at photographs, I'm struck by how old and motherly I look, usually with my arm around him. In some ways, I was much too precocious, protecting him and looking after him." Both her parents, Milton and Frances Anderson, worked in their wholesale grocery business in Atlantic City. Her father carried the major responsibilities of selling and managing, while her mother helped with the buying. Nursemaids took care of the children at home and Lulu is recalled very warmly by Sherry as a loving person during those years. Her father's brother, Bob, who was eleven years younger, lived with them, worked in the business and was very important to the children.

"We lived right in Atlantic City and it was a pretty scary place with bars on the corners and warehouses. I could sense my mother's fear at times. A lot of my childhood was about having a concern for Howard. It was a way of feeling strong and competent and there was someone who was afraid, but it was not I." By the time Sherry entered school, she had become a tough kid and the head of her 'gang'. She was Roy Rogers and when it was suggested that she be Dale Evans instead, she insisted she was Roy Rogers! Most of her memories are of playing with her brother and going to the nearby beach with him. On the weekends, the family trekked down to the beach which Sherry says was a place of great freedom. Her parents sat on the beach chairs and the children played in the sand at the water's edge. "Even today, when I have experiences of boundless states of being, they often begin sitting at the ocean's edge and feeling that wonderful expanse of the ocean and the morning light. Very wonderful!"

Sherry and Howard also went to day camp in the summers which she loved. She found her parents to be very restrictive at home and loved being with the other children. The family moved to Ventnor, a residential community on the island, when Sherry was in third grade. Their uncle Bob still lived with them and "it was fun having him at the dinner table. He made us laugh so much, teasing us and joking with my father." As soon as she had learned to read, books became an important part of her life. She discovered that books were her 'friends'. She would walk by herself on the boardwalk or the beach to the library, about ten blocks away, carrying ten or twelve books at a time. She read all the books in the children's section and by fifth grade, she was allowed to take out the 'grown up' books.

Sherry devoured novels and mysteries, looking for books that would tell her something about what was true about life. "I was looking for some kind of wisdom. My mother was not available and I didn't feel I had anyone to talk to about what I cared about. I was looking for that in books." In junior high school, Sherry found a boy with whom she could talk and then a group of best friends formed, ten boys and Sherry. They read Sartre and Camus and published a "literary magazine, *Genesis*," which was distributed to parents and other interested parties. "That was the first time I felt like being in a place with people who understood me. My mind was engaged and we listened to each other. I loved it."

Sherry speaks of her father as someone who listened to her as well. He would sit down and they would talk. Once, he discussed the book *The Status Seekers* with her when she spoke scornfully of the Cadillac in their driveway. He spoke honestly of his boyhood in Philadelphia in a family that was poor.

138

He had to quit high school in the last term before graduation to take a job. He said he looked out at his Cadillac and he would say to himself, *It's okay. You've made it and you can take it easy now.* And Sherry was very touched that he would share this with her.

She recalls another time when their Uncle Bob was married and Howard was given his room. Her father put down rose-colored carpet up the back stairs to the room and said, "When you walk up these stairs, imagine you are walking through roses!" She comments, "He was a big, gruff guy who could get very angry and my mother spent considerable time mollifying him. But every once in a while, he would say something tender and I would be very moved." Her father also recited Shakespeare to both children as bedtime stories almost every night.

In high school, Sherry was a high-achieving student. She loved chemistry because of the teacher who taught the table of elements as an 'exquisite design'. And there was an outstanding English teacher who continued her exposure to Shakespeare. "But high school was mostly about boys!" She was swept up into sorority life and dating as were most girls her age. Her mother had retired when a new baby, Richard, arrived and Sherry did her share of baby sitting. But the main interest in her life beyond the books was boys. She dated seniors rather than her classmates. And she had no close girlfriends except one in Philadelphia.

During the spring semester of her junior year, the family was torn asunder when her father suffered a massive heart attack. "My father had his attack when he was only 44. I remember very clearly seeing him carried out to the ambulance. My mother would go to the hospital every day and stay all day. I was home after school with the baby and the nurse. All our relatives were calling and I would talk to them on the phone. I thought I was fine and managing. But I had bottled up all my feelings."

In those years, coronary patients stayed in the hospital for weeks and were kept to a very quiet routine when they recovered at home. There was a special elevator chair installed to take her father up and down to the second floor. Most pressing was the approaching summer when most of the business was done in the resort community. Milton Anderson was sidelined and a daring plan was thought up and carried forth. Sherry, who had just received her driver's license, would take over her father's sales routes. She would drive to Wildwood and Howard, who was sixteen, would go with her. The two of them rose to the occasion. They took a crash course in the product and price book. They then covered the hotels, motels, restaurants and diners. They introduced themselves. They met with chefs in kitchens with temperatures in the 90s. They put in twelve- to fourteen-hour days. Together, they helped their father as he recovered. It was an important time of maturation for both of them.

Sherry had planned to go to college at Cornell, but there was concern about her father's health. Instead, she applied to Goucher College in Maryland, closer to home. She confides that Goucher had really been her first choice, a women's college because she felt she was much too interested in boys and needed to be serious about her studies. "In high school, I liked going out with older men, in college, or in the Army. Getting dressed up and going to cocktail lounges. My mother let me wear all her old dresses, cut down to my size. I started smoking at thirteen. I felt very sophisticated." Sherry, as most girls of her era, was terrified of getting pregnant. There was light and heavy 'necking' and 'petting' in the front or backseats of cars — but no further. Sherry's main goal was to go away to college and to be on her own. Her religious education had been rote to her and she had not found what she was looking for. "The questions that I had were not addressed in any way." She hoped to find the answers in college.

Sherry knew that she had to have an education to be independent. She worked for two summers in her father's business to earn part of the tuition. Having money for college was a concern to her throughout the four years. She also worried about her father's health. Yet, she describes college as the happiest time of her early years. "I felt a sense of adventure and freedom. I could choose my courses. But, I was afraid of subjects where I might not do well in, like astronomy or advanced chemistry." Instead, she majored in psychology and found many teachers "who loved to teach." There was still time for dating on weekend.

"I was besieged by boys from neighboring colleges." She dated whomever she wished without having to satisfy her parents' approval. She loved this freedom. "I grew up at Goucher. And we had a lot of strong women as role models. It was a time of great discovery and revelation for me." She also spent several summers at Johns Hopkins University, doing research and living in the medical residency hall. "Complete freedom!"

In Sherry's senior year, her senior thesis advisor recommended that she pursue graduate studies at The University of Toronto. "I had gone to a women's college near home which was a marvelous experience for me. The idea of going to Canada seemed like a great adventure. To a foreign country! I was from Atlantic City, New Jersey. It was all very exciting." An important part of Sherry's story was the cultural context of the time. She was in college when President Kennedy was assassinated in 1963. Like everyone else, she says she remembers that day very clearly. Yet, she also describes herself as "pretty unaware" in general when she was graduated in 1964. Many of her friends were already marching in front of the White House against nuclear bombs. Other people were sitting-in against the segregation in restaurants in Baltimore. There was a strong protest movement building in the United States, but Sherry recalls going to Canada and being unaffected at that time.

In her first year in Toronto, she concentrated on making friends and finding her way around the city. However, by the end of that year, she became involved in the peace movement in Canada against the war in Vietnam. "I was volunteering and took part in sit-ins. I remember the first demonstration I was part of. We lay down on the ground in front of the building where Dow Chemical was interviewing engineers. And they had to walk on top of us to go for their interviews — which they did. And we felt immensely self-righteous."

Sherry spent her first two years in a master's degree program followed by four more toward a doctorate in psychology. All during those years, she was active in the anti-Vietnam War movement. "I also went to demonstrations on the steps of the parliament in Ottawa. It was a very exciting time. There was a very strong sense then that we had something to contribute and that our voices mattered. We felt a really deep moral obligation to stop the war in Vietnam."

She pauses and then continues. "It was in the middle of that time that I met Lawlor Rochester. What impressed me about him was that he was a very good man. One of the most moral people with real integrity that I had ever met." Now she flashes the smile and laughs. "And very attractive. Very, very handsome." Lawlor was not in the movement. He was a construction engineer, a civil engineer who built bridges and dams. And he was in the process of being divorced.

Sherry was very active in helping draft dodgers and deserters cross the border from the United States to safety in Canada. She says as an aside, "I get goose pimples when I think of those times." She explains that the Canadian government's official policy was for the RCMP, the Royal Canadian Mounted Police, to return the men to the United States if they were discovered. "It was a policy for the deserters, and it wasn't supposed to happen for the draft dodgers. But it did anyway." She was part of a group who would drive across the border to Buffalo, New York, to pick the men up and drive back to Canada.

On her second date with Lawlor, she asked him if he wanted to help. He had graduated first in his class from the Royal Military Academy, the equivalent of West Point. Now, she smiles again. "He had short hair. He looked like an engineer. So straight! And he was perfect to bring deserters across the border. And not only that, but he was morally outraged about the war in Vietnam. When he had graduated, he was valedictorian, what they call Wing Commander. The following year, when Canada became heavily involved in the war, sending troops, he had sent atrocity pictures in the form of Easter cards to all his professors. So his heart was there, but he wasn't involved yet. With me, he got involved."

She related how Lawlor would drive a big borrowed car down to Buffalo and say to the crossing guards that he and Sherry were going to dinner. Then they would pick up the deserter or draft dodger who would get in the backseat. And on the return, say they were returning from dinner. Usually, they were waved right through. But even with Lawlor at the wheel, there were some nerve wracking moments. Some nights, they would go in at Niagara Falls and come back at a different border crossing. "One night, they wouldn't let us through. We were there until three in the morning. They couldn't find a category for the work the man in the backseat said he did. Finally, Lawlor helped them and we made it across." Sherry then backtracks to give a sense of how straight Lawlor looked. "The first time we returned to the safe house where the deserters and draft dodgers lived for a while — the first night we walked in — everyone took one look at Lawlor and froze! The conversation stopped. So he actually was a fabulous ally in the movement."

Sherry and Lawlor lived together for a year before they decided to marry. She was 25 and finishing her Ph.D. They were married in Atlantic City with a large-scale wedding and reception at one of the grand hotels. In her bridal picture, Sherry is wearing a very short elegant lace gown, the style of the day, and looks radiantly beautiful. She chuckles and says, "Then we got into the car and drove back to our little house in Canada." A few weeks later, one of their friends organized a small wedding celebration for them. She and Lawlor were downtown in Toronto the day of the party and passed a demonstration in front of the American Consulate. They saw a lot of their friends and decided to stop and march with them for a short while. They planned to then go home and dress for the party. Sherry describes what happened next.

"There were mounted police there. Then a sergeant arrives and says, 'All of you people will have to move on! You're blocking the sidewalk! You have to move on!' We keep standing there and somehow he picks out Lawlor. And he says to Lawlor, ' I order you to move on!' Lawlor says, 'These are our civil rights to stand here. I'm not blocking the sidewalk. We have a right to stand here.' To which the sergeant says, 'This is the third time I am ordering you to move on!' And then he says to a policeman, 'Arrest this man!'" At this point in her story, Sherry breaks into peals of laughter. "And Lawlor says, 'I think we should move on.'"

Then she becomes serious as she relates the next events. "So Lawlor starts to move on and the policeman runs and yanks his arm up behind him really hard. And Lawlor yells, 'Some bastard's trying to break my arm!' And the whole group of protesters like a Greek chorus, yells 'Some bastard's trying to break his arm!' Sherry, who was just married two weeks, reached over and grabbed the ear of the policeman and pulled it toward her and punched him. And the the policeman fell down and let go of Lawlor.

The sergeant yelled again, "Arrest that man!"

And Sherry cried, "Take me too! I don't want him to go alone."

The policeman, who was still on the ground, replied, "She's the one who hit me! Take her too."

They were taken in separate police cars to separate prisons. Lawlor and the men to one jail and Sherry and other women to another. Not even in the same complex. They found out later that 150 people were arrested and Lawlor was the first one released. Sherry was in prison for about eight hours. She says that during that time she really felt helpless. "I, of course, had seen American television. So I said, 'I have my rights and I demand a phone call.' I was acting angry but I was really scared. They said, 'You've watched too much television. You're not entitled to a phone call'. Then, I made up a story that I had small children at home and they let me make a call. I called my friend at the Civil Liberties Union and I said, 'Alan, I'm in prison!' So we got out on bail."

Lawlor's offense was disrupting the peace. But Sherry's offense was assaulting an officer and since she was in Canada on a student visa, the penalty could be deportation. The next day, Sherry recalls the heavy coverage in the newspapers, with emphasis upon Lawlor being arrested, since he had been the Wing Commander. "Lawlor's family was very upset!" She was still a graduate student and the trial dragged on for almost a year. They had to appear in court each morning. They were told if they weren't there when called, a bench warrant would be issued for their arrest. Of the 150 people, one man later became the mayor of Toronto.

When it was Lawlor's turn, and he went first, he made a very vociferous argument that he was entirely within his rights and it was an outrage that he had been arrested. The judge, who was a graduate of the Royal Military Academy, said, "I completely agree with you. The officers had gone outside their authority." And the charge was dismissed.

For Sherry's trial, her professors came to court to give character testimony. She was very worried about the possibility of being deported. And in her dreams, she was terrified they would put her back in jail. "It was so shocking to be there. Not to be free and to realize I didn't have all the entitlement I was used to. But I went on with my course work and showed up

143

every day at the court. The police were really angry. My trial went on for a few days and when I was called to speak, I said, 'I'm a pacifist. I really think the war is morally wrong.' The argument my lawyer made was that my husband, who had been a prize boxer in college, made no effort to defend himself."

And now, Sherry becomes very animated. Her voice rises and she throws her arms up in the air. "And I, as his wife, had acted in his defense, which was entirely proper , because unjust force had been used against him. And I got off completely!" After the trial, Sherry gave up her United States citizenship because of her opposition to the war in Vietnam. She became a Canadian citizen. Years later, when she wanted to emigrate back into the United States, there were no records in Canada of this event, since she had not been indicted. But she discovered that the FBI had pictures and records. This, however, did not block her return and at present Sherry holds dual citizenship.

Sherry completed her doctorate and moved to a position at the Clark Institute of Psychiatry, which was part of the University of Toronto Medical School. "It was exciting because this was an area I was most interested in, being with and talking to people. And they needed someone who knew how to do research. It seemed perfect. The Clark was the most prestigious psychiatric teaching hospital and research institute in Canada. At 30, I felt like I was in the cat-bird seat! This was all perfect. I had my Ph.D. I had this handsome and wonderful husband. I had a wonderful job, first nominal head and then actual head of the department I had total free rein of the kind of research I wanted to do. A very nice budget and office. I felt great! I remember having a photograph taken at my desk to send to my father to show him I had really done it right!"

About a year after the trial, Lawlor's former wife was no longer able to care for the children and they came to live with Sherry and Lawlor in their small bungalow. As Sherry looks back now, she says she didn't really understand what was happening. Lawlor had apparently decided that Daphne and Margo would live with them permanently. Sherry thought they were there for a short time until their mother was healthier again. After about a year, Sherry began to understand they were there full time. "And I was incredibly jealous and not prepared to be a stepmother to two girls. It felt like an intrusion. They were very needy and dependent upon their father, understandably of course. They were nine and eleven and very clingy to Lawlor and affectionate. And I felt like the wicked stepmother! The younger one, Daphne, would ask, 'When are you going to die? I hope you die soon.' I had no sophistication and no depth of understanding of child psychology even though I was head of the research department. I really needed some good therapy and I didn't get it. It wasn't as common as today to have a second family. I didn't know how to deal with their envy and jealousy. And I was enormously jealous of them and the way they were so close to Lawlor and intimate. Finally, I was appalled at myself that I was feeling this way."

At the same time, Sherry relates that Lawlor was not happy being an engineer and he enrolled in law school. Thus, she was supporting him and the girls as well as cooking the meals, shopping and trying to be a surrogate mother. "I was trying to live up to this image of myself as this wonderful, good stepmother. And I was really full of hatred and envy and resentment for the girls. But we didn't talk about any of this. Lawlor and I had only been married about a year and a half. He sensed the difficulty and his solution was to step in between, so he was the center of all this relating."

Lawlor was 38 and going to law school. Sherry's solution was to do more, to work harder which made her feel competent. She became very active in the women's movement and helped publish the first book in Canada on women's liberation. "It had a fist on the front! A woman's fist!" Now, Sherry illustrates with her outstretched arm and fist. "And it said, 'Women unite!'" She also took part in one of the first women's liberation groups in Toronto and chaired the board of the new women's counseling service and rape crisis center. There was little time or space at home for privacy or intimacy with her husband.

Lawlor added another floor to the bungalow with two large rooms for the girls upstairs, but the family problems persisted. Sherry says of those times, "There was just a coldness between Lawlor and me, and neither of us knew how to bridge it." Their lives changed when Sherry's friends in the women's liberation movement said they needed therapy and rejected the male psychiatrists, often Freudians, who were in the area. They wanted Sherry to be their therapist and she demurred since she had not been trained in that discipline.

Then, she found the Gestalt Institute of Toronto that had just started and joined the first class along with Lawlor's sister Judy. It was a three-year program, meeting one weekend a month and certain weekdays, a completely new experience for Sherry. "It was totally shocking to me because I had no idea how to feel my feelings! I remember trying to fathom how to know what someone is feeling if they're not shouting and angry or weeping. And, of course, I didn't know what I was feeling at all. After two years, I still had immense difficulty with being sensitive to myself. I was so, we say now, 'all armored up'. And shut down too. I didn't know my tender feelings from my vulnerable feelings. Or being afraid. I've only recently learned how to feel

145

that — to be afraid."

Sherry describes herself at this time as being very immature and self centered. At the end of the second year at the Institute, during a week-long retreat, she met a man and spent a night with him. "I was very attracted to him. I didn't even tell him my last name. It was very exciting! My sex life with Lawlor had been awful. He was very jealous of any male friends I had. I didn't feel guilty about that night. I had a splendid time!" She returned home and they were due to go to Singapore and Bali the next week. Then, the man called. He had found her name and number. When Lawlor demanded to know who he was, Sherry told him what had happened and declared that she wanted an 'open marriage'. "Lawlor said, 'Absolutely not!' And I replied, 'I need my freedom!'" On that fractious note, they left for Singapore and Balis.

The serious issues between them were not resolved on the vacation. And on their return, Sherry moved out of the house to her own apartment. She was 32 and relieved to be on her own. She saw Lawlor and the girls every other weekend. The meetings did not go well. "Lawlor was icy cold. We were like two people being in glass boxes. And the girls too. We were all in glass boxes. Stiff as could be. Trying to be together but not doing a good job at all."

Sherry pauses and says with quiet emphasis, "At this time in my life, there was a great turning, a great change." After hearing a speaker from Esalen, the human potential center in California, she signed up for a four-week program for doctors and other credentialed people. A fifth week was then recommended as an introduction, with a famous Zen master and his Dharma teachers. Sherry was very skeptical of Zen when she entered the program. "We all lived in a beautiful big house right on the edge of the Pacific separate from the rest of Esalen. The people who were the presenters are now the key people of the consciousness movement. Those five weeks were extraordinary!"

The Zen master was Korean, known as Soen Sa Nim, Revered Teacher. When Sherry entered the main room for the first time, she saw people sitting on cushions facing the wall. Through the windows that opened to the ocean and the sky, the air was filled with orange and black Monarch butterflies. "It was an exquisite scene, but I was in misery, as was almost everyone else who was in the room. We were not allowed to speak and we were left alone facing the wall, with those hornet nests that were our minds."

They were to remain in complete silence for the next seven days except for a fifteen-minute interview with the Zen master each day and a talk by him with time to ask questions. They could talk during some of the communal meals and during the visits to the famous hot tubs. No clothes were worn in the hot tubs. Sherry had experienced nudity during the Gestalt training and felt comfortable. "The truth is I did a lot of things and didn't feel any fear. *Oh, this is what's happening and I'm doing it.* There were bodies. A woman with a double mastectomy. Fat old men. Beautiful young women. It wasn't like a big thing. It felt very normal. And the relaxation in the tubs was wonderful after sitting for so many hours in formal postures on those cushions. The real pain was the psychic pain. Sitting facing a wall and not knowing if I was screaming out loud or just inside."

There was complete disciplined silence each day during the Zen sitting. The Zen master carried a large stick and if someone fell asleep, the stick was applied in a proscribed manner to bring wakefulness. During Sherry's first interview, the Zen master said, "Good morning. How are you?" At that point, Sherry burst into tears and cried for the entire fifteen minutes. When asked if any of the participants left the program, she replies, "Some people did leave. I felt constantly that I wanted to leave. But what I really wanted to do was to foment a revolution among the others. But I didn't know a soul there. I felt extremely trapped."

"I got through the first day by having profound sexual fantasies about the fellow sitting next to me. The second interview, I bawled again, but Soen Sa Nim was ready for me. He had a roll of toilet paper!" By the third interview, Sherry said, "Good morning. What is my path?" And then she cried for the rest of the fifteen minutes. She felt she had followed her trajectory and that she had done it all. She had the degree, the job, the husband, the status, the prestige. And yet she felt that her life was empty. And she was on the verge of divorce.

She sums it up. "I thought there's got to be more than this. I didn't know where to go. Or how to find my direction." The Zen master answered her question with Zen koans, puzzles to make the mind "go into spasm". An example would be: What is the sound of one hand clapping? The intent is to make the mind unable to think in conventional ways. To create an openness to a new way of experiencing the truth of reality. It is not meant to be answerable in any traditional terms. The Zen master also surprised the participants when he introduced wild and ribald humor into the morning question and answer time.

Sherry began to enjoy the sessions. "It was really fun and exciting and he was totally confounding the mind every time he could." On the fifth day, Sherry says her mind stopped. "My mind was silent. I could hear the slap of the waves outside. And I remember seeing this big, beautiful moth. I would have whole moments of silence through the next two days. It was a revelation that this was possible. It was astonishing! A feeling of incredible freshness and clarity, all through every part of my being. Not just my mind, but my body too. It felt like being alive for the first time! Being alive to life. And I felt, *I want more of this."*

Sherry calls her first experience with Zen at Esalen as one of the two major turning points in her life. It changed her direction, sense of values and sense of identity for the rest of her life. After the first week, the participants were allowed to talk and the building of the community began, what the Buddhists call the Sangha, the community of like-minded people. Sherry describes the people she was with as very intelligent, very thoughtful and very mature. There were psychiatrists, therapists and medical doctors. All different ages; she was the youngest. "We shared during meals, going for walks and in the hot tubs. We became quite a community. Fascinating people!"

She admired them greatly and stresses that having them as companions heightened the impact of the entire experience. They were introduced to an array of perspectives with visiting presenters and great teachers. Joseph Campbell, then a professor at Sarah Lawrence, told mythical stories from all traditions and religions. Sherry took notes and came to realize that he was talking about them and the transformation of the psyche and the soul. And about maturation to another level of consciousness. Successive teachers included a professor of anthropology who was an expert in Shamanism, a Buddhist monk just out of the monastery, and the Simontons, who were doing groundbreaking work on the relationship between cancer and consciousness. "Our minds were spinning! First, we think we have it. And then, the next ideas hit us. It was very exciting! The intellectual thrill and the experiential connection. I had never had that before. And the body included. We did Tai Chi in the morning. And the hot tubs in the evening. It was tumultuous!"

Sherry invited Lawlor to come to Esalen the final week and he came and immersed himself in it. They had a reconciliation and the "the iciness softened." As she prepared to go home, the Zen master suggested that she do two things: continue her 108 prostrations every day and sit with a Korean monk he knew in Toronto. Prostrations are a form of full body push-ups which Sherry hated to do. She asked why she should do them and his answer was, 'It means believing in your true self a hundred percent." She did not understand what he meant, but decided to try it anyway. She then returned to Toronto to her own apartment with her relationship to Lawlor somewhat improved.

And then, the second turning point in her life began to take shape. A few months earlier, Sherry had received a letter from a friend who said she was staying at "an amazing place called Findhorn" on Inverness bay in Northern Scotland. Her friend wrote, "You need to come. Buy a book, *The Magic of Findhorn* by Paul Hawken. The book told of a spiritual community of about 150, founded by three people, famous for their gardens. The Findhorn newsletter and other pieces of literature were also available and Sherry was drawn to what she read. She cut out a picture of the sanctuary and scotch-taped it to her wall. Another book by one of the founders explained how she received "guidance". She would sit in silence and "be open to hearing the still, small voice of God within me." then she would take a notepad and without thinking, let her hand write in answer to the question she would be trying to understand.

Sherry started following the same process and began to get answers to her questions. She was separated from Lawlor and had become very attracted to a man at work, who was interested in her as well. The 'guidance' told her not to get involved with him. "It was very good advice," Sherry says. "He was very handsome and very powerful. He said he was madly in love with me and would leave his wife. We took walks and had lunches. But I never had sex with him. I followed the guidance."

Other issues and questions arose and Sherry found the method was working well for her. And every night, she would look at the photograph on the wall and try to come up with a way to get to Findhorn. Then, she received an invitation to submit a paper for presentation at a conference to be held in Sterling, Scotland. As head of the research department, she was often asked to submit papers. This one, of course, she accepted. After the week-long conference, she left for Findhorn, "an impossibly difficult place to reach." It involved a long trip by train, bus and cab. When she finally arrived, she went first to the small sanctuary or chapel. She sat there and wept for hours. "I felt so relieved to be there. I didn't understand it. But I knew there was some incredible truth for me in that place. And I was so grateful to be there."

Findhorn consisted of an old hotel, Cluny Hill, and the Findhorn Trailer Park a few miles away. The first week at Cluny Hill, Sherry shared a large room with a "marvelous woman from Australia." There was an introduction to Findhorn coupled with learning about the plants. She felt very much at home. "I totally fit in. People constantly asked me for directions. I was perceived as fitting in. It was also astonishing and shocking!" For the introduction, there were big circles of people from all over the world. They were all speaking English and talking about how they were all connected — all one. They stressed forgiveness and not harboring hatred in one's heart. At that point, Sherry burst into tears. "I was just in a rage! And I said, 'Well, that's fine for all of you, but the Nazis burned my ancestors in their ovens and I am not going to forgive them!"

There were Germans in the group but they were young people. They all listened and then a woman with an Irish accent spoke about the burden of carrying hatred in one's soul. Sherry replied abruptly, "What do you know about that?"The woman answered that she was from Belfast and several of her relatives had been blown to pieces. And she had let go of her hatred. The group then joined hands and sat in silence. This was very different from Sherry's three years at the Gestalt Institute, where one acted one's feelings within the group. "I was feeling so immensely disturbed and angry and confounded by the woman from Belfast who did have good reason for hatred. Then, we just held hands and I felt this wonderful feeling of kindness come through my left hand and wash through my whole body and come out through my right hand. I was helpless to forgive but in the context of these people, my heart was washed clean."

During the next two weeks, Sherry reached a further understanding of new ideas of kindness and peace within an experiential base. She found an open atmosphere without people invalidating the other's feelings. Every morning, Sherry went to the sanctuary and asked for guidance about staying at Findhorn, which she loved. The guidance told her she had to return and fulfill her book contract to write about her five years of research on schizophrenia. She accepted that and asked every day about Lawlor and the children. On the last day, the guidance said she was to give up her apartment and move back into the house with Lawlor and the children. And she was to meet whatever came to her with love. If she was not able to do that, she was to go for a walk. And she was to meditate every day at work to prepare to come home.

"I was stunned and shocked. But I did it. I returned to Toronto and moved back with Lawlor and the girls. And the first thing I did was to meet with Daphne and Margo in their room. This was the hardest thing I had ever done in my life to that point. And I said to them, 'I've been really jealous of you and your relationship with your Dad. I want it to be different between us. I feel like I don't even know you. I want to learn to be with you. I want us to have a good relationship.' The girls listened. And they said, 'We've been really jealous of you too. And we haven't liked you one bit. But we'll try.'" They then all agreed to try. And to talk without Lawlor getting in the middle. Margo was fourteen and Daphne was twelve.

Sherry then realized that the girls had always wanted to be close to her. The break with their mother had been very traumatic and they did not want tenseness and jealousy with her. Within one week, there was an astonishing change in their relationship. Everything became easy with the girls. With

Lawlor, it took much longer. Sherry would tell him that she wanted to talk about what he wanted, what he hoped for. She discovered that one of the things he wanted was for the house to look beautiful. He wanted to redecorate and for Sherry to be involved. "It was a big deal for me. I wasn't interested in furniture and colors and drapes. But I agreed to take part. And I took a large role in redoing the house. The guidance had said, Do this for one year. If at the end of the year, you want to leave, you are free to leave and never go back. So, I did it for a year and at the end of the year, I was so happy that I didn't want to leave."

The final part of the turning points in Sherry's life came when her Zen master phoned to tell her that he was coming to Toronto to see her. He wanted her to invite all her friends and he would put on a Kido, a special kind of Korean Zen retreat. Drums and singing chants would be interwoven with his telling Dharma stories. There would be no sober sitting in silence in this Kido. At that time, none of Sherry's friends had ever heard of Zen. "We didn't understand in those days that it was a great honor for him to come. He was opening Zen centers all over the world and he wanted a Zen center in Toronto." Sherry laughs and says, "He was a Zen entrepreneur!"

The retreat was "exotic and successful" with Lawlor taking part as well as Sherry's friends. Later, the Zen master suggested that once a week a group sit Zen in their front room. Sherry was charmed and wanted to have their home be the center. And at that point, the guidance process that she had been following said there would be no more guidance. She was to learn from her Zen master for the next seven years. "And I did those prostrations every day for the next seven years without missing maybe one or two days a year. Sometimes, it was a thousand prostrations a day! And what he said was true. It developed a quality of will that was unbeatable. I learned something — that I could do anything! It developed a quality of trust in myself at a deep level."

The Zen group grew in numbers on Wednesday nights, with the Zen master visiting once or twice each year. And during the years that followed, Margo and Daphne became very close to Sherry. They talked through the problems that arose and worked them out without involving Lawlor. Sherry had decided that she did not want to have any children of her own. "I just loved Margo and Daphne. They became a blessing in my life. I didn't want children. And Lawlor didn't want any more children. If Margo and Daphne hadn't been in our lives, I might have wanted to. I was just so interested in finding out how to be a person."

Sherry and Lawlor lived together for seven years. As a lawyer and a civil engineer, he was in a strong position in his field as was Sherry at the Clark

Institute. He wanted to buy a bigger house and she did too in order to have more room for the Zen center. They bought a Victorian house with eight bedrooms in a beautiful residential section of Toronto. Sherry thought of it as an ideal Zen center and Lawlor threw himself into decorating the house. Margo and Daphne had left, with Margo in France and Daphne in Mexico. There was a top floor that they agreed would be used for the Zen meetings. And there were some people who wanted to live in the house, an idea which Lawlor accepted reluctantly.

After Esalen and Findhorn, the two turning points in her life, Sherry was guided by what had happened to her there. "What had value to me, what had meaning to me, what had a purpose to me, the measuring stick against which everything was assessed was a sense of spiritual connection. This was what was real to me." Lawlor was trying to live a fairly normal life as a father, a husband, a lawyer and to fit Zen in as one of the things in his life. For Sherry, Zen was the most important thing.

After several years in the new house, Sherry finished her book on schizophrenia, *Crazy Talk,* based on all the research she had done. When she returned from Findhorn, she had gone to the meditation room at the Clark Institute to seek the way to align a sense of larger purpose with her role as head of the research institute. Her decisions, how she voted on committees, how she worked with her colleagues, were all affected by her new view of life. She began looking beyond her department to the community as a whole for whom the institute had been created.

And she was also looking for what she would do next after her book was published. She asked for and was granted a year's sabbatical. "The book had been a great coup. They didn't have many coming out of the research institute." Sherry stayed at home, went for walks with the two dogs and sought clarity as to what to do next. And she continued her Zen prostrations and sitting. When the year ended, she was sill unsure of her direction.

On her return, Sherry received a promotion to Associate Professor of Psychiatry, rare for a young woman at that time. She was interested in geriatrics, since everyone would reach that stage eventually, and began work in that area. But, after less than a year, she realized that she didn't want to do research anymore. She retired from the Clark and her colleagues were aghast! She had just been promoted. She was a consultant for the National Institute of Mental Health, sat on editorial boards for some of the important journals and her book had been well received. She was there!

"It seems like in my life, I always have to be there before I leave. My achievement orientation. I said, 'I'm sorry. I have to go.'" Many of her senior colleagues came to see her. They sat in her office for hours and told her about their lives and what they had hoped for. She was saddened that she had never known this. They might have had a community there if she had known. And she had been so private about what was of value to her that they didn't know that about her either. It was a profound experience for Sherry. She knew them as "striving, political tough guys" and they probably had seen her the same way.

At that point, she and Lawlor had taken some major steps. They had sold the house. "He was fed up with the Zen center and had an interesting job offer in Vancouver. I went with my Zen master and several other people on a three-month trip around the world to teach Zen. And there was no emotion for me with this separation from Lawlor." Sherry had become a Dharma teacher by now and the head Dharma teacher of the Ontario Zen center. In each country, they would be joined by groups of people. They flew to California, Korea, Japan, Bangkok, all through India, Italy, France, Poland, Germany and England.

In Korea, they lived in mountain monasteries for a month, waking at three thirty in the morning to the eerie sound of the moktok, a hollow form of gong. They washed in cold water and wore the traditional Zen robes while at the monasteries. "Soen Sa Nim was always teaching and we were always learning. The teaching came from our experiences each day. Understanding ourselves and our minds. One of the great teaching was cultural teaching in each country. Our minds were expanding."

Before Sherry had left on the trip, she had taken her half of the money and bought a house to be a Zen center. It was a block from Lake Ontario with a boardwalk for her to run on. And it reminded her of the seashore house where she had grown up in Ventnor, New Jersey. She was 33 years old and imbued with the concept of the Sangha, the community of like-minded people. She was moving in with her friends to create that kind of Zen center. She was the head Dharma teacher and chose a very small room at the top of the house as her own. "I was in heaven!" She also wanted to work and gain experience with everyday life. "All my life had been lived through books. And I knew very little from direct experience with real life." She became a waitress and was fired after the first night. She asked Soen Sa Nim for guidance and he suggested that she do a three-month retreat in the Zen center.

Sherry followed this plan. She did 1000 prostrations a day, sat Zen and felt she was leading a life of great value. "It was like a great need was being filled in me." She then conceived of a radio show where people could call Zen teachers, ask questions and learn from them. Initially, she met skepticism and rejection when she approached people in the field. But her determination kept her on track and she recorded six interviews as a pilot program that was accepted by a small station in Toronto.

"I learned to do everything. Editing tapes with a razor blade makes you better at being an interviewer!" She had a tough spot, at 6:30 on Sunday nights. And she did this for free. One of her friends sent the tapes to larger stations in the area, and after six months, she received a call from one of the stations. "Since I was a psychologist, they wanted me to be a second Dr. Joyce Brothers. But I didn't want to do that! I wanted to have a call-in show after I interviewed someone substantial, as I had done before." That format was followed for several months until Sherry came up with the idea of a five-day a week show from nine thirty to eleven on serious subjects. The station was interested and Sherry called the show, 'Networking'. The station called it, 'The Dr. Sherry Rochester Show!'

Sherry interviewed many authors. "I was convinced if we could speak on topics where people had personal experiences, they would have wisdom to offer. We would have topics like, 'Saying Good-bye', 'Going Back to School' (returning adults), 'Intimacy'. Men who had been in World War II called in and talked about their buddies." Sherry found this work very satisfying and engrossing. At that time, Lawlor came back from Vancouver and asked Sherry to try again. They found a small apartment near the Zen center and he took a job with a law firm. She meditated at the Zen center and asked the people she interviewed, "What's important in life? What kind of support do we need to live the truth?" All parts of her life appeared to be fitting together. Yet, she felt a lack of zest and joy in life. She felt something was wrong in her life.

She reevaluated the rigidity with which she had been doing Zen and turned instead to a ten-day retreat in the San Bernadino Mountains in California. This was run by a healer who worked with energy systems in the body. She did not tell her Zen master where she was going. Sherry fasted. She skipped up and down the mountains, singing a Sufi song that brought her great joy. She felt a "great softening". Yet, when she returned to Toronto, she felt worse than before. Lawlor did not understand. And neither did Sherry. When Margo and Daphne came on weekends, Sherry felt as if she were outside, watching. "Everything was made out of cardboard."

At that point, Sherry attended a conference near Toronto, where she was introduced to the head of the Sufi Center in Ottawa, Paul Ray. "And I look at this guy with these huge dark eyes and think, *That's what a Sufi looks like.* And I ask him, 'Can you tell me what the words mean to this little song I've been singing?' And he says, after I sing the song, 'Oh, they mean, God is love, lover and the beloved.'"

Sherry had learned a healing technique at her retreat and needed to practice the method. She asked several people, among them Paul Ray, if she could do the spiral 'heart opening' technique and they agreed. That evening when she did this with him, he lying on a bed and she sitting on a chair, "an amazing thing happened. It felt like my heart and his heart had opened into a boundless space of love. And he said, 'If I weren't married, I think I would be in love with you.' To which I replied, 'Well, you are and I am. I'll see you later.'" And she left. Sherry describes Paul as quite pedantic and academic during their other meetings at the conference. She thought of him in a friendly way and sent him a copy of her Zen master's book.

On her return, her life felt as "flat" as before. Several months later, Paul Ray, who lived about 500 miles away in Ottawa, called Sherry. He told her he had seen her entire life one day on a Sufi retreat; Lawlor, the girls, her life and her unhappiness had all been shown to him in great detail. And Sherry never had told him anything about her life at all. He said he wanted to help her and he had two Sufi practices for her to follow in the three months ahead. By September, he said, she would be in "a different place." She didn't attach anything personal to his call. She followed his advice, and in September he came to Toronto.

They met for dinner and just seeing him had a powerful visceral effect upon Sherry. He then said to her, "I'm in love with you." And she felt a great love for him too. She did not eat her expensive salmon dinner. They both remember that. After dinner, he invited her to his hotel room and she refused. She said, "I'm not going to do anything that I can't tell my husband." Then, they walked until they reached a churchyard where they sat and talked for hours. They made vows of devotion to each other, to help each other in their spiritual paths and to love each other. Paul told Sherry he was going to tell his wife and they would separate. He said they had been on the verge of that for a long time. "We both felt sure. It was mystical and clear. I felt calm." At eight thirty, Sherry went home to Lawlor and her apartment. But she did not tell Lawlor.

The next morning, when Paul called, Lawlor demanded to know who he was. Sherry then told him and said they had to separate. Lawlor replied, "You're crazy!" But Sherry left him and went to live at the Zen center. She was sure. And Paul left his wife and came to Toronto within weeks. Sherry and Paul were married a year later.

Sherry describes her husband, "The thing that really opened the door for me to my relationship with Paul was through the heart. He has, through his own life experience, a capacity to open his heart to people he loves. And he's yearning to open it even more widely. It helps me to be able to open my heart. In the years that I've been with him, the thing that surprises me is that our communication and our intimacy and our sexual love and our friendship have deepened and grown. I had heard people say this was possible. But I didn't believe it because I didn't have that experience with my first husband.

"Paul had already been through certain profound experiences. He was quite brilliant, a professor at the University of Michigan, and married with two daughters. At age 35, he had been hospitalized with severe physical problems and told he needed to talk to a psychiatrist. That had never entered his life before. He went into Gestalt therapy, and intensive Buddhist therapy as well as meeting with Sufi teachers. He was very dubious and intellectual. Yet, to his amazement, the Sufi teachers quickly made him a teacher. He didn't want this to be known at the University, and when a research grant arose, he took a three-year leave of absence. He went to Ottawa for the Canadian government."

Sherry and Paul had followed similar paths to the point at which they met. Both had been high achievers in their academic pursuits, affiliated with major universities, holding positions of high status in research and scholarship. Then, they had both reached out beyond their disciplines, he to Sufi practices and she to Zen. Both had studied the Gestalt Therapy. "We had and have a lot in common. It's an amazing thing to me! Before I was with Paul, I traveled all over the world to fabulous places. But just walking around the block with him makes me happy. We enjoy life together. And he's a wonderful cook!"

Sherry also decided that if he had habits she disliked, such as taking his time getting up in the morning, she would try his approach before being critical. Thus, her routine of getting up at 4:30 according to Zen was something she was ready to alter. And she found that she liked getting up later. She describes herself as more "austere" than he, whereas he tends to indulge himself, as with food. He creates dishes with different spices and aromas in contrast to her more Spartan tastes. "He loves to feed me!"

They began their life together after the Ottawa grant ended. Both were associate professors but did not want to return to academic life. Instead, they applied for a Canadian Broadcasting Company (CBC) contract to do a four-part documentary, "Changing Our Minds". It was based on books they had read, and how the American consciousness was changing. They were awarded the contract and spent the next year traveling across the United States and Canada, interviewing people for the radio series. It was a continuation for Sherry of pursuing what was important and true in people's lives. They chose the people from the books they had read; writers, Nobel prize winners, scientists, psychologists and others on the cutting edge of thought and research. Often, they stayed with the people they were interviewing. One of the surprising things they discovered was that many of the people they wanted to see lived in the San Francisco Bay area.

They decided to marry and move to California. It also meant that Sherry would regain her American citizenship. Their wedding was small, simple and unrehearsed. "I made the cake. And Paul and I went to buy our clothes together. We wanted them to be beautiful and natural. Paul bought a white silk shirt and I had a white silk blouse with lace, and wore flowers in my hair." They lived for a time in the eastern Sierra mountains with a spiritual teacher who was 96 years old. Then, they moved to a small cottage in Mill Valley as house sitters with very little money left from their savings. Paul became acting director of the Association for Humanistic Psychology.

Sherry was not successful in the job search and joined a women's group where she met Pat Hopkins, who would become her co-author of *The Feminine Face of God.* She was drawn to Pat. "I felt a great excitement talking to her. There was nothing more fascinating than talking with Pat. And I said, one evening, 'Pat, we're going to write a book together. And it's going to be about women's spiritual development.'" Pat came up with the title — spontaneously. And they were to work together on the book for the next five years.

They began by going on a week's retreat, where they decided to first write a research proposal, based on asking women about their spiritual development. "We didn't know the answers. We had to create the questions." For six months, they drafted their proposal and gave it to many people they knew for criticism and input. Sherry meanwhile was doing workshops with groups of women on *The Feminine Face of God.* One woman, who attended one of the sessions, had also looked at the proposal. Sherry asked her, "What do you think of it, Marsha?"

And she replied, "I think it has merit. And here is a check for $20,000 to get it started." This was a personal donation, not from a philanthropy.

Sherry and Pat then sent the proposal out to their friends who in turn sent it to others. "Within the next six months, $90,000 had come in! Maybe, $10,000 from small foundations; all the rest from women. We got checks for $250 and $100 and $10. And another check for $20,000 from someone we didn't even know — in an envelope with blue tulips on it. And a note saying, 'Go for it, ladies!'" At that point, they knew they had the resources to do the research. Then, they wrote the book proposal.

They sent the book proposal to four publishing houses and within two weeks, all were interested. As well as other houses who had heard about the book. 'We went with Bantam, who made the best offer. A $40,000 advance that seemed just incredible to us! The aim was two years for the completion of the manuscript." Sherry and Pat traveled across the country and interviewed over one hundred women. Their individual stories tell of the "unfolding of the sacred in women". The book they wrote, *The Feminine Face of God,* eventually sold over 200,000 copies, a huge best seller by any standard in publishing. It is still in print and selling.

During the five years it took to write the book, Sherry and Pat found their own spiritual path. "We didn't want to follow any tradition led by a man. And I didn't want any ancient traditions. The diversity of women living today was where we wanted to concentrate. There were fundamentalist women, social activists, native American teachers, modern women — all different kinds of women." After they had done all the interviews, listened to the tapes and transcribed their notes, they were overwhelmed by the task of the writing that lay ahead of them. They were one year into the project.

Sherry and Pat were offered a cottage on the north coast of California on the ocean, where they went for a month to work. While they were away, Paul became involved with another woman. This came as a terrible shock to Sherry. "I was devastated!" It was ironic that she learned of this while she was writing a chapter entitled, "Leaving Home". And on her return, she left Paul and moved to a small apartment. His affair ended and he also lived alone. Sherry comments about this period in their lives, "I didn't see him at all."

She became deeply involved in the book, working with Pat every day, taking turns at each of their apartments. They found it very difficult to do the actual writing. "We didn't know the questions to ask." All the questions on the subject were in terms of a male perspective. They ended up becoming completely immersed in each woman's story. And the metaphor of a sacred garden grew out of the book, *The Secret Garden,* where the heroine is a little girl showing the way.

By the time the book was finished, Sherry and Paul had gradually come back together. "This happened very slowly and with great difficulty. It was hard. I was very distrustful. He really put himself out and I came to understand how he felt. I had not wanted to see how rejected he felt that I was doing with Pat what he hoped we would be doing together. He felt devastated." Sherry says that she still didn't fully understand that until they started to write a book together years later, based on his research.

"In the first three months that he and I started working together on our book, it was like making love with our minds! I had never really had this experience with him. Our minds would leap to new places together. One of us would be able to voice something new that was emerging from the two of us. And that kept happening in different ways. Then I understood what Paul felt I had been doing with Pat. And he was right. He had felt totally irrelevant at that time."

When Sherry moves to the present and how she feels about herself, her thoughts are set in an ever searching context. "I am aware of wanting to be invisible. I've done my work on the second book. I want to go off into the desert or some small town and just be on retreat. Not be known or seen. The promotion tour for the book which is coming up makes me feel inadequate. I have been very inner for the past eleven years since *The Feminine Face of God* was published. I do one-on-one with my patients. And meditation. And working on the book with Paul has been an inner process. It's been almost twenty years since I was on the radio."

She shares that she has been studying as a teacher in a spiritual school and could move in that direction. And that she made a private vow when she was 33 that she wanted to be a "world server". She does not see herself becoming active in different causes. She does hope that the new book, *The Cultural Creatives,* will empower the people who read it, who care about what is happening to our country and the planet — that they will have hope. "They will see how many others there are who care. And they will be more willing to reach out and speak out."

Sherry's eyes fill with tears as she continues, 'My prayer has been that my life would not just be for myself. That it would be a blessing for the people of the world in whatever way that might be, with the gifts and advantages I have been given. And that has really been my prayer since I was 33. Right now, I'm really just trying to listen for guidance." Sherry adds, "Pat and I asked Maya Angelou what was most important in her life and she answered fiercely, 'The most important thing in my life is to know the will of God and to do it!' And I think that's really true for me too. When I feel I am in alignment with a sense of larger purpose, then fulfillment is always there. It's a great blessing."

She looks back over her life, "When I was younger, the titles and the good jobs mattered. But when I finished *The Feminine Face of God,* it felt like I've done it. Everything else is frosting. And I keep being surprised at the fullness of life beyond anything I expected. I think it's splendid to be as old as I am. Fabulous! That it just gets better and better! For me, part of it is that life slows down. To see the drops of water on the branch of a tree in the morning and the way the sun glistens through — is fulfillment. And I am a thousand times more able to experience reality than I ever was when I was younger.

Sherry speaks of her friends in their 70s and 80s who are even more able than she to experience reality. Her many women friends in all the places she has lived. "Being a woman of a certain age is a plus. You can go one way or the other as you grow older. You can shut down more and more against the pain and limitations of life. Gnarled, bitter and twisted. Or you can let your heart open more and more. You can be more and more expansive, spontaneous and surprising. I feel like I'm learning how to be a human being."

Sherry emphasizes that it is the quality of presence with a person that matters. And the quality of listening — when something unexpected happens— that can be like free fall together! She becomes very animated as she goes on, "One of the fabulous things about women is that it can happen in whole groups of women. And it such fun! And older women can do and say whatever they want! That too is so very important."

Sherry's favorite time of day may be a metaphor for her life story. "Morning. Yes, morning. The way the light looks on the ocean. Spread out with that young blue sky. The sense of the possibility of the day. I can see the beginning. The challenge for me is life. To be fully alive. And to be free! That has been immensely important to me all my life. For me, it means not free from something, but free for something. Free to be human — completely. To let my heart break if it's breaking. To let myself be afraid if I'm afraid. To be present to life as it happens. To feel reality! To be fully alive! I am happiest when I feel I am being fully used. When all of what I am is being used — for a good purpose."

CHAPTER VIII
JEAN'S STORY*

"I think that serenity for me has a lot to do with religion. Growing up in the environment that I did means that I learned how important that was. I have always relied on religion. I draw on prayer. I carry rosary beads. They have never been away from me. I guess as a little girl, I always believed that holding the rosary brought me close to God. I don't say them every day. As long as I have them in my hand in times of crisis, that's all I need."

"We were setting up our four classrooms in a maximum-security men's prison in Virginia, when the guards started banging on the doors and the phones rang. The words were urgent, 'Get out! Now! The men are rioting in the pods!' Our classrooms were in a long rectangular building with offices and other facilities. We were directly across the yard from the three pods, huge cell blocks that housed a thousand inmates.

"We ran for the exit doors, through the gates and the outer walls to safety. The riot was not a complete surprise. Two weeks earlier, the newly elected Governor had sent out a list of prison policies that inmates statewide found restrictive. There had been widespread anger. We heard some violent talk. The policies were to take effect the next day.

"It took almost two days to contain the riot. In that time, the men had smashed the glass windows and thrown twisted burning sheets doused with gasoline through the bars into the main building that faced their pods. When we returned, we expected to find our classrooms covered in broken glass and filled with burnt furniture and books.

"We were stunned by what we discovered. Our four rooms were the only ones that had not been touched! On either side, rooms were gutted and black

---

* The names have been changed in this story.

163

with soot. Our classrooms were exactly as we had left them two days before. I learned a powerful lesson that day. I learned that the word must have gone out. 'Leave the classrooms alone! Off limits!'

"Some of the men were working for their GED, the high school equivalency diploma. Others, barely literate, were mastering basic reading skills. A few were enrolled in college level courses. But all clearly realized the value of education. And I was once more sure that I was doing very valuable work every day as a teacher in the prisons. Some of the men called me 'Miss Jean', in the southern way. Others 'Mrs. Kerns'. There was a common bond between us. If there hadn't been, the classrooms would have been in ruins."

* * *

Jean Kearns is a very private person, yet easy to talk with. She is a pretty woman with a natural hairstyle and a ready smile. With her calm demeanor and the soft tone of her voice, it is fascinating to imagine her teaching in the prisons — in dangerous surroundings. Yet, it is not hard to see that she would hold the respect of her students. She is open and candid about her life as well as her work. Her core of strength appears to emanate from inner serenity. Religion has played a formative role throughout her life.

Jean was born into a large Irish Catholic family and neighborhood in Brooklyn. She was the sixth child of Mary and Thomas Fitzgerald, the 'baby', nine years younger than her older brother. And unexpected. Her mother, who was 45, didn't realize she was pregnant until her seventh month. The next years were traumatic for the family. Within two years of Jean's birth, two of her sisters died, one of pneumonia and the other of acute appendicitis. They were 18 and 19 years old. Despite these tragic early deaths, Jean thinks of her extended family in terms of their long lives.

"My mother was the youngest of seventeen children. Her family emigrated from Ireland about the turn of the century. They came two by two. Her father came first to see if he wanted to stay. Then he went back and eventually the entire family came to an apartment on the lower East Side of New York. At that time, there was a lot of prejudice against the Irish. Several of Mary's sisters went to the local schools to try to lose their Irish brogue. They did not want people to know."

Jean remembers seven or eight of her aunts and uncles. Some had gone back to Ireland. Those who remained were in Brooklyn or New Jersey. Jean attributes her view of aging, as a positive time of life, to knowing them as she grew up. "The Irish stock, as my mother used to say, didn't go to doctors much, only if they really had to. They were hearty and lived long and healthy lives, into their 90s. The oldest of my mother's siblings, Uncle John, outlived three wives with whom he had children, and died at 98!"

As a child, Jean felt her mother was happy that she had arrived. In a traditional Catholic family, every baby was considered a blessing. But her mother had an enormous physical handicap. She was legally blind, a condition that had grown from a congenital eye problem. Eyeglasses helped as a child. "When she had the trauma in her life, when my sisters died, it affected her eyesight tremendously. The shock made the disease worse. At that time in her life, she basically lost her vision. Within two Christmases, my father died and my two sisters died!"

When Jean talks of her mother's blindness and then of her father's death in the same two years as her older sisters, the succession of tragic events sound overwhelming. When asked how she made it through, Jean stresses the importance of religion in her mother's life. "She was a deeply religious woman. She didn't run to church all the time. She wasn't outward in her religion. She was very private. And she had a hard time when this all happened. But she accepted it."

Thomas Fitzgerald had worked for New York City in the transportation department. He had come from "a nice family" and had graduated from high school. But he was, Jean states clearly and firmly — an alcoholic. This began between the time he finished school and he married and started a family. "He started to drink — the Irish way. We lived in an Irish enclave. The men would start drinking beer on Saturday morning. And keep drinking the entire weekend. That was the way it was." Her mother never drank , "not a drop", but some of Jean's aunts were also alcoholics. Jean relates this part of her story in a flat matter-of-fact tone.

Thomas Fitzgerald was unable to support his family at times. Yet, Jean says her mother told her, "I never want to poison your thinking against your father. It's never proper to do that." The family lost their home more than once. When the rent was not paid, they were evicted. Mary would pack up the children and move in with cousins. She did not go to her sisters for help. "She never felt sorry for herself. She deplored people who did that." One time she walked from First Street to 90th Street with one baby in the carriage, another sitting on the front of the carriage. And she was pregnant. She knocked on the door of a cousin and asked if she could stay. She never told Jean why she did not turn to her sisters at those times.

Jean was only two when her father died and she barely remembers him. She does not recall anyone ever telling her that he died. "He just wasn't there anymore." Yet, she says, "I was a very happy child. My mother was very

doting. And very conscious of education. She had only gone to fourth grade."
Jean liked school and was a strong student. She attended Catholic schools
through high school. They lived in a Catholic neighborhood and Jean's
friends attended the same church. "Everybody was Catholic!" Saturday night
they went to Confession and Sunday morning they went to Mass. Religion
was the binding fabric of their lives in every way. Jean adds with a smile,
"Saturday, if you were playing, you knew at five o'clock you stopped,
because you had to go and get cleaned up to go to Confession."

Mary Fitzgerald struggled to maintain her family after her husband died.
There was a small pension from the government, but no Social Security. Jean
speaks of the hard times. "She eked it out. She made do. We had meatless
meals. And hand-me-down clothes. It affects me to this day. It bothers me to
hear kids asking for things in stores. We never did that. We never even asked.
We knew not to ask. But we always had nice Christmases. She bought things
on the installment plan, fifty cents a week. We had Christmas!"

What Jean missed most of all as she grew up was not having a father.
"Everybody else had a father and I didn't. That bothered me tremendously.
I wished and idealized in my mind what a father would be." She describes
how the father of one of her friends came home from service in World War
II and included her in his family's activities. "I got to know him. He was a
wonderful man. A sweet man. And he always included me. I felt terrible,
years later, when he died."

Jean enrolled in a Catholic high school, a small girls school that prepared
the students to become nuns. Mercy Juniorate was a convent school whose
graduates entered the novitiate. They would become part of Sisters of Mercy,
a teaching order founded in Brooklyn by Catherine McCauley, who had
emigrated from Ireland. Jean had talked of becoming a nun during her
elementary years and her mother and brothers neither encouraged nor
discouraged her. It was just accepted that she would take her vows and enter
an order after graduation. "Jean wants to be a nun. That was it." Only 56 girls
were enrolled in the school, seven in Jean's class. They had all passed the
New York State Regents exams to qualify. In addition to their academic
studies, they had to take care of the school ,clean and dust and, at the end of
the day, put the chairs on the tables.

Jean recalls the nuns as teachers throughout her school years in a mixed
light. "Some of them were nice. But some of them were very rigid, very
authoritarian and mean. They instilled the fear in you of the Lord. They used
that term all the time. " Jean laughs and adds, "I never bought that. I used to
think there was something wrong with me. I just didn't buy all that stuff. But
I never told that in Confession." Jean had a close friend who was Lutheran

166

and she wanted to go with her to church although that was forbidden at that time. Catholics were not allowed to enter any other house of worship. However, her mother did not object and Jean did go with her friend to hear the services in English instead of Latin. She liked it and adds, "I didn't tell that in Confession either!"

Becoming an adolescent for Jean wasn't easy. "I was very small, very short, five feet. Didn't grow until I was in high school. And I didn't mature physically until I was fifteen or sixteen. Everything was late for me. I would lie about it to the other girls. And I was very Catholic, very timid." Jean's family didn't have television at home. She would pretend they did when the other girls talked about the programs they had seen. Like most teenagers, she did not want to be different. And she did not invite the other girls to visit her in her home.

On the subject of boys and dating, Jean's face lights up. "I loved boys! All the neighborhood boys went to the same church. There were dances once a week. I loved to dance the Lindy. We didn't actually date. We went in groups. We would go to the ice cream parlors too. I loved boys! I had a fun time with them." Jean talks about a "healthy boy-girl thing" at that time. Without the heavy emphasis on sex as there is today. There was kissing but little else. Since no one had a car, there was no steamy sitting in the back of cars. Jean shares that she had 'crushes' on boys from about the age of fourteen. She feels her growing up was a natural and healthy introduction to sexuality. "It was fun for all of us."

Jean began working in seventh grade, baby-sitting. Then she was a salesgirl at the 5 & 10 store. In the summers, she did filing at an insurance company. "I never kept a penny. It was all for the family. The money went to my mother. It wasn't your money. You handed the paycheck to your mother." Jean notes that everybody she knew did the same thing. Her friends also worked after school and in the summers to help at home. It was a given that they worked to add to the family's income. None of the money was theirs to keep. They didn't resent this. It was taken for granted that everyone worked for the family.

When Jean graduated from high school, she was seventeen, younger than the other girls, too young to be accepted as a novice and take her initial vows. This was to be an important turning point in her life. She tells what happened. "I took a job with AT&T. And once I got out working, I knew that becoming a nun was not what I wanted. I came out of my little shell, where everything was Catholic. The little parish world." Jean had taken a rigorous academic course in high school with 4 years of Latin, 4 years of French, Algebra, and Sciences. But she had also taken typing and was able to use it

167

in her new job. Now, Jean kept a quarter of her salary to pay for transportation and lunch and gave the rest to her mother. She commuted to Wall Street in downtown New York from Brooklyn. It was a completely new world for her. And she loved it.

Jean had applied for the job after hearing that AT&T wanted Catholic girls. She and two of her friends, who were not going on as novices, went at the same time. The company was interested in them because of their strong academic background. Jean started in filing and knew within three months that she needed to go on with her education. She never considered full-time college, since her earnings were essential at home. But she went to Pace University, nearby, to investigate taking courses part-time. "I don't know where I got the nerve because I was timid. But I went in there one day and told them I wanted to take classes in shorthand and typing." When the admissions official saw her grades on the transcript, he said, "You need to go to college full-time." Jean told him she couldn't do that and enrolled in the shorthand and typing classes. Within a year, she was promoted in her job to a shorthand pool and then to a private secretarial position. "I went up fast."

In the years that followed, Jean switched to Fordham University and began the academic college curriculum. She could only afford one course at a time. AT&T also sent her to Pace for additional business courses. And the company sent her to their own school as well in speed dictation and typing. She pursued education wherever she could find it. It would be nineteen years before she would complete her undergraduate college degree. Jean also made her first investment, buying AT&T stock when it was offered at a special rate to the employees. She laughs as she relates her entry into the stock market. "I bought it at fifty cents a week. And I still have it. I never touched it!" Jean had it taken out of her paycheck when friends advised her that it was the 'smart' thing to do. She says it was very good advice.

During the summers, Jean and her friends would get on the train Fridays after work and go to the New Jersey shore for the weekend. The second summer, she and one of her friends were sitting at a table in a cafe at the edge of the beach. Alan Kerns and one of his friends walked over and introduced themselves. When I ask Jean about her first impression of Alan, her eyes light up. "Both of us liked them right away. I knew what kind of man I was not looking for. From what I had seen growing up, I didn't want anybody who drank. And I wanted someone with a college degree. Alan was in his last year in college. He was tall, thin, athletic, with a crew cut. I liked the way he looked. And he was very polite. We had a good time from the moment we met." Jean also noticed that when he took money out of his pocket, he took out his rosary beads and she thought, "Oh, he's Catholic!" She was happy to see that.

In the succeeding weeks, they dated and Jean kept track of how Alan met her standards. He lived in New Jersey, less than an hour from her home. The two couples double-dated all summer. Dances. Greenwich Village night spots. Movies. "But I was still checking him out. I would not settle for a man without ambition. And Alan certainly had ambition. In fact, he had a vision." Alan planned to go on for advanced degrees and build a career in the business world. "I didn't want my life to be the same as everybody else's in my home environment. Alan was going a different way and that attracted me." Jean met his family and liked them. Their courtship progressed. On Christmas, they were engaged. Alan was 25 and Jean was 24.

They had a traditional wedding in November, a church ceremony followed by a reception and dinner for family and friends. Jean wore a beautiful long-sleeved white satin gown that she borrowed from a close friend. Luckily they were the same size. She wore a veil and carried white chrysanthemums with autumn leaves in the bridal bouquet. Two nieces and Jean's best friend were her attendants. Alan and Jean paid for the wedding with the presents they received. They even hired a limousine to make the occasion very special.

They were only married several weeks, when Alan received notice from the government that he was going to be drafted. He was working in his first job and this was a jolt to both of them. He left for Fort Dix and then was sent to an Army base in Oklahoma for a six-month stint of active duty. Jean went with him. "Oklahoma was an experience coming from Brooklyn. It was tornados. It was the West. You saw native Americans everywhere. It was culture shock! But I liked it. There were things I'd never seen before." They lived in a small apartment in the nearby town of Lawton. Jean had become pregnant before they left Brooklyn. Without a car, she walked, read and sewed. They would rent a car on weekends and drive to the nearby mountains. "It was hot, dusty and tumbleweeds were blowing down the middle of the street. It was definitely not Brooklyn!"

Theresa, their first baby, was born ten months after their marriage. Jean shares, "In some ways I regret that we had children right away. We had no time just to be together as a couple. We never really had time for ourselves." And she talks about being in labor. "In those years, the husband was not allowed to be with you. You did it all by yourself. A cold, dark room. All alone. It was barbaric! Hours and hours of labor." Theresa was a big, healthy baby and they were thrilled. When they returned from Oklahoma, they had moved in with Jean's mother. They then found a small apartment in New Jersey and Alan resumed his former position with an insurance company. He was enrolled in an MBA program and he urged Jean to continue her college courses as well. From the earliest days of their marriage, Alan said that the best insurance policy they could have for their future would be for both of them to have college degrees.

Jean took a course every semester at night while Alan would watch the baby. Their second daughter, Diane, was born thirteen months after Theresa. "I was pregnant, but I still went to school. I never missed a semester. I never stopped. They were good babies. No colic. And they were big. Eight and nine pounds." Jean then had several miscarriages before she had Claire, four years later. "Catholic mentality did not believe in birth control of any kind. No rhythm method. You didn't plan. There were huge Irish Catholic families. But your thinking changes over the years." Alan received his master's degree and was moving up in his company. Jean was a full-time homemaker and she loved it. "I was content with it, given our set of circumstances. Limited money, but I knew going to work would be a hassle. I enjoyed raising the children as long as I had my one night a week at the college."

On Theresa's fifth birthday, Jean's serenity was shattered when Theresa fell from her bicycle and hit her head. She was in intensive care, unconscious for three days with a double skull fracture. Her condition was critical. "It was a very traumatic time. We were so young and so frightened. It was awful! We were scared to death!" Alan never left the hospital. He never left her side. He sat with Theresa for three days. "That's when I knew the kind of strength that man had. Alan's strength got me through." Jean had to be home with Claire, who was an infant, and would visit for an hour at a time. She tells me about an older woman who was sitting with her in the waiting room. She told Jean, "Don't you worry. She's going to be fine." Then she left and returned with a small bag. She said, "I brought your daughter a present. You take this doll to her when she opens her eyes. You press the tummy and she sticks out her tongue. It will make her laugh!"

Jean says she did just that. When Theresa opened her eyes after three days, she saw the doll sticking out her tongue and she laughed! Jean never saw the woman again. And every time she tells the story she cries. Her eyes are filled with tears when she says, "It was such a beautiful thing for her to do." Theresa came home after two weeks and never had any aftereffects that the doctors warned might happen. No epilepsy. No palsy. But Jean still worried. "A mother worries."

She talks about Alan and the fact that he never gives up hope when hard times occur. "He never looks at the down side of any situation. He's always looking at the up side. That is how he is. He might worry, but he worries with the upbeat. He always says, 'It's going to turn out fine.' He said, 'When she opens her eyes, she has to see me.' Jean also shares that Alan lost his temper in the hospital when the doctors would not give him an answer about Theresa's condition. He demanded to see the doctor and talk to him about her prognosis. And he did. Jean was very unhappy that the Catholic priest never came to see Theresa, but the Protestant minister came to see her three times a day. "He brought her presents!"

Alan received a promotion within his company that brought a move to Pennsylvania for the family. As soon as they were settled in a small home, Jean enrolled at the local community college to continue her degree program. The children loved living in the suburbs with a big yard and many playmates nearby. Several years later, Jean and Alan suffered a terrible loss. A baby son died during childbirth. Jean says, "I can't talk about it because it has never left me." But she does go on. Her voice is choked up as she continues. "It was terrible. I had a normal pregnancy. And he was a perfect baby. It was traumatic! But that wasn't the terrible part. The terrible part was the planning — the hopes. To lose a baby is very painful. And people say the worst things, like, 'You'll get over it.' It's never gone. I can't talk about it. He would have been twenty-eight. The day of his birth is the worst day of the year for me. Every birthday."

The nurse brought a tranquilizer for Jean to take, to ease the emotional pain. Jean refused to take it. "There is nothing that will ever ease the pain. I have to go through this and come out of it. I'm not going to mask it and come out of it next year. So you tell the doctor where to put the pills!" It angered Jean that they were going to "dope me up." She asked to be left alone to deal with it. The doctor came in that night and talked with her. He said that she should consider what her life would have been if the baby had been born severely disabled. "Then you and your husband would have had to deal with that for the rest of your life." Jean never forgot what he said. "It helped me at the time. It was true. And I have seen that in other people's lives. The child has consumed their lives. The rest of the family suffers. Often the parents divorce."

"We just went on with our lives. We had the other children to take care of. We just got up and did what we had to do. That doesn't mean that you didn't feel the pain. And it was hard on the kids. Theresa couldn't handle it. She was nine and she thought of the baby as hers. She would say 'I have a baby brother.' She didn't accept that he had died." One of their friends came to visit and urged Jean to talk to Theresa and explain what had happened. She did and Theresa learned early in life what death meant.

Jean became pregnant again. "Best thing I ever did." Their fourth daughter, Marianne, was born when Jean was 35. "You have to go on the best way you can, because who knows what will happen next?" Jean cites a saying about life that she likes — "Dish it up, baby, and don't be stingy with the jalapeños!" She says it stresses the difference between being defeated and taking whatever life deals and going on. She thinks of the jalapeños as all the things in life that we don't want, but have no choice about. "The sour and bitter things that are going to happen. The death of a child is a horrible thing. Yet, I consider myself very lucky to have four kids. My life is good. Things that you have to go through, you go through. Depending on how you look at life affects how you react to the bad times."

Jean completed her two-year Associate degree and transferred to a nearby four-year state college to reach her Bachelor of Science degree with a major in sociology. She enjoyed the course work, the challenge. And she felt wonderful about reaching her goal. It was nineteen years since she had first enrolled in college. She and Alan were on course for their plan to make education their insurance for the future. After her graduation, Alan had another career opportunity with a large national firm. It meant moving to upstate New York and Jean agreed that he should take the job. Alan advanced to the position of Chief Financial Officer with the company. He also urged Jean to go on for her master's degree at the State University in Utica. The commute was short and Jean took her courses in the afternoons as well as at night. Marianne was starting kindergarten. Jean became a teaching assistant with a small salary. Her goal was a master's in Education: Curriculum Development and Instruction. "I went to school from day one." Jean liked living in the area. She found it a combination academic and ethnic atmosphere. There were three colleges nearby. She formed new friendships and also worked in the college center for two years, tutoring learning disabled students. She looks back on this as a good time in their lives. A growth time for her in particular. They stayed in New York for four years. "I earned my master's degree at graduation in May and we left in June for Alan's new position in Virginia."

Alan became the President of a branch of the company located in the southern part of the state, a position he holds today. Their home is about ninety miles from Richmond and as Jean describes it, almost 'another country' compared to the places they had lived before. After eighteen years, Jean still feels the enormous differences in the culture. "This is rural southern Virginia. There are parts that I like. I could leave my doors open whenever we go away. I still lock my doors because I'm a city person, but you don't have to. And if you have something you want done with your car, just leave it in the driveway and they will pick it up, take care of it and bring it back at the end of the day. That's what you have in a small town.

Everybody knows who you are. And the people are very generous with their time. That's the nice part."

Jean then shifts to the negative aspects of living in a small southern town with less than a thousand people. "It's rural and the ideas are narrow. It's an unbelievable backwardness, people don't know there are other cultures out there, other religions out there. There are no movie theaters in these little towns. If you want to see movies, you have to go to Richmond."

She speaks of the Civil War still referred to as 'The War Between The States.' "The whole Civil Rights Movement and changes haven't really gotten there. It's the Old South. There's a 'black section' of town. Desegregation does not exist. Many African-Americans are descendants of former slaves and unless they go north, they remain in menial jobs. White women do not clean their own homes. Even if they have very little money themselves. It's a status thing. They still say, 'The colored girl comes in to help me.'" Jean has found it hard to live in this culture, since the customs and behavior are directly opposed to what she believes in. "It's the way it is and everyone accepts it." But she has also seen that the African-Americans she and Alan have come to know are very close to them. "They want to be around us. As soon as they know who you are and where you are coming from, there is a different feeling. A good feeling."

Jean found her way through several jobs before she started teaching in a prison. "I didn't want to teach in the public schools. So, I volunteered in the hospital when I first got there. To get my feet on the ground. Then, I saw an advertisement in the paper for a job in the prison."

When she told Alan she was going to go for an interview, he said, "I don't want you working in a prison!"

After arguing, Jean said, "I just want to try. I haven't been on interviews. I need to do it." Alan then agreed. She went to the interview and got the job. It was a super-maximum security prison thirty miles from their home.

Alan then said, "You can't go into that prison!"

Jean replied, "I'll just go for one day." When she came home, she said she was a 'zombie'. "It was traumatic! To see these stone walls and walk through all these gates and hear the clank behind you. You see brick buildings with bars. And you hear men howling! Some of it is moaning. Yelling back and forth to one another."

Jean was taken around by another teacher and stayed a full eight-hour day. She thought it was like a 'den', a horrible experience. There had been a riot three months before and there was a total lock-down still in effect. There were no classes taking place. They walked by the 'pods', the cell blocks. The men were locked in their separate cells. "You could also hear men crying. It was very sad. You could see two levels of cells. That was my first day!" Alan, of course, did not want her to return. Jean chuckles when she says, "And the next day, I went back. Alan knew that I would make my own decision." She describes two weeks of grounding and then she reached an important point in her life. "Something inside of me said, *This could be a career.* I can make some changes in this place. I can bring education here."

The prison had been built as a model super-maximum security prison in the state. It housed 'lifers' and other hardened inmates serving long terms. It was supposed to be the 'prison of all prisons' built in the United States. A completely foolproof prison. But the model had not worked as planned. First, there had been a major riot. And then — an escape. Six inmates had walked out the front doors! Jean comments, "It was a disgrace to the state. And the Governor. Six death row inmates were loose. There were road blocks all over. It was a frightening thing!" The men were captured and the federal government was called in to investigate. They found "deplorable conditions" at the prison and gave a consent decree with fifteen actions that were to take place and be monitored for a period of ten years. An entire new administration came in with more humane conditions spelled out in the decree. And there was to be a full-fledged educational program.

Jean came into the prison at this time. "I knew that I could do it. There were a few teachers doing very little. I was thinking that these men are locked up behind bars under terrible conditions. They weren't in there forever. Some were kids in there under protective custody. They were young, white, with behavior problems. Most of the inmates were black. And there were men on death row. All of those men I knew then have been executed. Somewhere in those two weeks when I was walking around, I knew that I could create a program to help some of them." She told Alan she was going to stay.

First, she went out to buy books. "There were no books. The classroom was inside the housing unit. At first, I didn't even know there was a classroom. I was told that there was no place to teach." The former warden was fired and there was support from the new administration. The new warden said to her, "This is an embarrassment to the state!" He gave her carte blanche. Jean was one of the four teachers hired. There was no principal and they each taught in their own way. The inmates ranged from non-readers to high school level. First, Jean and the other teachers had to establish rapport with the students. The inmates had to see that something worthwhile was happening in the classes. This took time. There were about fifteen students in a class for morning and afternoon sessions. Jean introduced herself in a direct way. She said to the men, "This is going to be a learning environment. There will be no smoking in this classroom. I am here to teach and you are here to learn." When she had first discovered the classroom, the floor was thick with cigarette butts. It was scrubbed and ready when she began her classes.

Schooling was not mandatory. Jean describes how she would go with the guards and round up the students in the beginning. "You had to go bring them in. We would knock on the cell doors and say, 'We're going to recruit you for school.' I had their records and chose one or two to get it started. I tried to sell them. Then three or four would come and gradually the word got out. I would see them in the yard or at a window and say, 'Why don't you come to the classes?' We would talk. They have to trust you and they don't trust anybody. They would say, 'You're an honest person and we're going to come to school.'"

Guards were outside the door when classes were in session, not in the room. Jean explained that there were very few discipline problems and if they happened, she handled them. "You develop a relationship with some of the men who become teacher aides. They become leaders. It's almost like a line of defense. They're the ones that run interference. They're very protective without saying it." There were two separate classes enrolled, morning and afternoon, five days a week. There were 'counts' in the prison every two hours that interrupted the sessions. "It was not a simple thing. It's counts. It's loudspeakers. People being pulled out." When asked how she felt working in the prison, Jean says, "I felt fine. I felt good. I felt I was contributing something really good. Some kind of purpose. When I got home, I felt tired but good." She describes how growing up as a Catholic affected this part of her life. "There are spiritual works of mercy and corporal works of mercy. Spiritual things you do every day and physical things you do. And one of the things you do is to visit people in hospitals and prisoners as Christ did. To emulate his life. So I felt I was doing something that's part of what I believe in my core."

Jean taught for six years at that prison. Was she ever afraid? She pauses and says, "No. I almost felt like Mother Theresa when I walked in there. I really felt that way. The respect is there. And some of the inmates would ask, 'Why do you come in here every day ?' And I would say, 'Because I'm a professional.'" She describes one of the aides who still keeps in touch with her. He is in prison for life, but she never asked why he had that sentence. "I never asked any of them. You don't ask." They called Jean, 'Mrs. Kerns'. Some used the southern way, 'Miss Jean'. She called them by their first names. She talks about a young man who was about 25 when he first came into her class. He told her, "The only word I ever heard of kindness in prison was from you. You treated me like a human being." He completed his high school GED degree and went on to take college courses. He is still in prison.

Jean faced a strong challenge when 'lifers' entered her classes. More than once, students would complete the GED degree and see no purpose in going on to college courses. They would say, "What is the point of doing that? I'm never going to get out of here!" She tells me about one of these men whom she first encountered walking across the yard in handcuffs and leg irons with a guard on each side. "And I said, 'Excuse, me. Would you like to go to school?' He told me where to go! Next time I saw him, I asked him the same question. Finally, one day, he showed up in school. He went through the GED inside of a month. He had been in prison from the time he was twelve. Then he said, 'Why would I bother to go to college? I'm going to be here for the rest of my life. I'm never getting out!' And I said, 'That's the point. You have the rest of your life. You could study and influence other men. And you could write. And do you want to be an interesting person? Do you want to stop growing?' He's the one who graduated with a 4.0 average from college."

Certain prisoners were segregated from the other men. Jean would teach them one-on-one, in a room where the guards would bring the men in leg irons to sit at a desk. Some had manacles as well and would write with both wrists together. She also taught certain men through the bars of their cells, passing assignment papers in to them. She would sit in a chair outside their cells and teach. In some cells, the only opening in the door was the slot where the food tray was passed in. She would shove papers through the slot to those men. Her purpose was to reach the inmates and she devised many ways to do this. She was completely dedicated to her daily pursuit of 'corporal mercy'.

After six years, Jean decided she wanted to move on and influence other teachers. She was interested in a position in administering an entire educational system. "I wanted to go on. There was an opening as a principal in another maximum-security prison. Three prisons within one wall, the largest prison on the East Coast." Jean applied and got the job. It was a new prison and Jean would be able to set up the system as she thought it should be. "I wanted to do it the way I knew it could be done. I wanted a pretty place with pretty pictures on the stone walls. I wanted flowers in the classrooms. Nothing stuck on the walls with scotch tape." She knew she would only be there for three or four years since another prison was being built closer to her home. When she was hired, it was with the understanding that she would transfer there when the second prison opened. There were twelve teachers, a library and ample space. Jean also was given the responsibility for closing down the old state penitentiary in Richmond. Before her new job started she spent two months evaluating what could be salvaged from the physical plant. The furniture. The books. What might be useful in the new prison was saved. When she returned, she tackled the new job.

"I knew what had to be done. I put beautiful posters on the walls. Marathon posters. Posters with bright colors. I hated the stone walls and bars. How can you come into that environment and learn? Bulletin boards were changed every month. And everybody got into it. And the men loved it!" Several years later, after the program had been well established, Jean and the other teachers learned in a dramatic way how important their classes were to the inmates. Their classrooms were in a long rectangular building with offices and other facilities. They were directly across the yard from the three 'pods', huge cell blocks that housed a thousand inmates. "We were setting up our classrooms for the day when the guards started banging on the doors and the phones rang. The words were urgent, 'Get out! Now! The men are rioting in the pods!' We ran for the exit doors, through the gates and the outer walls to safety."

It took almost two days to contain the riot. During that time, the men smashed the glass windows and threw burning sheets doused in gasoline through the bars into the main building. When Jean and the other teachers returned, they expected to find the classrooms covered in broken glass and filled with burnt furniture and books. "We were stunned by what we discovered. Our classrooms were the only ones that had not been touched! On either side, rooms were gutted and black with soot. Our classrooms were exactly as we had left them two days before. I learned a powerful lesson that day. I learned that the word must have gone out. 'Leave the school alone! Off limits!' They never touched my school!"

During the years that Jean was building her career in the prison education system, Alan was growing his company. He became CEO of the Virginia organization and a vice-president of the national corporation. He liked the work and the challenge. There was some traveling involved, but most of his time was spent at his home base. The girls did well in their high school years and Theresa, Diane and Claire went on to college. Marianne was seventeen and had just been graduated from high school when something happened that changed her life and affected her parents and the entire family. She was a very pretty girl in her teens, tall and softspoken with the southern charm that is legendary. She was going out with a boy in her class whom Jean and Alan knew and liked. One evening when Jean was watching the presidential debates on television, she went into the kitchen and found a note propped up on the table. Alan was out of town and Marianne was out with her boyfriend.

In the note, Marianne had written that she was seven months pregnant.

Jean was stunned! "I couldn't believe what I was reading. I was numb. The girls wore those big, baggy sweatshirts and I had never noticed anything different about her. I wasn't looking. I picked up the phone and called Alan. Then I called all the girls. Alan came home the next day. Diane was there by 7 o'clock the next morning. They all came. Marianne had not come home. We found out later she was at her boyfriend's house. And his parents had known about this and never told us!"

Jean had been awake all night. In the early morning, she sat in the living room and stared out the picture window. She tried to figure out what to do. As she looked out, she remembered that the couple across the street had a son who was killed in a car accident that past summer. "And the woman was just coming out of the house. I looked at her and thought, *How could a baby have a bad effect on our lives? That woman lost her only child. He's dead.* And that was it for me. I got up. Diane came. And I was fine. I said, 'Marianne is having a baby. This is the way it is. We can deal with this.'"

Diane then called Marianne and talked to her. She told her not to be afraid to come home. When Marianne did come home, her boyfriend waited outside in the car. She cried as Jean held her in her arms. Jean told her, 'You have choices. This is purely your decision.'

"We didn't want her to feel she had to give the baby up." When Alan came home, he also comforted Marianne. However, he felt very strongly that she should not give up the baby. He said, "There's no way she's going to give away that baby!" Theresa and Diane, on the other hand, were adamant that she should. Jean felt she should keep the baby but did not express it forcefully as Alan did.

Jean and Alan did not want Marianne to marry her boyfriend, who was as young and immature as she. They both felt such a marriage would be a "disaster". Marianne agreed. Jean describes how they went through the next nine weeks. "She and I and Alan, together. I took her places, to Catholic Charities to talk to counselors. And to other places to get a whole spectrum of opinions. But it wasn't until she actually had the baby and held him in her arms, that she made her decision to keep him." Most of Marianne's friends did not remain close to her or give her support. She was, of course, very hurt by this. Jean was most unhappy with the local parish church that she felt did not help Marianne at all. She had expected the priest to understand that Marianne had not had an abortion and therefore was taking a path that should have been approved.

Jean only went back to the church once, when the new baby named Steven was about six weeks old. "We went to church and took him with us. We used to take turns reading from the Bible and I went up to the priest before the service and said, 'I'm going to have the last word here.' During the Mass, they ask if there is anyone who has anyone special they want to pray for. And I got up and said, 'I want to pray for a girl who had a lot of courage to do what she did.'" Jean's voice becomes husky with emotion as she goes on. "I said, 'Sometimes decisions are made that are the best decisions. You have to admire courage when you see it!" Alan was there with Marianne and Steven when Jean spoke. They left and never returned to that church again.

Steven was born in December and the community college semester was to start in January. Marianne said that she could not go back to school and face all the other students. Jean told her, "You're going to school! You're not going to miss a step. That's the first day of the rest of your life! I'm going to take you to get a new hairstyle and treat you to new makeup. And you're going to have a new outfit and you're going to school!" Marianne protested that she could not do it. She begged her mother not to make her do it. Jean was firm. "You have a beautiful child. You did the right thing as we saw fit. You hold your head up high! Everybody's got their own choices in life. You made this choice. We made this choice. We're partners. This is it!'" And Marianne went back to school. Jean took pictures of her on the first day of her return to college.

Marianne attended the community college for two years. She lived at home and took courses at night and during the summers. She was enrolled in classes four nights of the week and Jean and Alan took care of the baby. "I would walk in the door from work and take over. Every night, we took care of him until we put him to bed. He was an infant. And we woke up with him during the night too." Marianne completed her two-year degree and went on for a four-year degree. She drove to college in Richmond to complete the next two years, a 90-mile commute. She would take Steven with her to day care at the college pre-school and then attend classes. Jean pays her great tribute for what she accomplished. "She put a big part of her life and soul into that. An enormous effort. I'll never forget that. It was a lot of work. She had our support, but she did it!" Marianne was graduated and then found an apartment in Richmond where she would go on for a master's degree in Education.

During this six-year time period, the other Kearns daughters were also moving ahead in their lives. Diane and Claire married. Diane became the mother of a son and Claire of a son and daughter. Diane's marriage was a good one. Claire's was not and she went through a very hard time of betrayal and divorce. Jean and Alan gave her all the support they could. She was alone with two small children, but she did have her education and a teaching position. They had encouraged all the girls to go for graduate degrees, a continuation of Alan's theory that education was the best insurance in life. They moved Claire and the children twice to relocate in Richmond and to find a new teaching job there as well. "We moved her twice within four months. It's been all the difference in the world for her. She got her bearings. She's in a new life. She's doing very well." Jean talks about what it has meant to be there for her children as they have faced very serious problems and hard times in their lives. She refers to what it means to be a mature person. "A mature person sees what has to be done and does it. Our girls needed our help and we gave it. That's what you do."

There would be another kind of help and support Jean and Alan would be called upon to give. Theresa, their oldest daughter, has followed her father as a role model into the business world. She holds a master's degree in Finance and combines, in her mother's words, "talent, drive and savvy" to achieve a vice-presidency at an investment banking firm. She is single and lives in Boston. They were visiting with her one weekend, sitting at her kitchen table having coffee after dinner, when Theresa suddenly said, "I'm gay." Jean recalls that there was no lead-in. "She didn't say, Mom and Dad, I have something to tell you. She just said it. Alan and I had talked about this possibility between us, but it still came as a shock when she just blurted it out." Jean feels now that it was the only way Theresa could tell them. She trusted them to understand and accept who she was. She was right in her trust. Jean and Alan hugged her and told her they loved her as they always had.

On the long drive home to Virginia, they talked for hours about how they felt. It was not what they had hoped for their daughter, but they realized they had to accept it and go on with their family life. "Theresa was still the Theresa we loved." All her sisters were completely supportive and loving when they were told. The Kearns family bonds are strong.

Jean's career in the Virginia prison system grew through different stages. She stayed at the 'model' prison for five years. She talks about some of the mistakes she made along the way. "Some of the mistakes were in the staff I picked. Probably from inexperience on my part. I needed to be tougher, more selective. As an administrator, you're not getting the best people in the world wanting to work in a prison. You have to make it Tom Sawyer's fence. This is exciting to work in a prison! I don't think I did enough of that. That was my first job as a principal." When Jean moved to her next position, it was a new medium-security prison for 1200 men. The turn-over rate was 45 men a month. She wanted to work with men who would be going home. "Their thinking is that they are going home. It's a different environment. The day they walk in the prison, we say, "You have to plan to be leaving." Most of the offenses are drug-related. Robbery. Assault. We work on their thinking. The trend in correctional education is away from purely academic to teaching life skills. How to think things out critically. Show them a simple process to avoid making a mistake and thinking about it later. We say, 'Think about it first!' And we offer vocational education as well as the academic GED. Classes in such areas as carpentry, masonry, electrical maintenance and horticulture. We prepare the men to reenter the outside world with a way to earn an honest living."

An opportunity arose for Jean to become a regional principal, with two additional prisons to administer. Alan and one of her close colleagues advised against it, but Jean rose to the challenge. She comments, "Biggest career disaster in my life! That was a big mistake." One of the prisons had been locked down for two and a half years; the other had major problems. The superintendent wanted her to completely restructure the teaching systems and staffs in both prisons. Jean created her plans for change, but found that she did not have support from the top when the teachers in both prisons resisted the changes. "The problem was sabotage from the bottom. The teachers went running to the superintendent. And he didn't stand behind me." She decided to leave the regional position after a year and a half of frustration and inability to meet her goals. "I fixed some of the problems at one of the prisons. And I did put a structure in place. But I thought, this is not going anywhere! It had me crazy! And I decided there was nothing that would convince me to stay." Jean wrote a letter to the superintendent spelling out five things she would do before she left. And she told him she would continue as principal in her original position. He accepted her offer.

Jean, in reflecting on her long career in the prisons, recalls a significant incident that occurred in the super maximum-security prison years ago. It epitomizes for me the courage she has displayed working with the inmates. She was setting up her classroom early one Friday and several teacher aides had walked in. An inmate, who had been distraught, came in and attacked her from behind. "I struggled and fought back. I broke one of his ribs with my elbow before the aides subdued him. Then, I fled to my home. On Monday, I went back. I knew if I didn't go back then, I would never go back." When she returned, she thanked the inmates who had helped her. They, in turn, told her they were surprised she had come back. They never thought they would see her again. "I said, 'Why? Just because of one person?' He was transferred out of the prison. And that was it." Jean adds that she does not carry fear of other inmates because of this one event.

When Jean is asked how she feels about herself, she replies, "I feel very content with myself. I really do. I feel very content with my life and my family involvement, which is the way I like it. I have a hard time understanding how other people don't want to feel that way about their family. I work very hard at making sure our family stays close. " Jean plans days together. Shopping or having lunch in Richmond with her daughters. And weekend trips to visit. Thanksgiving, Christmas and Easter, all the major holidays are times when the entire family gathers. Sometimes at her daughters' homes as well as at Jean and Alan's. They have taken vacations as a group as well.

The most unusual vacation Jean and Alan have taken was dog-sledding in Canada for two successive years in 2000 and 2001. They joined other couples and embarked on the first numbing wilderness trip that Jean describes in vivid terms. "The six of us were really naïve about what was awaiting us in North Bay, Ontario. As Dickens said, 'It was the best of times. It was the worst of times.' When we arrived at the airport, at six a.m., the temperature was around 5 degrees and we knew we were going to be further tortured on this trip!" There were only six of them at the airport in Toronto bound for North Bay. They each brought arctic gear: anoraks, layers and layers of clothing, face masks, thick hats and mittens. Special boots and protective sun glasses. They were met by their guide, who drove them through semi-wilderness to the Rock Pine Motel and Restaurant, their first home base. They had to hold onto the railing with two hands in order to walk up the ramp that was covered with ice and snow.

Jean laughs heartily as she continues her story, "The inside of the motel looked like a scene from a Klondike movie where the fur traders come in and hurl their pelts on the counter. We asked the Canadians who came in if they had ever dog-sledded up there. Their answer was the same, a blank stare accompanied by the question, 'Dog-sledding?'"They settled in to see a video and hear a lecture on their adventure to come. The next day, the sleds and dogs arrived. Each person had a separate sled and six dogs that they were to take care of on the trip. "They were beautiful dogs," Jean says. "Huskies. Perfectly trained. We were the beginners." They took off that day, each standing with the reins in hand and the brake to stop the sled by their side. They sledded for hours through snow and ice landscapes as well as wooded areas. Despite the sub-zero temperature, Jean loved it! When they stopped for the night, it was at a rude shelter with no heat and a slab of ice as the support for their sleeping bags. They rested after they fed and watered the dogs! "We all slept lined up next to each other like sardines to stay warm. The ice slab was supposed to be an insulator! If you had to get up to use the bathroom during the night, it was outside and you had to crawl over all the others. I stayed put!"

Despite the rigor of their trip, Jean and Alan returned to Canada the following year and this time their trip was even more challenging than the first. Only one other couple went with them to a section of Canada that was separated from the North Pole by only an Indian village! When asked why they went back a second time, Jean tries to explain what the attraction was. "It is a marvelous adventure. To be up there in the wilderness and to stand on the sled, holding the reins of those six amazing dogs. It was exhilarating! I felt free!" On their second trip, Alan had an extra chapter in his adventure. As the four were getting ready to embark with a guide, who spoke no English — and they spoke no French— Alan fell off his sled and his dogs took off ahead of the others. Alan was dragged several hundred yards before the dogs stopped. He suffered some bruises to his body as well as his pride. Jean is convulsed with laughter as she describes what happened. "He just went flying by all of us! It was one of the funniest things you ever could imagine! Alan was a good sport and joined in the laughter — after the dogs stopped." Jean adds that they are planning a third trip next year to a remote area of Alaska.

On the subject of regrets, Jean speaks poignantly. "The regret is that I wish I had waited to have children. You deprive yourself of a chance to have time, just the two of you. Since we didn't know each other that long before we were married, it would have been good to have that time." Jean and Alan were not to be alone as a couple until Marianne finished college and moved to Richmond with Steven. Jean appreciates the freedom she and Alan have now. "To come and go as we please. It's a good feeling. Maybe, that's the reason we take these adventuresome trips. It's a good feeling to be free. Free from responsibility. Since I was little kid helping my mother read because her eyesight was failing, I was always responsible for someone."

Jean says she is happiest when she is with family and good friends. When there is harmony in the family. "I try to massage that and nurture it. I write letters sometimes when there is a problem." She talks about what happened before Marianne's recent marriage. Marianne met her future husband after she moved to Richmond. The wedding plans were underway. "Everybody was going in different directions. The girls couldn't seem to get together to pick out their dresses. So, I wrote her sisters a letter at three o'clock in the morning, that it was important for them to come together and pick out the dresses. It was a nice letter. I wanted the three sisters to see that it would be supportive to Marianne to do this. And it worked. They never mentioned the letter. They just did it."

Jean looks back over the years of her marriage to Alan. "Alan is strong.

A very loyal friend. His loyalty is incredible. He would never cross the line of loyalty to his wife and his children. He is devoted to them. He is devoted to me. I know that when I need him, he's there. We both feel that way." She adds that he is a lot of fun to be with. That he's funny and has the ability to laugh at himself. "He does things that he knows he won't be good at— such as dog-sledding. And falling off the sled!" She says that he would have much preferred being on snow shoes. That he dreaded getting back on the sled, but he was a good sport and climbed back on. She adds, "I also know what not to ask him to do. He does not like to shop. So I pick a day when he is doing something else. That is a good thing in a marriage. To respect each others likes and dislikes. Sometimes, I think young people today think they have to do everything together and if you don't, they just split."

Jean's two passions in life have emerged clearly during the hours of our interviews: her work and her family. "I feel passionate about my job. I feel passionate about my family. I know what has to be done at work. And I know I can do it. I love going there! Planning. Seeing it happen is very fulfilling for me. Where I go with it at some point, I don't know. But, I know for now, I love going there! And my family. I feel very passionate about wanting to see harmony at any cost. At times, I tell my daughters that the choices they make in life should include our family values." Jean notes that Claire's ex-husband did not share many of their family values, such as the importance of continuing one's education. She and Alan were concerned about the marriage from the beginning. Jean sees the overall family harmony as based on the values they all share.

Jean feels fulfilled as a person and a woman. "I feel I am at the point in my life where I can say what I want. Without hurting people's feelings, of course. And I can do what I want. And I have confidence in what I'm doing. That also comes from being successful. It's because you have accomplished certain things." Jean tells how she made the break from her family in New York and moved away. She feels that some of her relatives never forgave her for doing that. "They feel there is nothing outside of living in New York. It's like the New Yorker magazine cover with only the East and West Coasts and nothing in between!" She sees certain turning points in her life as the "devastating times" that caused her to stop and pay attention. To review her perspective and put things in proportion. "You're thrown back and you're speechless. You're jolted! But then, you work through it."

Jean thinks of herself as a religious person, although she did stop going to church after Marianne had her baby. "I'm not outwardly religious. The hypocrisy of organized religion came out to me at that time. I did stop going to church out of utter disgust! But that parish and that priest are not the whole church and I do intend to start going again. And praying is very important to me in my life. The only thing that saves me is to pray." She has little tolerance for people and groups that use religion for political purposes. Jean is also strongly pro-choice and believes it is a private matter for a woman to decide what is right for her. She says, fiercely, "How dare we ever intrude on that!" She is not in favor of the 'Jesus movement' which she sees as proselytizing and aimed at converting people of other faiths. She respects the beliefs of other religions and does not see hers as the only way.

Jean says that she does think about death. But she adds that she does not dwell on it. Rather, it comes with reaching a certain stage of life. She feels it is more important to "embrace every day." She believes in an after life and that one has to live to the fullest. She only wants to live a long life if she is healthy and fully functioning. To meet this, she follows a regimen of exercise, walking three to four miles daily in the woods with her dogs, rest and healthy food. She tries to keep her mental balance, seeking periods of "solitude and peace." She does not fear serious illness, even though her mother died of cancer. "I don't fear things. I don't fear walking alone in the woods. I don't fear going into the prisons. Maybe it's good. Maybe it's bad. That's how I am."

Jean gets up every day at five. She describes herself as a 'morning person' who gradually runs down during the afternoon. No upswing in the evening. She is in bed most nights at nine. "I'm out!" she says with a laugh. And she does not enjoy cooking. "I do it because we have to eat. I get very bored with people discussing recipes. What you put in a certain dish. How could you talk about that?"

She has very definite ideas about dealing with the aging process. "I think physically, you have to ignore the normal things that come with aging. I have a hard time listening to people talk about their ailments. At work, I just tune it out. I have my aches and pains. We all do. Whatever they are, you just take care of them." In terms of a beauty regimen, Jean uses creams on her face. She feels her appearance is very important. She applies makeup skillfully, with a frosted eyeshadow highlighting her eyebrows. Her hair is cut, layered and colored every four weeks. Her nails are manicured. And the right clothes are also important to her. She considered a face lift, but decided against it. "You should be the best you can feel. Look the best you can look. When you look in the mirror, you feel good. But you shouldn't try to be what you're not. You should be the best you can be as you age."

Jean stresses that she will never retire. She may move into a different kind of work some day, but she will stay in the work force because she feels it is very important to do so. She does interject, "I might change my mind, but for now I feel very strongly about it." She refers back to her mother's family. They were all older and everybody worked. She had one aunt who worked until she was 85 and even lied about her age to stay on the job. "I feel that they kept young mentally by being engaged rather than disengaged. What I've seen from people who literally retire and don't do anything, they just fade away. So, I will not retire! I want to work. I don't want to retire."

Women friends are very important to Jean. She has childhood friends and friends she has made across the years. "Having these connections, being able to talk openly and honestly is very important in my life." She has many colleagues she likes and respects, but she does not consider them friends in the same sense. They are professionals she works with and shares many experiences with. Special bonds are formed, but she does not discuss personal matters with them. Jean and Alan have a quiet social life. They attend certain business related dinners and functions related to Alan's position in the company. But Jean prefers to spend the weekends with her family, doing things together. When Alan is away, Jean enjoys the solitude. "I love it! I'll cook a simple meal and sit down with candles on the table. I play music, maybe read a book. I enjoy being alone." She says that she plays music every day when she comes home from work. Her choices cover a wide range from the classics to current day groups. "I love to listen to Italian recording artists and I joined the classical music club. I just started this in the last few years. And, of course, I love to listen to Frank Sinatra favorites. Alan and I danced to his records years ago and we still love to dance. We go dancing whenever we have a chance."

Possessions do not play an important part in Jean's life. She likes "nice clothes and real jewelry, like pearls," but owning things is not high on her list of priorities. The possessions she values the most were given to her by people close to her. "Things that were my mother's or belonged to Alan's mother. If there were a fire and I had to grab something, that's what I would grab." The big ticket items like a car are not important to her. "I go by the color of a car." She and Alan feel financially secure. They have planned carefully for their future. Alan's original concept of education as their insurance has proved to be very significant. Jean looks back at the hard times her mother endured with little money and no security. She cites the famous line from *Gone With The Wind*, when Scarlett stands on the hill at Tara, clutching a carrot and waving it at the sky. "She swears, 'I'll never be hungry again!' And I could identify with that as a child when I saw the movie. That is how I feel. I could never go through being poor again."

Eleanor Roosevelt is at the top of the list of people Jean admires. Most, but not all are women. Louis Armstrong is on her list for what he contributed to the music and jazz world as well as his way of handling adversity. She talks about Eleanor Roosevelt's qualities and contributions. "Her humanity shines out. It didn't matter what her station in life was. She was a wealthy woman, came from the upper class and still was able to identify with those of us who didn't have what she had. She did for other people and changed things in the world. Her concerns for children and poverty were real and she did something about it." Jean also cites Martin Luther King and the other leaders of The Civil Rights Movement as people she greatly admires. "I lived through that period. I remember what they fought through and what they accomplished." Jean adds Oprah Winfrey as a person who has not lost her connection to people. And the authors Toni Morrison and Maya Angelou, whose books she reads and enjoys. "I like to read about the struggle of the human spirit as it rises above adversity. "

Jean speaks of missing her mother. "She died in 1976 and I still think of her — every day. She was a strong woman. She was tough. She was amazing! When I think about her life, there was strength that was unbelievable. All the things she overcame. And I never saw her cry that much." Jean says that when her daughters have gone through problems, she always refers to her mother and all that she faced in life. "Think of your Nana." The three older girls knew her well and Marianne has learned from the stories she heard about her. 'Nana' has been an important role model for Jean's daughters as well as for Jean herself.

Jean feels she is a resolute person, not easily influenced by others. Once she thinks things through, she does not usually change her course. She smiles when she recalls a remark, one of her bosses made several years ago. He said, "Nobody supervises Jean! I wouldn't try." She is softspoken, but admits to "yelling at times." She says she can usually control her temper, but has found living in the 'Old South' for eighteen years to be a matter of "survival". The small town they live in has 980 people and 35 churches. The Catholic Church is the only one that is integrated. "When you first meet someone, they ask, 'What church do you go to?' And my wall goes up!" Jean describes 'jack-leg preachers', when a man decides he is a preacher, buys a suit and becomes a traveling minister. "It is really another country. There are rebel flags flying everywhere. There are bumper stickers that say, 'I shoot possums and Yankees.' And here I am — still a New Yorker in my soul!"

Jean looks ahead to the future in an open and positive way. She believes that she has strong genes in her family. All her relatives have lived long, healthy lives. She also thinks that one's mindset and attitude influence one's physical condition. "You have to will it. You have to make the decision that you will not be sick. I will myself to be healthy. I will not give in to things.

When I'm older, I want to get where I'm going under my own steam. I don't want anyone pushing me in a wheelchair. Every relative I had has walked to wherever they were going until they died! " Jean has taken part in half-marathons and has set a goal to run a full marathon in the years ahead. She also adds that if she finds she is seriously ill, she does not want extraordinary measures taken. She has warned Alan, "Don't you dare do that!" They both are preparing living wills.

Jean Kearns' story has come full circle. The little girl who was going to become a nun, faces life each day with inner strength and serenity. She says, "I think that serenity for me has a lot to do with religion. Growing up in the environment that I did means that I learned how important that was. I have always relied on religion. I draw on prayer. I carry rosary beads." She then takes the beads out of her handbag and holds them in her palm. They make a gentle sound as she does this. "They have never been away from me. If I move anywhere, if I go on a dog-sledding trip, they're with me. I never go anywhere without them! If I touch them — if I put them in my hand — my whole body relaxes. If I'm having a fretful night, I reach out and hold them. I have a second rosary that Alan gave me next to my bed."

She continues, "I guess as a little girl, I always believed that holding the rosary brought me close to God. I don't say them every day. As long as I have them in my hand, that's all I need. I must have them with me. Last year, I had a cancer scare. The doctor wanted to give me a lot of information. But I said to him, 'I'll be fine. And I'm going someplace else right now.' He knew what I meant. I had to go home, meditate and hold the rosary beads." Jean refers back to high school when there was a yearly retreat. They would spend five days in the large walled-in garden at the convent in complete silence. It was to be a time of deep contemplation and meditation. They were allowed to read. "I read Thomas Acquinas, tried to concentrate and understand it. I learned from the retreat and the priests who came to talk, about the good that religion could do. I learned self-control. And to know that there was a higher being. Now, when I am alone with nature, even with dog-sledding, it is a spiritual experience. At night, I go out and look up at the stars and see the Northern Lights. You can feel a spiritual connection. It reminds me of when we were kids. We would go up on the roof of the apartment building and lie down and look up at the stars. It was very dark and quiet up there. And you could feel the connection!"

A sense of mystery and wonder for Jean Kearns. Then and now — full circle.

EPILOGUE

For some years, I have been intrigued by the phrase, 'a woman of a certain age' when I hear it in conversation or read it in articles. And now that I'm there, I am still trying to figure out what it means. Of course, in French where it originated, it sounds sexier, 'femme d'un certain age'. An air of mystery. I like that.

We live in a youth-besotted culture. Movies, music, clothes, commercials seem to be pitched at the youngest common denominator. Yet, scientists talk of the 'graying' of America. More of us are living longer and healthier lives — women in particular. So, what does it really mean to be an older woman today — 'a woman of a certain age'?

For me, being a woman of a certain age means that my exact birth date and age are my own affair. The cosmetic companies tell us, with the billions they spend, that we are "as young as we feel." Yet, they hawk the myriad anti-wrinkle creams to rescue our skin from telltale crows feet and laugh lines. I have news for them. I've earned these lines. Besides, we can't all look like Catherine Deneuve!

It does take real discipline to exercise, eat right and ward off the body's aging process. Gravity pulls relentlessly at the chin line. I considered a face lift, did some research and decided that route was not for me. I was afraid of emerging with a better chin line, but not quite looking like myself, after all. So, my hairstyle keeps getting shorter. And like Katherine Hepburn, I wear scarves and turtle necks. It seems to be working so far.

For many women, and I am certainly among them, the advantages of being a woman of a certain age outweigh the disadvantages. There is the wonderful freedom of saying exactly what I want, when I want and to whom I want. I've taken a leaf from the Boomer generation who like to let it all hang out. I do try to modify the possible hurtful effects of being outspoken. I've learned to do that from the years of living in a family and raising children.

In her provocative book *Wisdom and The Senses*, Joan Erikson wrote, "Love, intimacy and work provide life with its essential meaning." A strong statement in a book that stresses creativity as a key to healthy human growth

189

and development. Erikson, a psychologist, wrote this book when she was well into her 70s. As for me, I've worked hard and well in two careers. Writing is now my full-time endeavor. And I'm loving it.

Does love translate into baby-sitting with the grandchildren? Sure. Sometimes. But not to excess. It is a delight to watch them grow and take part in their childhood. To enjoy the birthday parties and the Sunday School programs. To feel a sense of pride in their successes.

But the central focus of life, as a woman of a certain age, has to be with my own life. What are the measures of my days? Am I counting them out with T.S. Eliot's "coffee spoons"? Am I finding intimacy and love in my human relationships? With my husband, my children and my friends? Am I giving as well as receiving?

These are existential questions for a woman of a certain age. The 50-plus years are behind me. I know that. It doesn't make me sad. I don't dwell on it in a morbid sense. The number of years ahead is unknown. And that is the wonder. The mystery. The excitement of savoring each day. And creating something new. What Elizabeth Cady Stanton, the 19th century philosopher of the Women's Movement, called "The Solitude Of Self."

The essence to me of being a woman of a certain age is having a glimpse into what the human condition is all about. That glimpse has three parts: wisdom gained through the years of living, a strong dose of humility, and the absolute necessity of a sense of humor. After all, reaching a certain age should entitle women to certain rewards. Some tangible, of course. But perhaps the intangible are just as important. Such as deference and admiration. We've earned the right to a place of respect in our families and in our society.

For this book, I interviewed eight remarkable women of a certain age — in their 50s, 60s, 70s and 80s. They have passed through the same life stages that all women traverse. What makes them different? And why are their lives inspiring and interesting to read about? When they shared their life stories with me, I discovered that each woman has overcome daunting obstacles in life and has landed on her feet. Each has displayed enormous courage and resilience. In a real sense, these women have climbed mountains and have come through triumphant. They give new depth and rich meaning to the phrase, 'a woman of a certain age'.

Joyce S. Anderson
Linwood, New Jersey
June, 2001

190

QUESTIONS FOR DISCUSSION

1. How do you define courage? Does it differ with time and circumstance? Is it an inherent quality or can it be developed?

2. Which of the women's lives interested you the most? Why?

3. Were there decisions that some of these women made that were courageous? Explain why.

4. Have you had any similar experiences to any of the women in the book? How did you deal with the challenges or hardships when you faced them in your life?

5. Do you know women whom you would describe as courageous? If so, explain why.

6. How do you feel about this book? And has it changed your concept of courage? If so, how?

7. Has courage been considered largely a male characteristic in our society? Give examples to support your answer.

8. Should courage be a value that we encourage our children to develop? If so, how can we do that?

9. "Speaking truth to power" is one way to think of courage. Did any women in the book display this? Who and in what circumstance? Can you give any examples of that happening in your life? Or in our society?

*

Printed in the United States
15701LVS00005B/298-303